STO ✓

ALLEN COUNTY PUBLIC LI

3 1833 03877

D0149295

DEC 2 1 2000

A Mystery of Errors

A
Mystery
OF Errors

Simon Hawke

A Tom Doherty Associates Book

NEW YORK

This is a work of fiction. All the characters and events portrayed in this novel are either fictitious or are used fictitiously.

A MYSTERY OF ERRORS

Copyright © 2000 by Simon Hawke and Bill Fawcett & Associates

All rights reserved, including the right to reproduce this book, or portions thereof, in any form.

This book is printed on acid-free paper.

A Forge Book
Published by Tom Doherty Associates, LLC
175 Fifth Avenue
New York, NY 10010

www.tor.com

Forge® is a registered trademark of Tom Doherty Associates, LLC.

Library of Congress Cataloging-in-Publication Data

Hawke, Simon.
    Mystery of errors / Simon Hawke.—1st ed.
        p. cm.
    "A Tom Doherty Associates book."
    ISBN 0-312-87372-7 (acid-free paper)
    1. Shakespeare, William, 1564–1616—Fiction. 2. London (England)—History—16th century—Fiction. 3. Dramatists—Fiction 4. Actors—Fiction. I. Title.

    PS3558.A8167 M9 2000
    813'.54—dc21   00-031809

First Edition: December 2000

Printed in the United States of America

0 9 8 7 6 5 4 3 2 1

To

Deborah and Josh,

my family,

with special thanks to

Brian Thomsen,

Cindy Davis,

and Dr. Jo Ann Buck

A
Mystery
of Errors

1

$\mathcal{T}$HERE WAS NOTHING QUITE SO invigorating to the senses, Smythe decided, as ending a long and dusty day by being robbed.

The mounted highwayman came plunging out of the thick underbrush at the side of the road like a specter rising from the mist as he reined in with one hand and drew his wheel-lock with the other. His black courser reared and neighed loudly as the masked man shouted out, "Stand and deliver!"

Even under such startling and intimidating circumstances, Smythe could not help an instinctual assessment of the brigand's mount. A powerful and heavily muscled Hungarian with a proud carriage and admirable conformation, the courser pawed at the ground and pranced in place, responding to the knee pressure of its rider. The hooked head and bushy tail were characteristic of the breed, as was the long, thick mane that reached below the knees and would require a good deal of loving curry-combing to look so splendid and silky. A magnificent animal, thought Smythe, well-schooled and obviously well cared for. And the horse's master had a sense of the dramatic, too, something else Smythe could not help appreciating, despite the pistol aimed squarely at his chest.

The brigand was clad from head to toe in black, with a silk mask that covered the entire lower portion of his face. He wore a black quilted leather doublet, tight breeches, high boots, and a long black riding cloak that billowed out behind him. No ordinary road agent this, thought Smythe, but a man with a true sense of style. And apparently some substance, judging by his steed and his apparel. A flamboyant highwayman who was evidently successful at his trade and clearly understood the impact made by a good entrance.

"Did you hear me, man, or are you deaf? I *said*, stand and deliver!"

"Deliver what, my friend?" asked Smythe, with a shrug. "I haven't a brass farthing to my name."

"What, *nothing*?" said the highwayman through the black silk scarf covering most of his face. "Come, come, let's see your purse!"

Smythe took hold of the small brown leather pouch at his belt and gave it a shake, to demonstrate that it was empty. "You may dismount and search me if you like," he said, "but you shall find that I haven't a tuppence or ha'penny anywhere about my person."

"Dismount and search a strapping young drayhorse like yourself? Methinks not. You look like you could pose some difficulty if I gave you half a chance."

"Spoken with a pistol in your hand and a rapier and main gauche at your belt," said Smythe, wryly. "And me with nothing but a staff and poor man's bodkin."

"Aye, well, one cannot take too many chances," said the highwayman. "The roads are not very safe these days." He chuckled and looked Smythe over, then tucked his pistol in his belt. "So, no money, eh?"

"None, sir."

"And how will you be paying for your next meal?"

"If I shan't be catching it tonight with a snare or hook and line, then I fear that I shall not be eating," Smythe said.

"Oh, well, we cannot have that," the highwayman replied.

"Here's a silver crown for you. Buy yourself an ordinary and a night's rest at the next crossroads."

Surprised, Smythe almost missed catching the coin the robber tossed to him. "You are a strange sort of highwayman, indeed," he said, perplexed. "You demand money and end up giving it away, instead!"

"Ah, you look as if you need it more than I do. No matter. I shall make it up and then some with the next fat merchantman who comes along."

"However that may be, I am nevertheless grateful," Smythe replied. "I shall be sure to say a prayer tonight that they do not catch and hang you very soon."

"Most kind of you. What a splendid young fellow you are. I take it you are bound for London?"

"I am," said Smythe, nodding.

"In search of work." It was less a question than a statement. More than half the travelers on the road were starving beggars, making their way toward London in hopes of finding a better life. Or any kind of life at all.

"Aye," said Smythe. "And God willing, I shall I find it."

"You have a trade? You have the look of a blacksmith, with those shoulders."

"My uncle is a farrier and a smith," said Smythe. "I apprenticed at his forge. But I hope to be an actor on the stage."

"An *actor*?" The man snorted. "You had best stick to shoeing horses, lad. 'Tis a much more respectable profession."

"So says the brigand."

"Indeed, it takes one mountebank to know another," the highwayman replied. "But then, each to the devil after his own fashion. I wish you good fortune, young man. And if you care to, you can remember Black Billy in your prayers tonight. A word from an innocent like you might do some good, you never know. The Almighty bloody well stopped listening to me long since."

The highwayman touched the brim of his black hat in salute

and then spurred off into the woods. The sound of his mount's hoofbeats quickly receded in the distance. Smythe decided that he probably wouldn't need to worry about hanging, riding through the thickets like that. He'd likely break his neck long before some magistrate could stretch it for him.

It was certainly an interesting conclusion to a rather dreary and otherwise uneventful day, although it was his fourth time being robbed in as many days since he had left the midlands. Well, attempt at being robbed, in any event, he thought. The first three had been unsuccessful and this last one hardly seemed to count, seeing as how the highwayman had left him better off than he had been before. That was certainly a switch. He had never heard the like of it.

The first attempted robbery had taken place shortly after sundown on his first day out, as he had made his way toward London. Two men brandishing clubs had leaped out at him from under the cover of the woods. They had been more desperate than dangerous and he had made short work of them with his staff and left them both insensible in the middle of the road, or what passed for a road, at any rate, in that part of the country. It was little more than a pair of muddy ruts running side by side through the forest, tracks made by peddlers' carts as they made their way from one small village to another, passing news and trying to sell their wares.

The second attempt took place the very next day, but in broad daylight. Well, not quite daylight, perhaps, for little daylight had actually penetrated the thick canopy of branches overhead. This time, three surly and bedraggled men had accosted him, looking a bit more competent, armed with staves and daggers and demanding that he surrender all his money. The trouble was, he didn't have any. He had tried explaining that to them, in a reasonable fashion, but for some reason, highwaymen seemed a rather skeptical lot. They had insisted on searching him. Smythe had complied with their demand, seeing no harm in proving his point by demonstration and taking no unnecessary risks. On seeing that he was, in fact, as penniless as they, without even any decent clothes or weapons worth stealing, the disgusted robbers had let him go his way.

The third attempt had taken place early in the morning, proving to Smythe that there was actually no safe time to travel at all. He had been walking through the woods when an arrow from a longbow thudded into a tree trunk just to his left, passing so closely that he had felt its breeze. Immediately, he ducked behind that very tree trunk, so as not to give the unseen archer a target for a second shot, then wasted no time in slipping back further into the woods and putting some distance between himself and the bowman. He had left the unseen archer behind him, the sound of his cursing receding in the distance, and took his time before he ventured out upon the road again. He then continued on his way without further incident, until the mounted highwayman accosted him . . . only instead of robbing him or trying to kill him, the brigand had given him a silver crown. It was a singular occurrence, indeed. All in all, Smythe had to admit that he had met more interesting people in the past four days on the road than he had during all the years that he had spent in the village of his birth . . . save for the time the actors had come through.

The Queen's Players, featuring the famous Dick Tarleton, had put on a performance in the courtyard of The Goose and Gander. With the open sky above them, they had erected a small stage in the courtyard of the inn, with several screens behind the stage to make a tiring-room where costumes could be changed, and the entire village had attended their performance. Smythe had never seen anything like it. Somehow, that little group of men had managed to turn a small wooden platform supported by several barrels into another world, another place and time. Tarleton and Will Kemp, the two comedians of the troupe, had everyone helpless with laughter at their jigs and capers and from that moment on, Smythe had wanted nothing more than to be among those men and on that stage himself.

His father disapproved, of course. A life as a player was totally unsuitable and utterly out of the question. While working at his uncle's forge was no more a fit occupation for a gentleman, his father had believed that it could do a lad no harm to learn a bit of industry and develop an eye for iron, steel, and horseflesh. Those would certainly be useful things to know for a man of standing and position. But acting? The very mention of it had driven his father to apoplexy. Actors were nothing but immoral vagabonds whose careers were built on lies and fancy. He had stormed and thundered and threatened to disown him. The dream of acting, it had seemed, was destined to wither on the vine. Instead, it was his father's dream which had died before ever bearing fruit.

Symington Smythe's great, ambitious dream had been the achievement of a peerage. To this end, he had worked ceaselessly for most of his adult life. He had inherited and married well, but it was not enough to be a man of means and property. That property needed to be increased and increase in the means, in turn, begat more property. An improved estate could bring improved position and, these days, an improved position could bring a state of knighthood.

In the old days, titled blood had needed to be blue and preferably spilt in the name of king and country over several generations. But though the glory days of armor had, except for tournaments of sport, largely passed away, arms were still in very great demand. It was not unheard of for a prosperous merchant or a privateer to attain a peerage through some service to the Crown, or someone close to it. And becoming a gentleman with a claim to an established lineage was a necessary first step. Nowadays, every successful glover, stationer, and vintner who fancied himself a gentleman applied to Derby House for an escutcheon with which to grace his mantelpiece.

Even a man with blood less venous than venial could petition the offices of arms for the design of a device he could engrave on silver bowls to grace his dining room or have glazed into the leaded windows to lend an air of stature to his home. He could have a local glover embroider the arms upon his gauntlets and commission a goldsmith to craft a handsome seal ring to be worn upon the thumb as a sigil of importance. And if the fees were promptly paid and embellished with a few gratuities, then the heralds' inquiries into oft exaggerated claims to bear the port and charge and countenance of rank were not particularly scrupulous.

Thus, Symington Smythe II had applied for and received a coat of arms, so elaborate as to be positively tasteless, with engrailed crosses, lions passant, sable this and purpure that and argent every which way, which device he had then proceeded to emblazon on everything from the arched entryway over the front doorway of their country house to the handkerchiefs he had elaborately embroidered, apparently not seeing the irony of blowing his nose into his prized, dearly bought escutcheon.

A coat of arms, however, did not yet a knighthood make, so much more had needed to be done to curry influence and favor and prove merit. And in his rashly injudicious pursuit of that vainglorious ambition, Symington Smythe II had thoroughly bankrupted himself. In the process, he had denied his son any inheritance at all save for his name, to which he could append a lofty "III," if he so wished.

He did not wish. The appellation was, in his consideration, a bit too grand for a young man whose menial skills so far surpassed his means. Symington Smythe alone was cumbersome enough for a man with an uncertain future. He could, in all likelihood, secure an apprenticeship with some smith or farrier in London, for he had some good experience of those crafts, thanks to his uncle, who had taught him well. Thomas Smythe had not, by virtue of his later birth, inherited any part of the family estate, save for what his brother chose to settle on him. However, if he bore any resentment for his older brother's preferment, then he had never shown it.

As loathe as his would-be aristocratic brother was to get his hands dirty, Thomas Smythe was never quite so happy as when he labored at his forge. He loved working with his hands, and while he was kept busy as a smith and farrier, on occasion he would pursue his true love, which was the forging of a blade. He alone had lent support to his nephew's dream of acting, even if he had not entirely understood it. It seemed to him much too intangible and frivolous a way to make a living. Nevertheless, he had not opposed the notion.

"Your father has ruined your future in pursuit of his ambition," Uncle Tom had said, "so it would only serve him right if you lent rancor to his future in pursuit of yours. His threats to disown you have no weight now, for he has squandered his estate. He will count himself lucky to avoid the debtor's prison. He is my brother, and I will help to what extent I can, even if he is a thoroughgoing ass. But as for you, if what you truly want to do is act, lad, why then go and be an actor. Odds blood, life is short enough. Go live it as you like it."

It seemed like sound advice, so Smythe had taken it. And it was all that he had taken, for he'd left home with nothing more than the clothing on his back, a wooden staff, and a plain-handled, serviceable, if unpolished bodkin that his Uncle Tom had made and given to him as a present on his fifteenth birthday. The thieves who had accosted him had not even deemed the sturdy blade worth stealing. But though there were prettier daggers, to be sure, there were none so strong or sharp. And it was the only thing Smythe had that truly meant anything to him. He would have defended that ugly dagger to the death.

His mother had died shortly after he was born, so he had

never known her, and though he had spent his childhood years in the same house with his father and his stepmother, he had never truly known them, either. He had known his wet nurse, Nan, much better. While still a boy, he had been sent to his Uncle Tom's to be raised and educated and taught the value of hard work while his father chased his lofty dreams. But he felt that it was not as if his father and stepmother were alone or even necessarily at fault for being so distant. Smythe knew that it was not unusual for children to be sent away to live with other families. Children often did not survive and convention held that if parents became overly attached, then the grief over a dead child would be too difficult to bear. In his case, there had been no siblings, either alive or dead, because his father's second marriage had not been blessed with offspring. He would have been the heir, therefore, had his father left him something to inherit. Now there was nothing to hold him to the life he'd lived before, nothing to stop him from seeking the life that he so earnestly desired. The question was, how to make the transition from the one life to the other?

He was not even sure how one went about trying to join an acting company. Was there a waiting list for openings? He imagined there probably had to be, for he knew that most companies had only a few regular players who were shareholders and the rest were hired men who might be taken on for no more than one production, or even one performance. There would likely be apprentices that the senior actors would take into their homes and train in stagecraft, just as was done with apprentices in every craft and guild, but these would be young boys who would play the female roles in the productions until their voices changed or until they grew too big. And he was already too old for such consideration, to say nothing of his being much too large of frame to play a woman, and too deep of voice.

So what if there were no openings, he wondered as he proceeded on his way. What then? It was not as if there were an unlimited number of opportunities. There were only a few acting companies in London. Much like his father, the London city council did not look very favorably upon actors. The Act for the Punishment of Vagabonds, passed in 1572, stipulated that all fencers, bear-wards, common players in interludes, and minstrels not belonging to any baron of the realm or other honorable personage of greater degree would be taken, adjudged, and deemed rogues, vagabonds, and sturdy beggars. And the punishments were harsh.

A man so charged and then found guilty would be whipped and then burned through the ear with a hot poker. This was done in order to discourage gypsies and others of their ilk from wandering the countryside and making their living dishonestly at the expense of others, or cozenage, as it was known. And such idlers and masterless men were not tolerated within the London city limits, where they could at best make a nuisance of themselves or, at worst, instigate a riot that could cause damage to property and loss of life.

What the law meant for actors was that they had to be members of a company that had a noble for a patron, so they would then be "in service" to that lord, rather than masterless men. Thus, Lord Strange had his own company of players who bore his name, and then there were the Admiral's Men, under the patronage of Lord Howard of Effingham, as well as Lord Worcester's Men, and the Queen's Players, under Her Majesty's Master of the Revels. But there were not many more established companies than that and taking up with some itinerant band that merely claimed a noble's patronage was only courting trouble.

Performances still took place in the courtyards of inns in the city and the surrounding countryside, with the audience of groundlings gathered around a stage erected in the courtyard and the wealthier people who had rooms at the inn watching the productions from the galleries. However, in 1576, a former carpenter named Burbage had built a playhouse where the old Holywell Priory had been in Shoreditch and the Theatre, as he called it, became the first permanent building for the purposes of staging plays. With the patronage of the Earl of Leicester, Burbage had secured a royal warrant, granting him permission to perform comedies, tragedies, interludes, and stage plays, subject to the approval of the Master of the Revels. And in the decade since, the Theatre had become famous throughout England.

Ever since he had seen his first play, acted in the courtyard of the local inn, Smythe had obsessively collected every bit of news and information he could glean from travelers and peddlers about the players and their world. He knew, or at least he could imagine, what the Theatre looked like in its arrangement, how James Burbage had departed from the inn-yard layout by designing a building that was circular instead, similar to the rings where bear- and bull-baitings were staged. And while performances continued to be held at some of the larger inns in London, such as the White Hart and the Bell-Savage, this new arena for the production of the drama had spawned similar buildings, such as The Curtin and, most recently, the new Rose Theatre, which had been built by a man named Henslowe in Bankside, just west of London Bridge, primarily as a home for the Lord Admiral's Men. And it was this distinguished company, Smythe knew, that boasted the greatest actor of them all, the legendary Edward Alleyn.

He had never seen Alleyn perform, but he had heard the name often enough. One could not talk of players without hearing Alleyn's name invoked. Only some twenty years of age, scarcely two years older than himself, and already he boasted such renown. Smythe imagined what it must be like to achieve fame. Symington Smythe, the actor? Ah, yes, of course, we saw him in that new play by Greene. He could not walk out on stage without all eyes being riveted upon him! Such intensity! Such fervor! *Such horsedroppings*, Smythe thought, shaking himself out of his reverie. Daydreaming would certainly not get him there.

*   *   *

True to the brigand's word, there was an inn at the next cross-roads, only a few miles from the spot where Smythe encountered him. And there was not much more there than that. It was just a crossroads marked by a small, two-storied building that was the inn, a barn and stables to the side, and several small cottages clustered around a sign that showed the way to London.

He would probably reach the city by tomorrow night if he made good time and started out bright and early in the morning, well rested after a hearty meal and a good night's sleep in a warm straw bed. The thought filled him with eager anticipation. Strange that he would owe it all to a man who'd meant to rob him! Perhaps it was a good omen, Smythe thought, a potentially bad situation resolved to his advantage. It would be nice to think it was a harbinger of better things to come.

The Hawk and Mouse was an unpretentious roadside inn with a large green-painted sign over the front door that showed a hungry raptor stooping over a panic-stricken rodent. An ironic sight, thought Smythe, to greet the weary traveler, especially with conditions on the road being as precarious as they were. No one paid him any mind as he walked up to the front door, but as he was about to enter, the sound of rapid hoofbeats coming up behind him made him turn back to face the darkening road.

A horseman galloped up to the front door and, immediately, several servants came running out to meet him. One held his horse—a well-lathered, dark bay barb, Smythe noticed—and after the rider had dismounted, the servant proceeded to walk the hard-ridden animal around to cool it before he would lead it to the stable for a rub and feed. The other servant followed, or at least tried to keep pace with the rider as the man swept up the steps past Smythe without giving him a glance, flung open the door, and stepped inside. Smythe entered behind them.

"Call out your servants!" the flushed rider demanded loudly, as the innkeeper approached. "Tell them to arm themselves and mount pursuit! We have been robbed!"

"Robbed, did you say?"

"Aye, robbed! By a mounted brigand dressed in black from head to foot, the ill-omened knave! The coach with my master follows hard upon. If you send your men out now, you might still manage to catch the god-cursed ruffian!"

It seemed, thought Smythe, that Black Billy had made back his silver crown and then some.

"I have no men to send chasing after outlaws," the innkeeper replied.

"What? Preposterous! What about your servants?"

"They are needed here," the innkeeper insisted, maintaining his calm in the face of the other's agitation. "This is not one of your larger inns, sir, and I have but a small staff of servants and a few post horses to serve my guests. I have no men that I can spare to go gallivanting off into the night on a wild goose chase. Leastwise after the likes of Black Billy, unless I miss my guess. He'll be long gone by now, and if he wasn't, I would not envy the man who found him. And what men I do have must remain here to look after my guests."

The already red-faced man turned positively crimson. "This is an outrage! Someone will surely be held responsible for this!"

"As an innkeeper, sir, I am held responsible solely for losses that travelers may sustain while they remain as guests under my roof. That, sir, is the law, and the full extent of the law. Whatever happens while they are *not* beneath my roof is quite out of my control; thus, I cannot be held responsible."

Before the angry rider could reply, there came the sounds of a coach pulling up outside and the servants at once ran out to greet it. The man looked toward the door, his lips compressed into a tight grimace, then apparently decided not to pursue the argument. "Well . . . we shall need four of your best rooms for the night," he said, curtly.

"Very well, sir. And how, if I might ask, sir, shall you be paying for them?"

"What the devil do you mean, how shall we be paying for them?"

"Well, sir, you did say you had been robbed."

The man turned beet red and his eyes bulged with outrage. "Why, you impertinent, cheeky bastard! I ought to thrash you!"

The red-faced man pulled out his riding quirt and looked quite prepared to make good on his threat, but the innkeeper countered by reaching down to his boot and pulling out a dagger. At the same time, he called out, "*Duff*!" and a man the size of an oak tree appeared in the doorway behind him. The bearded giant wore an apron, but he did not look terribly domestic, Smythe thought.

"Trouble, Master Martin?" the giant said, in a voice that sounded like the crack of doom.

"No trouble," said a new voice, and Smythe turned to see a group of men who had just come through the door. There were three of them, two apparently servants, for they were not as well-dressed and were carrying bags. The man in front wore a brown velvet hat with a large red plume and a floppy brim, which he removed as he came toward them with a steady, purposeful stride, his long cloak hanging open and fanning out behind him slightly. A gentleman, by his look and his demeanor, Smythe thought. Elegant hose and boots and a dark brown damask doublet of a shade to match his dark brown hair, worked with gold and silver that looked rather too frail and expensive for traveling. "Put away your pigsticker, innkeeper," he said, "and call off your colossus. There will be no bloodletting here tonight."

"Your man here threatened to thrash me," the innkeeper replied, truculently. But the commanding demeanor of the new arrival had its effect. He put away the knife, albeit reluctantly.

"Did you do that, Andrew?" the gentleman inquired casually, as he removed his lace-trimmed and gauntleted calfskin gloves.

"The scoundrel is impertinent, milord. He presumes to question our ability to pay." At the mention of the word "milord," the innkeeper instantly assumed a more respectful posture.

"Did you inform him that we were robbed back there on the road?"

"Indeed, I did, milord, and the wretch refused to send men in pursuit of that damned brigand."

"Doubtless because he had nothing to gain by it. And if you told him we were robbed, then it seems entirely understandable that he might assume we lack the means to pay for our accommodations. You can scarce blame the man for reaching that conclusion."

"His manner was offensive."

"Well, if you went around thrashing everyone who offended you, Andrew, you would be bloody well exhausted all the time. Now put away your quirt, there's a good lad, and go see to our belongings, or what remains of them." He turned to the innkeeper. "As it happens, the highwayman did not make off with *all* our money, though he did manage an uncomfortably good take for his trouble. We are quite able to pay, thanks to some judicious foresight, and in good English gold, at that. As soon as Andrew sees to your servants bringing in the remainder of our baggage and mine making proper disposition, we shall then be able to secure our accommodations for the night. I trust that will be acceptable?"

"Oh aye, of course, certainly, milord," the innkeeper replied, all sudden subservience. "Four of our best rooms, as your man said. It will be done. They shall be prepared for you at once." He clapped his hands and another servant appeared. The innkeeper barked orders and the gentleman was led upstairs, with Andrew and the rest of his retinue following.

Smythe cleared his throat. "If 'twould not be too much trouble, innkeeper, I would like a room as well. And an ordinary for my supper."

"I have no rooms left," the innkeeper replied.

Taken aback, Smythe assumed that it was his appearance that

made the man balk at giving him accommodation, so he held up the coin the brigand gave him. "But I can pay," he said.

"It matters not. I have no rooms left to give you. That gentleman took the last. We are now full up. I can let you make a bed of some clean straw in the barn and I shall let you sleep there without charge if you pay for your supper. That is the best that I can do."

Smythe sighed. "Well, I shall take your offer, then. A bed in the barn is better than no bed at all."

"Perhaps I can make you a slightly better offer," said a stranger, sitting at one of the nearby tables. Smythe turned to face him. "As it happens," the stranger continued, "I already have a room, having arrived earlier tonight. But I am also somewhat short of funds. If you are not too proud to share a bed, then mayhap we could split the expense of our accommodation and both benefit."

Smythe looked the stranger over carefully. He was not richly dressed, so the claim of being short of funds did not seem hard to credit. He wore a short, dark cloak over a plain russet cloth doublet with a falling collar and simple, inexpensive pewter buttons, loose, country galligaskins, and sensible, sturdy, side strap shoes. Good kidskin gloves, almost new, well made. He wore no gold or silver rings, no enameled chains, no bracelets; his one affectation was a golden earring worn in the left ear. His hair was a dark brown, with a wispy, slightly pointed beard and mournful eyes to match, eyes that bespoke intelligence, alertness, and a touch of sadness, but not—to Smythe's perception, anyway—corruption. There was a softness about the face that suggested femininity, but did not proclaim it. The forehead was high, like his Uncle Tom's, a prophecy, some said, of wisdom, but more often merely a harbinger of baldness coming early. He looked between twenty-two and twenty-five years old, too old for a roaring boy, too young for a settled ancient, and yet, somehow, there was an unsettled ancientness about him.

The stranger flushed at Smythe's coldly appraising gaze. "It was, I should perhaps make plain, merely my room and bed that I proposed to share . . . and nothing more. My frugality, born of necessity in this event, led me to speak perhaps too boldly. Forgive me, I did not mean to presume."

"No, 'twas not taken as presumption," Smythe replied. He approached the stranger and perceived he had been drinking. "You have an honest face. And I, too, am short of funds and would benefit from a sharing of expense." He held out his hand. "My name is Smythe. Symington Smythe."

The stranger stood only a bit unsteadily and took his hand. "Will Shakespeare, at your service."

Over a hearty ordinary of meat stew, bread, and ale, they began to know each other. Smythe told his story, without any elaborations or embellishments, not making much of it, and when he reached the part about his traveling to London in hopes of joining a company of players, his companion smiled and his dark eyes sparkled with amusement.

"You think it is a foolish notion," Smythe said, in anticipation of some moralizing lecture.

"Nothing of the sort," Shakespeare replied, with a grin. He tapped his temple with his index finger. "That is my plan, exactly."

"You jest."

"Not at all. Save that it is not acting that is my main ambition, so much as the writing of the plays. I fancy myself something of a decent hand with verses. It is a small conceit of mine, but I do love to write. But acting, writing, prompting, helping with the props and scenery, helping mend the costumes, I would perform whatever tasks were asked of me to get on and make a start."

"That is my intent, as well," said Smythe. "Though I must admit," he added, uncertainly, "I did not think that writing might be asked of me."

"You cannot write?"

"Oh, I can read and write," said Smythe. "I was given my first hornbook early and my uncle saw to it that I attended grammar school and had some Latin. But I am no hand at all with verses. I could no more write a song nor concoct a story for a play than I could fly. I had never even thought that such would be expected of me."

"Nor shall it be," his new friend assured him. "Never fear, most men in a company of players are not poets. Each player may, from time to time, contribute a line or two or an idea, perhaps even a speech, but no one expects every man to write. The Benchers and the Masters of the Arts residing at the Inns of Court have written, in their spare time, many of the plays they act today. Indeed, many plays were first performed there by the young barristers for the better class of people."

"That is much as I would have assumed," said Smythe, "that one would have to be a learned scholar in order to write a play. It would seem quite an undertaking."

"Aye, well, that is what all the academic gentlemen would have you think," said Shakespeare, with a grimace. "But herein lies the truth of it: No amount of academic training can bestow the gift of words, my friend. It can add to one's vocabulary, as indeed can a sojourn among Bristol whores and seamen, but it cannot teach the skill of putting words together in novel and surprising patterns which reflect some previously unguessed truth of life. A proper scholar from the Inns of Court might pepper his dramatic stew with references to the Greek classics or to Holinshed, but all the learning in the world will bring him no true insight into the soul of man."

He set his tankard down upon the table a bit more solidly than necessary and then belched. "Bollocks. We need more ale. And you have scarce touched yours."

"I have no head for it, nor stomach," Smythe replied.

"You know, they say you cannot trust a man who will not drink."

"Well, I think I would hesitate to trust one who drinks too much."

"Aye, well, there's the rub," said Shakespeare, as he signaled for another pot of ale with a raising of his tankard. "*In vino veritas* . . . and so truth served, in his cups, did he like Caesar *vidi, vici, veni* and then hoisted on his own petard into the bloody state of matrimony . . ."

Smythe frowned. "I have but a little Latin learning, Will." What was he babbling? Something about truth in wine and Caesar? What was it? "I saw, I conquered, I came?" That did not sound quite right. It seemed that his new friend had not the head for drinking, either, and yet he drank to rapid stupefaction, as if all in a rush to get there. He found it difficult to follow the man's cant.

" 'Tis nevermind to thee, Symington, old sport." A frown. He had rather badly slurred the name. "We shall need another name with which to call you, Smythe, old sod, one that trips more off the tongue than trips it up. What shall it be, then? Faith, an' you barely touch your ale, an' I am on my fourth pot, or is't my fifth or sixth? Yet you inhale your food as if Hephaestus himself did hammer in your belly, tucking into it like some ravening beast withal . . . *Ha!* There we have it! *Tuck!* You shall be Tuck!" He raised his tankard. "A toast to you, my new friend Tuck! Tuck Smythe, my friend and fellow player!"

"Tuck?" said Smythe. He considered briefly, then he shrugged. "Why not?" It was, to be sure, a lot less cumbersome and high-flown than Symington, and he had always despised having his Christian name shortened to some horrid and cloying familiarity as Symie or Simmie, as they used to do back home. Symington he was christened, and Symington his name would stay, but Tuck his friends would call him. Tuck Smythe. It even sounded like a player's name. Ned Alleyn and Tuck Smythe. "Why not, indeed?" he said.

"Well, Tuck, my new old friend, I fear I am inebriated."

"Come on, then, poet," he said, rising and reaching out to help Shakespeare to his feet. "Let us go and find our room, before we have to lay you out right here, beneath the table."

"Ah, I have laid beneath the table once or twice before. And lustily upon it, too."

Smythe wrapped Shakespeare's arm around his shoulders to support his weight as he staggered toward the stairs, dragging his feet. "Oh, bloody hell," said Smythe, "hang on. 'Twill be much easier to carry you."

"Nay, I am too heavy . . ."

Smythe hoisted him up onto his shoulder effortlessly.

"Zounds! You are strong as an ox!"

"And you are drunk as a lord," said Smythe, with a grin as he climbed up the stairs.

" 'Tis my only lordly ambition."

"Well, before you swoon, milord, be so kind as to inform me which room is yours."

"Second door from the top of the stairs."

"Second door it is."

"Or perhaps 'twas the third."

"Well, which is it?"

"Second. Aye, second door."

Smythe came to the second door and opened it. However, the room was already occupied. The gentleman who had arrived in the coach earlier that night stood bare-headed and without his cloak in the center of the room and opposite him stood a dark-haired woman Smythe had not seen before. They both turned, startled, at the intrusion, and Smythe caught only a brief glance of them before the servant, Andrew, stepped in front of him, scowling, and slammed the door in his face.

"I think you meant the third door," Smythe said.

"Third. Aye, third door," slurred the dead weight on his shoulder.

Smythe sighed and shook his head. He found the right room,

entered, and deposited his burden on the bed. The poet rolled over onto his back and promptly started snoring.

"Wonderful," said Smythe, with a grimace. He sighed. "I start out on my new life and my first bedmate is a drunken poet. But I suppose it does beat sleeping with the horses in the barn." Though perhaps, he thought, not by very much.

2

HEY GOT AN EARLY START the next day, leaving the inn as the first grayness of the dawn began to lighten the sky. Having paid for their lodging and victuals the previous evening, they had no accounts left to settle, so they simply packed what few possessions they had (which in Smythe's case amounted to nothing more than the clothes upon his back, his staff, and the dagger on his belt, and in Shakespeare's, merely the contents of a small leather satchel) and set off to resume their journey before most of the other travelers were awake.

The road ahead of them was quiet and deserted, and they proceeded without incident, for which Smythe was rather grateful. He observed that the road had grown somewhat wider since they had left the inn, and was clearly more traveled and in better condition, which was a sure sign that they were approaching London. It made him feel excited to know that they would reach the city soon. A new life beckoned.

As they ambled down the road, with the early morning mist undulating lazy tendrils at their feet, they compared their knowledge about the different companies of players and which might be the best one for them to join. They were both in agreement about the Queen's Players, also known as the Queen's Men. They had each seen that company perform, and Shakespeare had some contact with the players when they had visited Stratford-upon-Avon while on tour, as they did every season.

"The Queen's Men are, without a doubt, a most estimable company of players," the poet said, apparently none the worse for wear from the previous night's tippling. "And as they were assembled on the orders of Her Majesty, membership in their company would, of course, provide the opportunity to display one's talents in performances at court, and there can be no more prestigious audience."

"I saw Dick Tarleton and Will Kemp perform with the Queen's Players while they were on tour," said Smythe. " 'Twas then that I decided to become a player myself. And I thought from the first that was the very company that I would wish to join."

Shakespeare smiled. "Well, I felt much the same when they played the Stratford Guildhall. In truth, I was of a mind to leave with them right then and there, and though they did not seem unwilling to take me on as a hired man till I could prove my worth to them, circumstances for my leaving were not favorable at the time. And perhaps 'twas just as well. One should never make such decisions without proper planning and consideration. Choices made on impulse often have unfortunate results. As for Dick Tarleton, he is an amiable clown, if you like that sort of thing. He is famous for his drollery, but Kemp isn't half the man that Tarleton is. He can never seem to remember his lines, probably because he does not bother overmuch to learn them in the first place. From what I've seen, he fills in what he forgets with extempore or some silly piece of clowning. Some of your more dull-witted groundlings may like that sort of thing, but it is not my meat. I have never cared much for pratfalls and silly prancing and whatall myself. I believe that audiences respond much better to a *story*, not clowning, jigs, pratfalls and posturing, and silly prancing. And while it is true that a play is a thing to which the entire company usually contributes, a poet labors much too hard over his words to have some clownish player disregard them altogether."

"You do not like Kemp?" asked Smythe, with some surprise, recalling that he had quite enjoyed Will Kemp's performance, pratfalls and all. "Is it merely because he cannot measure up to Tarleton or is it something more personal?"

"Oh, I have no personal quarrel with him, if that is what you mean, although I think he is an ass," said Shakespeare. "Tarleton is no longer young, and his energies are clearly waning. You can see the difference from one performance to another. And as his successor, Kemp is clearly champing at the bit. He thinks rather well of himself, and is not hesitant to inform anyone within earshot just how well of himself he thinks. Yet if Tarleton should retire from the stage, I fear the Queen's Men would lose much of their luster, despite their bombast to the contrary, much of which, I fear, has been inspired by Kemp himself."

"Bombast?" Smythe said. "What do you mean?"

"Oh, why, they are the best actors in the world, you know." Shakespeare's voice took on a mocking, portentous tone. "For tragedy, comedy, history, pastoral, pastoral-comical, historical-pastoral, tragical-historical, tragical-comical-historical-pastoral, scene individable, or poem unlimited, *these* are the only men! Or at least," he added, pulling out a piece of paper and unfolding it, "so they themselves inform us, by virtue of this bill they post."

He passed the playbill to Smythe. "Tragedy, comedy, history, pastoral, pastoral-comical . . ." read Smythe, aloud. He raised his eyebrows. "They seem to have counted all the points of the dramatic compass."

"Save for bawdry and pederasty, and those points they doubtless count offstage. However, Tuck, old bean, we shall forgive them their trespasses if they forgive ours and enlist us among them."

Smythe glanced at him and shook his head, not certain whether he was more astonished or amused. "That remark verges either on blasphemy or slander, I am not sure which."

"Blasphemous slander, then. Or slanderous blasphemy. Or slanderous-blasphemous-tragical-comical-what-have-you. Either way, those are more the province of Christopher Marlowe than myself. I prefer to remain somewhat less controversial and contentious. 'Twill be easier to avoid prison that way. Damn me, I need a drink. Hold up a moment." He stopped in the middle of the road, leaning on his staff, and pulled out a small wineskin from underneath his cloak. He squeezed a stream into his mouth and didn't miss a drop.

"I should have thought you would have had enough last night," said Smythe, shaking his head at the thought of drinking wine so early in the day. The birds were barely even up.

"There is no such thing as 'enough,' my friend. Life is thirst and hunger, and then you die. So drink your fill while you yet live."

"That reminds me somewhat of what my Uncle Tom said. 'Life is short, so live it as you like it.' 'Twas his parting advice to me."

"Indeed," said the poet, nodding. "Your uncle is a wise man. Live life . . . as you like it. I must remember that. 'Tis pithy."

"Do you never feel the morning aftermath of drink, Will?"

"What? No, never. Well . . . Hardly ever. Hair 'o the dog, y'know. And experience. A veritable cornucopia of experience." He squeezed another stream of wine into his mouth.

"*Veritas in vino?*"

"Oh, dear me. Not again. Was I spouting poor man's Latin in my cups again last night?"

"A bit. I caught a little of it, but then I am no scholar."

"Tell me, for my memory of recent events seems somewhat hazy for some peculiar reason . . . last night, was I angry drunk or maudlin drunk?"

Smythe considered for a moment. "Somewhere in between, I'd say, with a little touch of each."

They started walking once again, keeping an easy pace. "Well, 'tis all right, I suppose," the poet said, with resignation. "I simply cannot stand it when I become unutterably maudlin. That is to say, I cannot stand hearing about it later. Howsoever, unlike my sweet Anne, at least you have the grace not to throw it up at me when I am sober."

"Belike you're the one who does the throwing up," said Smythe, grinning.

"Odds' blood, I did no such thing! A man who throws up his drink is naught but a profligate wastrel. If you are likely to throw it up, then at least have the good grace not to throw it down. Save it for a man who can hold onto it."

"Anne is your wife then?"

"Were we speaking of my wife?"

"You were, I think, just now."

"Ah. Careless of me. Remind me not to do it again."

"I shall make note of that. You do not love your wife?"

"Well . . . ." The poet grimaced, wryly. "I love her well enough to tup her, I suppose. A dangerous bit of business, that. She is as fertile as a bloody alluvial plain. She swells with child merely at a sidelong glance."

"It seems to me that you would have to do some swelling of your own to aid in that," said Smythe, with a chuckle.

"You swine! You *dare* banter with me?" Shakespeare smiled, rising to the bait. The poet in him, Smythe saw with amusement, could not resist the challenge. "Aye, young Tuck, you prick me to the quick! And I, alas, have pricked too quickly. But 'tis hard to refrain from hardness at such a tempting pair of bosoms and such well rounded buttocks." He grinned. "Damn me, but her arse is a wondrous piece of work. And thus have I worked my piece. Thrice have we increased the population of the realm and so I have fled Stratford before we further swelled the ranks of the Queen's subjects and placed a further burden on the land's resources."

Smythe was taken aback. "You have not *abandoned* her, surely? With children?"

"Nay, I would not do so mean a thing." The poet shook his head. "That is to say, I have left her back in Stratford with the children, aye, that is true, but I have not abandoned her. Even though the marriage was not of my own choosing, 'twas surely of my own making. Had I but held my piece, so to speak, instead of being too quick to dip my quill in her all-too-willing and inviting inkwell, I would have written a different scene entirely and married better and more wisely. And for love, unfashionable as that may seem. But for want of better timing, 'twas another Anne I would have married."

"You loved another, also by the name of Anne?"

"Aye. For while a rose may be a rose, and while by another other name it may still smell as sweet, it is only once the bloom is off the rose, my friend, that you discover what is truly at the root. The Anne I loved was young and innocent; the Anne I got was older, more experienced and much craftier. And relentless, untamed shrew though she may be, she is nevertheless *my* shrew and the mother of my children, who could have done better, certainly, than to have a besotted, weak-willed poet for a father, though perhaps they could not have done much worse."

"So then you loved a younger woman whom you wanted to keep chaste for marriage, and thus your unquenched ardor made you succumb to an older woman who seduced you," said Smythe. "And you got her with child, which forced the marriage, is that it?"

"Aye, but somehow, it sounds much worse the way you put it," said the poet, frowning.

"Well, 'twas the way you put it that got you into trouble in the first place," Smythe replied, with a grin.

Shakespeare grimaced. "If you were not so large, my friend, I would give you sound drubbing for that remark." He chuckled.

"But prudence and my desire for survival dictate that I hold my temper."

"Forgive me, I do not mean to make fun at your expense," said Smythe, sympathetically.

"Yes, you do, confound you, but you do it well, so I forgive you. In any event, to resume my narrative, I knew that I could not, on a mere glover's takings, make any sort of decent life for us in Stratford. I recall only too well how my father worked his fingers to the bone, cutting tranks and sewing stitches, and doing what else he could withal, but there never was enough. That is to say, we neither starved, nor did we prosper. We survived, after a fashion. He rose as high as alderman for his ambition, did old John Shakespeare, and then he fell from grace when his debts exceeded his ability to pay. I had hoped for rather more than that. Times are hard and people have less money now. And making gloves did not, by any means, ignite my fire."

"So you decided to forego the glover's trade and make your way to London to seek your fortune as a player?"

"As a poet, actually. At any rate, that would be my preference. Mind you, I shall take work as a player, if I can get it, for one must eat, after all, and working as player will allow me also to write plays. And writing plays and selling them will bring more profit, if the audiences come and I make a reputation for myself and become a shareholder of the company. And then, if I am fortunate enough to find a noble patron, that too can bring increase."

"How so?"

"How? Why, through poetry, of course. Poetry that extols the virtues of your noble patron, or a nobleman that you hope to have as patron. You make a dedication—it is considered proper to ask permission, of course, usually through some friendly intermediary—and then you find some scrivener to make fair copies for them for distribution to their friends, or else have it bound and printed, if 'tis a longer work, although it seems that short Italian sonnets are all the rage among the fashionable nobility these days."

"And for this they give you money?"

"Aye, if the work should please them. Which is to say, if it proves popular and reflects upon them favorably. Many of your honorable Masters of the Arts, such as Marlowe, whom I mentioned, receive small stipends for their laudatory scribblings about Lord This or Earl That or Duke The Other. It is a common enough practice."

"But . . . why?" asked Smythe, puzzled. "Why would anyone pay money merely for being complimented in verse form?"

"They contend with poets nowadays as they once used to contend with arms in tournaments. Mine turns a sweeter rhyme than yours and what not. 'Tis not, perhaps, such manly sport, but 'tis considerably safer. Besides, what do you mean, 'merely' complimented in verse form, you great lout? Can *you* write a poem?"

"No. Well, that is to say, I have never tried writing any verses." He shrugged. "But then, it does not seem so very difficult."

"Oh, you think so, do you? Right, then. Give me a rhyme for 'orange.' "

"Orange? Very well." Smythe thought a moment. "Let me see . . . Orange . . . orange . . ."

"Well? Come on."

"Hold on, I'm thinking." Smythe frowned, concentrating. "Orange . . ."

"Mmmmm?" The poet raised his eyebrows. "Well? I am still waiting."

"I . . . uh . . . that is . . . uh . . ."

"Ummm?"

"Hmpf! I cannot seem to think of one."

"Indeed? I thought you said it was not so very difficult?"

"Bah! It is a trick. I'll warrant there *is* no rhyme for orange."

"Are you quite sure?"

"Well, you come up with one, then!"

"Door hinge."

"Door hinge?"

"Orange, door hinge . . . it rhymes."

"And you call yourself a poet? What sort of rhyme is that?"

"A perfectly serviceable one."

"Indeed? I would like to see what sort of poem you'd write with that!"

"Well, you merely asked me for a rhyme, not an entire poem."

" 'Twas *you* who asked me for the rhyme! Knowing all the while a better one could not be found. Is that what poets do, then, sit up all night drinking and thinking of such things?"

Shakespeare nodded. "More or less, aye."

"And they *pay* you for this?"

"Not nearly well enough, if you ask me."

The sound of rapid hoofbeats from behind them caused them both to turn in time to see a coach come barreling around the bend, bearing straight for them. The driver made absolutely no effort to rein in and there was no place for him to turn, not that he showed the slightest inclination for so doing. It was only by diving off to the side of the road, into the thorny brush, that they avoided being run down.

"Aaaaaahhhh! You pox-ridden, misbegotten son of a sheep tupper!" Shakespeare cried out.

Smythe winced as he extricated himself from the thorn bushes and then helped the poet out.

"God's bollocks! I'll be picking thorns out of my arse for the next two weeks!"

"Oh, stop it, you will not," said Smythe. "A few scratches, a thorny splinter here and there . . . you will survive."

"No thanks to that miserable cur! What in God's name was he thinking, careering down the road at such a pace? The fool will shake that fancy coach of his to pieces!"

"That was our friend from the inn last night, unless I miss my guess," said Smythe. "The one who took the last few rooms."

"What, the grand, well-spoken gentleman with his retinue of servants?" Shakespeare asked.

"The same, I think. He rose much later than we did, but makes much better time. He seems in quite a hurry."

"Well, I hope he puts that shiny new coach of his into a ditch and breaks his gentlemanly neck, the blackguard!"

"If he keeps up like that, he might well do that," said Smythe. "Although the road here is much wider and more level, he still goes at an unsafe pace."

"*Blast!* Look at this! I am pricked with stickers like a pincushion!"

"Here, let me see."

"Have a care now . . . *ouch!*"

"Oh, come on, now. I'll not pull these out if you go squirming like a wench upon a haystack. Screw your courage to the sticking place and stop your twitching."

" 'Tis the infernal stickers that are screwed in, not my courage."

"Will you hold still?"

"Aaah-owww!"

"Such bravery! Such mettle!" Smythe laughed. "Look at you. A thorn or two and you are all undone."

"Oh, sod off! *Yowwwww!* Have a care, Tuck, curse you!"

"Oh, don't be such a mewling infant. It is not so bad. Only a few more."

"*Ouch! Ow!* Damn it! I shall take *my* turn next and then we shall see who is more the mewling infant!"

"I'll not cry over a few thorns. But I *shall* remember that gentleman from last night. That's twice now he's inconvenienced me."

"Oh, indeed? And just what do you intend to do about it, your lordship? The man is not someone you can address on equal standing, you know. Or did you fail to note the arms blazoned on the side of his coach?"

"No. Why? Did you recognize them?"

"Nay, I caught but a glimpse of sable and some fleury crosses. I would not know those arms from any other scutcheon save that they mark him for a gentleman of rank. Not exactly someone you can give one of your country thumpings to, young blacksmith."

"Perhaps not, but I will remember that gentleman just the same."

The poet snorted. "You would do better to remember your place, my friend, if you do not wish to get clapped into the Marshalsea."

Smythe was tempted to point out to the poet that he could claim an escutcheon of his own, thanks to his father's efforts, but he decided at the last moment not to bring it up. It meant nothing to him, really, and he liked Will Shakespeare and did not wish him to think that he might in any way hold himself above him. Aside from which, his father might now be a gentleman, but he was in debt up to his ears, for all the good it did him.

"Well, I suppose you're right," he said. "But it still rankles, just the same."

"So then send an oath or two his way, as I do, and have done with it. There is little to be served in dwelling upon matters that one cannot resolve. Now bend over and I'll pull your stickers for you."

"Why, Will, I bet you say that to all the sweet young boys."

"Look, you want me to pull those thorns from out your bum or put my muddy boot into it?"

Smythe laughed. "Very well. You may dethorn me, but be gentle."

"I'll give every one at least three twists for your impertinence!"

"Well, best be quick about it then, or we shall not reach London until nightfall."

"Just as well," said Shakespeare, with a scowl, "for I shall very likely be much too sore to sit down until then."

3

"BUT FATHER, I DON'T *WANT* to marry him!" Elizabeth Darcie stamped her foot in exasperation, gritting her teeth with anger and frustration. She turned away to hide the tears that suddenly welled up in her eyes.

"Want? *Want?* Good God, girl, who in blazes asked you what you *want?*" Her father stared at her with open-mouthed astonishment. "What does what you *want* have to do with anything? You shall do as you are told!"

"I shall *not!*" In her exasperation, Elizabeth spoke before she thought and she caught her breath as soon as the words were out. She had never spoken back to her father in such a manner before, and was shocked at her own boldness.

Her father was no less astonished. "You bloody well shall, girl, or I shall take my crop to you, so help me!"

"But Father, please! I do not *love* him! I do not even *know* him!"

"*Love?* Who the devil spoke of love? We were speaking of *marriage!*" He turned with indignation to his wife. "This is what comes of your silly notions about education! 'She ought to *read,*' you said. 'She ought to know how to keep household accounts! She ought to have a tutor!' A tutor! God's wounds! That silly, mincing fop just filled her head with foolishness, if you ask me! Love poems and sonnets and romances . . . what does any of that have to do with the practical matters of life? A tutor, indeed! What a monstrous waste of money!"

"A proper lady should be well accomplished, Henry . . ." Edwina Darcie began tentatively, but her husband was in no mood to listen and simply went on as if she hadn't spoken.

"Music, yes, I can see music, I suppose," Darcie went on, working himself up into a fine state of pontifical righteousness. "A woman ought to know how to play upon the lute or the harp or the virginals, so that she can properly entertain her husband and his guests. And embroidery, aye, that is a useful craft, and dancing, I suppose, has much to recommend it as a skill, but . . . *reading*? 'Tis a thing for idlers. The only reading that is useful and fitting for anyone is the *Book of Common Prayer*. What value is to be found in your foreign Greeks and Romans, your windbag philosophers, or your absurd ballads and your penny broadsheets for the lower classes to while away their time with instead of doing something more productive? What waste! What utter nonsense! You see the sort of thing that comes of it! I tell you, giving an education to a woman makes about as much sense as giving an education to a horse!"

"The queen is a woman," Elizabeth said, hesitantly, invoking her royal namesake as the color came rising to her cheeks. She knew that she was being impertinent past all bearing, but she could not help herself. "And she is well educated and speaks several tongues. *And* reads and writes in Latin, too. Would you compare *her* to a horse, Father?"

Henry Darcie's eyes grew wide with outrage. "Silence! What monumental impudence! The queen is different. She is not an ordinary woman. She is the queen. She has, by virtue of her birth and divine right, given herself in marriage to the realm and thereof she has always done her duty. As you, young woman, are going to do yours and there's the end of it! 'Tis done! The matter is settled! I shall say no more!"

He stabbed his forefinger in the air to emphasize his point, then quickly turned and left the room, effectively bringing an end to the discussion. Not that it had been much of a discussion in the first place, Elizabeth thought. He wasn't the least bit interested in what she felt or had to say.

" 'Tis not fair," she said to her mother, fighting back the tears.

" 'Tis how things are done, my dear," her mother replied, in a tone of resigned sympathy. "I, too, was betrothed to your father before I ever really knew him. But I came to love him . . . in time."

"Yes, and I see how well he loves *you*, Mother," Elizabeth said, sadly. "He does not listen to you any more than he listens to me."

"That is not so, Bess!" her mother responded defensively. "Your father listens. In his own way."

"Which is to say, only when he so chooses," Elizabeth said, bitterly. "Where is the fault in me that he should treat me so? What have I done that was so wrong? Where have I failed to please him? How have I offended? Why does he wish to punish me?"

"Bess, you must try to understand," her mother replied, patiently. "This marriage is not meant as punishment for you at all. That was never your father's intention. The arrangement was made to benefit both families, to unite the two estates so as to make both stronger. 'Tis the way these things are done. 'Twas ever so."

"And what of love, Mother? What of a woman's feelings? What of a woman's heart?" Elizabeth asked, blinking back tears. "Or is that considered of no import?"

Her mother sighed. "Bess, 'tis not only women who have their marriages arranged for them, you know. 'Tis common practice among the gentry and men of the nobility, much for the same reasons. 'Tis only the poor, lowly, working-class folk who marry for love, for all the good it does them, the poor souls. Does it improve their lot in life? Does it secure a better future for their

children? Does it allow their parents to be cared for in their do-
tage, and in turn, for them to be cared for in their own advancing
years? Nay, such things require more practical considerations, such
as estates with income, land and holdings, things in which love
plays no part at all, unless it be the sort of love a husband and a
wife grow into with the fullness of time. And such a love is a
contented, *settled* love, mature in its composition and refinement.
The sort of love of which the romantic poets write is truly a mere
thing of fancy, naught but a brief fluttering of the heart, a momentary aching in the loins, a transitory desire which, if one gives
into it, can only lead to sin and degradation. For a woman, more
often than not, it leads to a belly swollen with an unwanted, bastard child and a bleak future of utter ruin and hopeless depriva-
tion. Your father and I did not wish that for you."

Elizabeth shut her eyes tightly. She wanted to scream. Not so
much with anger as with desperation, because she saw that there
was nowhere left to turn. It was as if the walls of her own home
were closing in on her and sealing her inside a box from which
there would be no escape. She felt as if she were suffocating. She
felt a pressure in her chest that did not come from the constricting
whalebone stiffeners in her embroidered bodice or the tight, hard
stomacher that extended down below her hips, squeezing her
body into the idealized figure of the fashionable woman, the adult
clothing in which her parents had started dressing her when she
was still a child of five or six, as if to create a grown woman in
miniature, like the tiny portraits of well-known lords and ladies
sold in the artist's stalls down by St. Paul's, an advertisement for
the marketable goods she would become. See? Look, you can see
already how well this flower will bloom, how plump the fruit shall
be! But not too plump, for we must look wide only in some places
and properly narrow in the others, padded here and stiffened there
just so, according to the dictates of the latest fashions.

The so-called "lowly working-class folk" whom her mother
so disparaged and despised seemed as unrestricted in their mode

of dress as they were in their mode of marriage. And though it was their lot to curtsy or else bow and tug their forelocks when confronted with a lady or a gentleman, by contrast, at least in some respects, they seemed so much more free than she was. A common serving wench employed in some tavern would work long hours and labor hard at tasks that I would never have to do, Elizabeth thought, morosely, but at the same time, she could wear simple clothing that would not restrict her movements and would let her breathe without feeling faint on a hot and muggy summer's day. And if she fell in love with some poor cook or tavernkeeper or apprentice, why then, no one would tell her that her love had naught to do with marriage and that her deepest feelings were but a momentary fancy brought on by too much indulgence in romances, and that she should take as husband someone who had been selected for her by those who knew much better, someone whom she had never even seen.

"If my belly were to be swollen with a child, even if it *were* a bastard, then I would sooner it were put there by a man I chose to love, rather than by one who had been chosen for me," she said.

"Elizabeth! Really! You forget yourself!" Her mother stiffened and the color rose to her cheeks. "I cannot imagine where you get such outrageous notions! I can scarcely believe that tutor was responsible for putting such ideas in your head, but if he was at fault, then he should be whipped! Honestly! If you were to speak so in your father's presence, I shudder to think what he would do!"

"What would he do, then? Whip me? Disown me? Turn me out? How could that be any worse than what he already proposes to do?"

"Oh, Bess, I simply do not know what has gotten into you! This is sheer folly! You needn't act as if 'twere such an awful thing! Anthony Gresham is, by all accounts, an excellent young gentleman! He comes of a good family and there has been talk of a peerage for his father, for his service to the Crown, which would certainly assure your future and the future of your children! I simply do not know why you bridle so at such an excellent prospect. Why, most girls your age would gladly trade places with you in an instant and consider themselves fortune's darlings!"

So there it was again, Elizabeth thought, bleakly, as her mother huffed out of the room in indignation. The Parthian shot. The same old, tired refrain. Most girls *her age*. Nineteen years old and still unwed. Soon twenty and a spinster. Unwanted, a burden to her parents. A girl *her age* could not afford to put on airs or be so choosy. A girl *her age* would be fortunate to find any sort of match at all, much less one that was so eminently suitable. A girl *her age* should be grateful that anyone would have her, when she was past her prime and there were plenty of fresh, young, wellborn girls for eligible suitors to choose from. She had heard every possible variation on the theme. Just the words "your age" were enough to set her teeth on edge.

They acted as if it were her fault to begin with, and that simply wasn't so. At twelve or thirteen, she could easily have been married off to any of a dozen suitors. There had surely been no shortage. She was young and pretty and the promise of the beauty that would come with more maturity had already been quite evident. Even then, her long, flaxen blonde hair, high cheekbones, deep blue eyes, and soft, creamy, nearly translucent skin had attracted plenty of suitors. But no one had been suitable enough. Each prospective husband was found wanting in some area, and each time it had been something different, but the truth, as Elizabeth now knew, was that none of them had been of the right class.

Henry Darcie had worked hard all his life and had succeeded in becoming a very prosperous merchant. But although he had changed his fortune, the one thing he could not change was that he had been born as common as a dirt clod. Elizabeth knew that he wanted, more than anything, to be a gentleman and gain admittance to the ranks of polite society. The problem was, as things stood, his application to the Heralds' College for a coat of arms would, of necessity, be based upon the thinnest of claims, claims that were mere, transparent fiction. However, an alliance by marriage to a family of rank and long-standing position could go a long way toward ensuring more favorable consideration by the heralds and, more importantly, acceptance by the upper classes. Or at least, so her father felt.

Elizabeth, for her part, had always felt as if she were less cherished as a daughter than as an expedient means to an end and nothing more, a Judas goat staked out as bait to attract the right sort of suitor. And like a huntsman sweeping through the forest with his beaters, her father had relentlessly pursued the cultivation of an ever-widening social circle, the better to increase the odds that the right sort of husband might be flushed and driven to the bait.

From the time that she was twelve, he had regularly attended the entertainments at the Paris Garden, not so much for his enjoyment of the bear baiting itself as to widen his circle of influential acquaintances, especially among the better class of people. Despite her protests, he had brought her along on several occasions, dressed in her finest clothing, to parade her before the gentry and the aristocracy. In her largest and most elaborate linen and lace ruffs, embroidered with gold and silver and sprinkled with a dusting of little moons and stars, and her widest, stiffest farthingales with waist frills and brocade skirts, and her best and most revealing stiff-pointed, padded bodices with slashed leg-of-mutton sleeves sewn liberally with jewels, she had felt awkward and uncomfortable, as if she were some gaudy ornament put on display. Worse still, the grim and brutal sight of the savage, ravening mastiffs tearing at a maddened bear or panic-stricken ape chained down in the arena was more than she could stand. The blood and the noise and the awful smells had made her ill and her father soon stopped taking her, realizing that even the prettiest and best dressed of daughters lost a considerable degree of her appeal while she was retching on her dress.

Still, there were other avenues of social contact that were open to him, many of which did not necessitate her being present, and he had pursued them with a vengeance. He had participated in investment ventures with various projectors, often losing money, but occasionally turning a profit. However, he had measured his gains in such investments not so much in financial terms, but social ones. Shared gains were often not so useful as shared losses, when commiseration could lead, under the right circumstances, to the offer of a loan to help surmount some unexpected and, of course, temporary reverses. There was nothing quite so useful as a social superior who was inconveniently short of funds . . . and therefore more than willing to grant favors. Especially if such requests were couched in soothing, diplomatic terms.

Among the ventures that her father had invested in through several such contacts was a playhouse called The Theater, constructed by a man named Burbage. Some of the money that had been raised for the construction had come from Henry Darcie, and he had also financed several of the productions. He was not the sole investor who had been involved, and so the risk was spread out somewhat, and in this case, there seemed a better than average chance of making a profit, for the playhouse proved to be quite popular.

There was competition from the Rose Theatre, where the Admiral's Men held court, and some of the other companies who mounted their productions at the inns, and then there was the children's company at Blackfriers, which was proving to be quite a draw and had the advantage of being fashionable because it was an indoor venue. On the other hand, The Theatre could accommodate a larger audience and had, overall, higher standards of production. Here, Henry Darcie could bring his daughter to show her off before whatever members of the gentry were in attendance without fear of having her get sick and ruin the effect of the expensive clothing he had bought for her by vomiting upon them. And it was the one venue for her display to which Elizabeth did not object. Indeed, she looked forward eagerly to going.

From her seat up in the galleries, Elizabeth could look down upon the teeming groundlings in the yard, jostling one another and boisterously calling to the vendors as they waited for the play to start. The early arrivals would have already heard the first fanfare of the trumpets, and as the rest of the audience came streaming into the theatre, Elizabeth would revel in the energetic, cacophonous spectacle, allowing herself to get caught up in it so that she would forget that, as far as her father was concerned, she was on exhibit for everybody else, and not the other way around. She would gape at the ostentatious fashions that were on display up in the galleries around her as the members of the gentry attempted to outdo one another in their finery.

Men in elaborate saffron ruffs and scarlet doublets, puffed at the shoulders, slashed at the sleeves, and padded at the chest, with matching breeches and contrasting hose in hues of periwinkle, marigold, and popinjay vied for attention with gold pomander-sniffing ladies attired in elegant gowns of Venetian satin or taffeta, festooned with precious stones and shot through with gold and silver thread, or else sewn from rich, three-piled-piece Genoan velvets, with dainty leather or satin shoes that were pinked, raced, and rosetted, their hair dyed in fantastic colors and braided with pearls or tucked beneath elaborate caps with large gold and silver brooches holding flowing plumes and feathers to set off the carcanet collars of small, linked enameled plates adorned with jewels and tiny pendants, wrists languidly displayed bracelets of gold or enameled silver with beads of amber, coral, or agate, rings everywhere, on every finger of both men and women . . . it was a visual feast, a writhing tableau of endless fascination.

And then the play would begin.

From the moment that the first player stepped out onto the

stage, Elizabeth became transported to another world, one that seemed even more real than the romances that she read, for these were living, breathing people bringing to life real characters upon the stage. And if, much of the time, these characters seemed less real than stagy, she did not mind and nevertheless allowed herself to be carried away by the illusion. For as long as the play would last, her gaze would remain riveted upon the stage, and if there were other gazes riveted upon her from some other vantage point, she was unaware of them and could thus forget them.

But now, there was a new drama unfolding that she wished she could avert her gaze from, for it was *her* drama and the ending she foresaw was not a happy one. Somewhere along the way, someone had gazed at her particularly long and hard, and favorably, and unbeknownst to her, her father had been approached, discussions had been initiated, and a marriage had been arranged.

She had no idea who Anthony Gresham was. Apparently, it was not really her concern, so she hadn't been consulted. What little knowledge she had was painfully sketchy. The mysterious Anthony Gresham was young, supposedly well set up, and handsome, although she had long since realized that, to her father, any eligible young man from a socially prominent family was certain to be "well set up and handsome." His father was a privateer, one of Drake's celebrated Sea Hawks, who was in line, so it was said, to receive a knighthood. She knew next to nothing of such things, but she knew that the idea of marrying his daughter to the son of a knight would send her father off into transports of ecstasy. There was little else that he would need to know or care about.

Chances were, she thought, that she was just as much a mystery to this young Anthony Gresham as he was to her, although it was certainly possible, even probable, that he had at least seen her, perhaps during one of her visits to The Theatre with her father. Yes, she thought, that had to be how it must have happened. The socially prominent son of a knight, or knight-to-be, could certainly not be expected to marry a young woman sight unseen, regardless of her father's wealth. She, on the other hand, was expected to do her filial duty to her parents and marry someone whom she not only did not love, but had never even seen.

And if, as her mother claimed, most girls "her age" would gladly trade places with her in an instant, Elizabeth felt equally certain that she would trade places with them just as readily, even if they were of the poorest and most common stock. As she sat alone in her room, feeling miserable and lost, she entertained the notion of what it would be like to run away somewhere and find a job in some distant town or village, working in a tavern or an inn, or as a seamstress with threadworn fingers or a laundress with waterlogged skirts and wrinkled hands. Perhaps that was precisely what she should do, she thought, dramatically. Pack up a few belongings and then run away in the middle of the night. That would certainly teach them a lesson. And it would serve them right.

The only trouble was, she had no idea where to go or how to get there. And so she sat, and wept in anger and frustration.

4

ONDON WAS EVERYTHING HE HAD expected and much more. A recent census had reported the city's population as over 120,000 and it seemed to Smythe as if they were all out on the streets at once. Cobblers, drapers, merchant tailors, younkers, ironmongers, weavers, goldsmiths and ropemakers, skinners, saddlers, tanners, vintners and apothecaries, discharged soldiers, dyers, pewterers and cutlers, hosiers, stationers, haberdashers, whores and grocers, barbers, balladeers and barristers, scriveners, booksellers, pickpockets and portrait painters and cozeners of every stripe, everywhere he looked, a different walk of life was represented, often loudly, sometimes repellantly, but always interestingly.

Dominating the city was the massive, gothic Cathedral of St. Paul's, where people gathered in Paul's Walk among the open stalls and bookshops to post bills or hire servants or be regaled by lurid tales of far-off lands from seamen—some of whom might even have been sober as they passed their hats—or else receive forecasts from robed and long-bearded astrologers, who were listened to with wary fascination and respect because they were believed by many to consort with demons. Here also was Paul's Cross, where Sunday sermons could be heard preached from the outdoor pulpit on those mornings when it didn't rain and turn the cobbled streets even more dangerously slippery with muck and slime than they usually were.

With so many carriers' carts and carriages and horse litters and coaches clogging up the narrow streets and alleyways, making passage hazardous for those who rode and walked alike, the Thames was the main thoroughfare for many, with the watermen plying their way up and down the river and across in their small rowboats, ferrying those who chose not to use the crowded London Bridge, which was the only bridge across the undulating river to Bankside.

Downstream, to the east, stood the famous Tower of London, built as a palace citadel to guard the city from invasion from the sea. The Tower was an armory, as well as a prison for the most dangerous offenders, and the only place of coinage for the realm, in addition to being a treasury for the Crown Jewels and home of a menagerie that included several lions. To the west, roughly two miles from the city of London and connected to it by the Strand, was the Royal City of Westminster, which contained the Palace of Whitehall, the main residence of the queen, and the Abbey of St. Peter, where the monarchs of the realm were crowned and often buried.

In the city streets, Smythe noticed that many if not most men went armed, although a recent proclamation had reduced the allowable length of swords to no more than three feet and daggers to twelve inches. The fast, slim rapiers were more and more coming into vogue and fashionable ladies carried little bodkins tucked away somewhere discreetly. Those less concerned with fashion wore their poignards or stilettos openly, the better to defend themselves in the event of one of the frequent brawls or riots that broke out from time to time, often the result of young apprentices swaggering about in raucous gangs, needing little more excuse than youth and drunkenness, always an incendiary combination, to start a sudden, bloody street fight.

And drunkenness was less the exception than the rule. Smythe had long since learned that his habit of making an infusion of boiling water with dried clover flowers, mint, and raspberry leaves with honey, a healthful and revitalizing recipe meant to clarify the mind, taught him in his boyhood by old Mary, the village cunning woman, would be considered quite the eccentricity. Water, as everybody knew, was merely for washing up and cooking, certainly not for drinking. Ale was the universal beverage, imbibed at breakfast, dinner, supper, and all throughout the day, save by the more affluent citizens of London, who drank wine, all of which created a constant state of ferment where violence could brew and street fights could erupt at any time.

Shakespeare and Smythe stumbled into just such a street fight shortly after they had entered the city, passing through one of the large, arched gates in the encircling stone wall. For Smythe, it had felt like passing through a gate from one world into another. They were assailed by a dizzying cacophony of smells, from the market stalls selling fish, meats, produce, breads, and cheeses, to the heady, pungent odor of the horse droppings and the still fouler stench of human waste and garbage that was simply dumped into the streets, to be picked at by the crows and ravens who nested in the trees and made their meals out of whatever refuse they could find, in addition to the fleshy morsels that they tore from the severed heads stuck up on the spikes outside the law courts.

There was noise and tumult assailing them from every quarter, with the squeaking, clomping sounds of ungreased cart wheels jouncing by on cobblestones, the snorting and neighing of the horses and the jingling of their tack, the clacking of the beggars' clap-dishes, the ringing of shopkeepers' bells, and the cries of the peddlers and costermongers—"Hot oakcake! Hot oatcake! Come an' buy! Come an' buy!" "New brooms 'ere! New brooms!" "Whaddyalack-whaddyalack-whaddyalack now?" "Rock samphires! Getchyer fresh rock samphires!"

As they moved through the streets, another cry suddenly went up with great alacrity, rising over and above the din they heard around them as it was taken up by many other voices. *"Clubs! Clubs! Clubs!"*

"Clubs?" said Smythe, frowning with puzzlement.

No sooner had he spoken than they found themselves engulfed by a stampeding mob that came streaming out from around the corner like the abruptly released waters of a sluiceway, forcing them back toward the gutter that held all the filth and garbage that would ferment there like an odious, swampy brew until the next rain washed it down into Fleet Ditch.

"Street riot!" Shakespeare cried out, pulling hard at Smythe's arm in an effort to drag him back out of the way, but the crowd had already surged around them and they found themselves caught up in its momentum and carried back the way they came.

It was impossible to tell who was fighting whom or how the whole thing had started. All they knew was that they were suddenly caught up in a crush of people trying to get away from the rising and falling clubs and flashing blades that were at the heart of it. Smythe slipped and tried to keep his footing on the slimy cobblestones near the gutter running down the center of the street, where most of the noxious muck had gathered and where people, forced into it by the press of bodies all around them, were falling down into the stinking, toxic ooze and being trampled. Someone bumped into him and Smythe pushed the man away roughly, sending him sprawling as he glanced around quickly for the poet.

"Will! Will!"

"Tuck!"

He spotted him, reaching out for help, being jostled repeatedly and trying desperately to keep his footing. He had lost his staff and he looked panic-stricken. Smythe stretched out his arm and, just at that instant, the poet lost his footing, slipped, and fell.

"Got you!" Smythe said, seizing his wrist and yanking him up and back from the filthy mire at the center of the street.

"Odd's blood!" said Shakespeare, gasping for breath as

Smythe shoved their way roughly through the crowd to the nearest wall. "A man could get himself hurt around here."

"Watch out, the City Marshal's men!" somebody cried.

The sound of hoofbeats on cobblestones rose over the shouting and the clanging of steel as the marshal's men came galloping upon the scene, responding to the riot that had been moving through the streets and causing considerable damage. There was a rather large group of young men, in various styles of dress, going at it with a vengeance with both clubs and swords, though Smythe had no way of telling who was on whose side. It looked like a wild melee. The combatants, however, either did not seem to suffer from that problem, or else they were simply fighting with anyone within reach.

As Smythe pressed back against the wall with Shakespeare, he saw the mounted men come galloping around the corner, an unwise thing to do, it seemed to him, considering the uneven surface of the streets and the slick condition of the cobblestones. And sure enough, even as they watched, one of the lead horses went down, pitching its rider off as its hooves slipped on the cobbles, and the rider coming up behind it was brought down, as well. The others did not even slow down as they rode down the rioters, laying about them indiscriminately with their swords and truncheons. One young rioter's head was split open like a melon in a spray of blood and brains. Another screamed hoarsely as he had his arm and most of his shoulder chopped clean through. Unlike some of the fashionable, rapier-toting toughs, the City Marshal's men were armed with broadswords. Not as quick, perhaps, but devastatingly effective, especially from horseback.

"We had best get inside someplace and quickly," Smythe said, "before we get caught up in all that."

"Aye, they do not seem to care much whom they chop down, do they?" said Shakespeare. "They are a most profligate bunch of butchers."

"Over there," said Smythe, pointing out a painted wooden sign for a tavern just a few doors down.

Shakespeare glanced up at the sign. "The Swan and Maiden, eh? Well, by Zeus, it seems like just the place. If we can make it there."

They made it through the door mere seconds before the carnage would have caught up with them, plunging through it so quickly that they tripped upon the threshold and fell sprawling to the rush-strewn floor. A group of men had gathered at the windows to watch and they were heartily cheering each brutal stroke, raising their tankards, slapping one another on the back, laughing boisterously, and toasting the slaughter outside in the street as if it were being staged purely for their benefit.

"Hah! Well struck!"

"Again! Get him!"

"Kill him!"

"Run him through!"

"Mow down the bloody bastards!"

"Look! Here's two of them come bursting in here, trying to flee! What do you say, lads? Shall we toss them back out into the street to get their just desserts? Or should we carve them up in here ourselves and save the marshal's men some trouble?"

Smythe turned, fixed the speaker with a glare, and rose to his feet. The man's eyes widened and he swallowed nervously, backing off a step. His hand went to his sword hilt. Smythe hefted his staff. The man who'd spoken hesitated, suddenly uncertain if he wanted to draw steel and commit himself to a fight he might not win. He looked to his comrades for support, his gaze quickly flicking from Smythe to them and back again, as if seeking a prompt for action.

Smythe made a quick assessment of his potential opponent. He had the look of a tradesman, middle-aged and bearded, as they all were, in his early to mid-thirties, and fashionably, if not ostentatiously dressed in a brown leather doublet with the rough side out and buttons of polished brass set close together. Slashed sleeves, showing touches of red cloth underneath, were in conformity with the latest style. The sword, too, looked more worn for fashion than for function. Doubtless, it was reasonably functional, but the hilt and scabbard looked a bit too ornamental for serious work to Smythe's trained eye. The workmanship was gaudy, but strictly second-rate. The man was a barroom bravo, a loudmouthed bully with a few tankards of ale under his belt, but judging by his weapon, he was not a real swordsman.

"Oh, we've got ourselves a roaring boy," one of the others said. This one, Smythe noted, was a larger man, but soft around the middle and bleary-eyed with drink. His large and red-veined nose betrayed his fondness for the cask. His gut-stuffed, ale-stained, blue and buff striped doublet confirmed it. "I think this one wants a fight, lads," he added, with ale-fueled belligerence.

"He's a strapping big bugger," the first one said, uneasily.

"Aye, but he's only got a staff," the third man replied. "And the other one's just a skinny little bloke, and there's five of us."

Smythe glanced at the man in the dark green doublet with the puffed shoulders and black-slashed sleeves. He was beefy, though not as heavy as the one in blue and gold. He wore a short black cloak that made it difficult to tell his true dimensions, particularly with the latest padded and puffed fashions. But he did not seem quite as drunk as his fat friend. A more serious threat, perhaps.

"Please, gentlemen," Shakespeare said, rising to his feet unsteadily and holding out his hands, "we wish to cause no trouble. We are not roaring boys or duelists. As you can see, we have no swords. I am but a poor poet and my friend, here, is an aspiring actor. We were merely caught up in that commotion out there in the street. We had no part in it ourselves, I assure you."

"Oh, you assure us, do you?" the fourth man replied, mockingly. "Well, a pox on your assurances!"

Medium height, medium build, but not muscular looking, Smythe observed, as he appraised the man in the red and gold doublet and floppy, plumed red cap. He seemed more drunk than his compatriots, and even less of a threat on his own. There was nothing about any of them or their weapons from what Smythe could see that indicated serious fighters, but then five drunkards armed with swords and egging one another on were still nothing to be sneezed at. He made a quick determination. If it came to a fight, and he saw that it was looking more and more that way, then he could not be sure if he could count on Shakespeare for much help. Glovemaking and poetry did not normally develop strength or fast responses. And the poet was neither a large nor a strong man. Best look to the one with the brown leather doublet first, Smythe thought, because he seemed the most sober of the bunch and therefore, perhaps, the greatest threat. Then the one in dark green, and then the fat one in the buff and blue, and then the fourth. . . .

"And a pox on bleedin' poets, too," the fifth man said contemptuously, staring at Shakespeare with an ugly scowl. As Smythe turned his attention to him, he immediately revised his estimation. No, this one would be the greater threat, he thought, looking him over. He seemed more fit than any of the others, and though he had a large pewter tankard in his hand, he did not look drunk at all. His eyes seemed clear and more alert, like those of the first man, only more so. He also filled out the chest of his brown and black quartered doublet with more thick muscle than the others had, and his shoulders looked more massive, too. This one was a craftsman or a laborer, Smythe thought. A man who did work with his hands and would not shy from getting them dirty. A cooper, or an ironmonger, or perhaps a farrier . . .

"A pox on *poets*, did you say?"

The new voice came from one of the tables behind them. Smythe glanced over his shoulder quickly to see a strikingly handsome young man in an elegantly jeweled burgundy doublet of

three-piled velvet rise to his feet with the lightness of a dancer.
His hair was a light auburn hue and shoulder-length, and his eyes
were large, expressive, and a bit dreamy, yet mockingly insolent.
A poet's eyes, Smythe thought, at once. He had a small moustache
that curled up slightly over thin, bemused lips and a spare chin
beard that framed his well-formed oval face, which had a delicate,
boyish, somewhat effeminate cast.

Wonderful, was his first thought. Just what we need. Another
drunkard with a blade. Things were liable to get dangerous at any
moment.

Another man sat at the same table, but this one kept his seat,
resting his elbows on the tabletop and steepling his gloved fingers
in front of his face as he watched his young friend with amusement. Smythe had little time to take much note of him, save that
he was dark-haired and exquisitely dressed in black brocade and
silk. His handsome young friend came sauntering around the table
and, in a smooth, lazy-looking, yet deceptively quick motion, drew
his rapier before the others could react.

" 'Ere now!" the tavernkeeper called out. "I'll have none o'
that in my place!"

The handsome young man's dark friend, still seated at the
table, merely raised his elegantly gloved hand, without even turning around, and the tavernkeeper fell silent at once.

"You *did* say a pox on poets," the young man said, "or were
my ears deceiving me? I mean, I could scarcely credit what I heard!
It simply seems impossible!"

"What concern is this of yours?" said the man in brown, who
had disparaged poets. His hand was still on his swordhilt, but he
remained undecided as to whether to draw steel or not. A blade
had already been drawn, and the young man wielding it looked
very relaxed and confident, indeed. Not in the least bit intimidated
by the odds. Smythe could see Leather Doublet calculating. Was
this merely some drink-addled young fool looking for trouble, or
did he know his business? Smythe was wondering the same thing

himself. He glanced over at Shakespeare, who simply looked at him and rolled his eyes.

"As it happens, I too am a poet," the young man said, as he approached the group, with a casual swagger. "As is my friend, there, who dabbles with a sonnet or two upon occasion. And so, you see, you have cursed not only this excellent young man here, and his friend, the actor, but you have wished a pox upon the two of us, as well, as you have also cursed all those who labor nobly in the dark and lonely hours with quill and parchment to produce some small bit of transitory beauty for an ugly, often unappreciative world. Yet, much more importantly, do you know who *else* writes poetry, and has thus been cursed by you? Well? *Do* you?"

Frowning, and looking decidedly uncertain about this new development or the flow of verbiage, the man in the brown and black quartered doublet shook his head. "No, who?"

"Why, the queen!" the young man said. "The queen writes poetry! Now I happen to know this for a certain fact, you see." He brought up his rapier and delicately played its point around the man's throat. "And I cannot very well stand by and do nothing while you wish a pox upon Her Royal Majesty, our good Queen Bess, now can I?"

"Here, you'd better put that rapier down, lad, before you go and do something rash," the one in the dark green said.

"Or what?" the young man asked without even glancing his way. His gaze was locked with the man in brown and black, with the swordpoint playing lightly at his throat. And that man was breathing shallowly, eyes narrow, his own gaze unblinking and alert. And very cold.

"Or you'll have to be taught a lesson in minding your own damn bloody business, you impudent fop." The man in green began to draw his blade.

Smythe reacted quickly, but the young man was even quicker. Before the man in green could clear his scabbard, the young man's blade flicked over like an adder's tongue and slashed across his face, opening up his cheek from temple to jaw. At the same time, the young man smashed the back of his fist into the face of the man in brown and black, who had begun to draw his blade, as well.

By this time, Smythe was moving, but so was the young man. He danced lightly back out of the way to engage the others as the man in green screamed, dropped his sword, and sank to his knees, bringing his hands up to his ruined face. He was clearly out of the fight now, and the odds had been reduced by one.

With a quick glance toward Shakespeare, to make sure he was not immediately in harm's way, Smythe targeted the man in the brown leather doublet, who was drawing steel as the man in brown and black recovered from the punch and also drew his blade. There was blood running from his nose and he had cold fury in his eyes. As he and the young man engaged, Smythe brought the end of his staff down hard upon his opponent's wrist. With a cry of pain, the man in the leather doublet dropped his fancy-hilted blade and had little time for anything save a wide-eyed stare of alarm as Smythe brought the other end of his staff up and cracked it hard against his temple. He crumpled to the floor, senseless.

The fat one in the buff and blue was slow to react to the outbreak of hostilities, his wits doubtless dulled by drink, but by the time Smythe's leather-clad opponent crumpled to the floor, he had realized there was a brawl in progress and rushed forward with a roar, ignoring the blade at his side, instinctively counting on his size to work for him as he launched himself at Smythe and wrapped his arms around him in a bear hug, driving him backward. They crashed into the table where the young man's elegant friend was sitting, but he simply got up in the nick of time and stepped casually back out of the way with his goblet as Smythe and the fat man fell to the floor, splintering the table beneath them.

Knowing that if the fat man fell on top of him, it would drive the wind right out of him, Smythe wrapped his own arms around his antagonist and twisted hard as they fell, with the result that the fat man took the brunt of their crash into the table and fell with the not inconsiderable bulk of Smythe on top of him. His thick layers of fat, however, absorbed much of the impact and kept him from getting the wind knocked out of him. He managed to dislodge Smythe, breaking his hold and tossing him aside, into another table. With an angry roar, he started to get back up, but never made it. Hoisting a bench high above his head with both hands, Shakespeare brought it down hard on top of the man's head, splintering the wood, and quite possibly bone, as well. Leaning back against the bar, the elegant man in black raised his goblet in a toast, which Shakespeare acknowledged with a bow.

Smythe got up to see the young man hotly engaged with two opponents, the man in red and gold and the man in brown and black. And he was being driven back under their combined assault. However, before he could do anything, Smythe saw the situation resolved neatly by the young man's black-garbed friend.

It happened very quickly. As the young man backed away, parrying furiously, his opponents passed the spot where the man in black was standing, leaning back against the bar. Moving in a casual, easy manner, the man in black unsheathed his dagger, flipped it so that he could grasp the blade with his gloved hand, then brought it down hard upon the skull of the man in red and gold. He crumpled to the floor as the man in black brought up his booted foot and kicked the other man right in the groin. The man in brown and black made a sound like a pig being stuck with a skewer, then collapsed as the elegant man in black brought the heavy pommel of his dagger down upon his head, knocking him unconscious.

The young man stepped back with an irritated look and shrugged, spreading his arms and sweeping his rapier out to the side in an elaborately expressive gesture. "I could have handled them, you know."

The man in black glanced at him and grimaced. "The trouble with you, Kit, is that you are not nearly as good as you think you are."

"I was doing bloody well all right till you stepped in!" the handsome young man protested.

"You had help," the man in black said, indicating Smythe.

" 'Twas he who helped us," said Smythe, "for which, sir," he added, turning to the young man, "I am profoundly grateful. We have only just arrived in London, seeking employment, and our first day in town was very nearly our last."

"Well, we cannot have louts and bumpkins abusing poets out in public, now can we? No, no, that would never do." The handsome young man grinned, adding, "We artists have to stick together, you know."

"Indeed," said Shakespeare. "Though for my part, I would prefer to do so in a manner somewhat less bellicose."

"Ah, but you must admit, it was a grand little set-to, was it not?" the young man said. "Just the sort of thing to get a man's blood up!"

The man in black shook his head with resignation. "If you persist in this sort of foolishness, Marlowe, then I strongly suggest you take more fencing lessons, else I shall find some other young, deserving poet to favor with my patronage. These tavern brawls are going to be the death of you, and I would hate to see my money wasted. You still have many years of decent work in you, Kit. Assuming you survive, of course."

The young man bowed with an exaggerated, courtly gesture. "I am properly chastised, milord. I shall make an appointment with your fencing master at the earliest opportunity."

"And I shall have to pay for that, too, I suppose," the man in black said, with a wry grimace.

"Kit Marlowe?" Shakespeare said. "Do I have the pleasure of addressing Christopher Marlowe, the author of *Tamburlane*?"

The young man smiled, obviously pleased at the recognition.

"At your service, sir. And now I fear you have the advantage of me."

"William Shakespeare is my name. And this is my friend, Tuck . . . that is, Mr. Symington Smythe. I know your work, Mr. Marlowe. I admire it very much. 'Tis a great pleasure to meet you, indeed."

"Well, you are most kind. And now it seems you have the advantage of me once again, for I fear that I am not yet familiar with your work, sir. Perhaps I will have the opportunity to become acquainted with it in due time." He turned to the man in black. "Milord, allow me to present Mr. William Shakespeare and Mr. Symington Smythe. Gentlemen, my esteemed patron, the honorable Sir William Worley."

The man in black inclined his head slightly and touched the brim of his hat. Smythe met his gaze and, in that instant, struck as if by lightning, he realized he knew this man, although he could scarcely believe it. "I am indebted to you, milord," he said. "Once again."

"Again?" said Worley, raising an eyebrow. "Have we met before?"

"Perhaps I am mistaken," Smythe replied. "It is possible that I took you for someone else, milord. Mayhap some chance resemblance to another gentleman in black."

"Indeed? Well, I shall have to speak to my tailor, then. He swore to me that no one else had clothes like these. If I find he has been selling copies, I shall have the fellow flogged."

"In any event, we are both indebted to you, milord," said Smythe. "Had Mr. Marlowe and yourself not intervened, I fear things would have turned out rather badly for us."

"Perhaps. Though you seem quite capable with that staff, I suggest you get yourself a more serious weapon, Mr. Smythe. This is London, after all, not some small village in the Midlands. A man needs to look out for himself around here. You know how to use one of these?"

He drew his sword and tossed it to Smythe. Smythe caught it by the hilt. Worley smiled slightly, seeing his quick reaction. Smythe examined it and felt its balance.

" 'Tis a good blade, milord."

"You seem to know the way to hold it. Keep it as a loan. You shall return it to me when you obtain one of your own." He unbuckled his swordbelt and handed it to Smythe. "And if you do not return it in good time, and in good condition, mind you, then I shall have you found post haste and beaten mercilessly."

"If I can get access to a forge, milord, then I shall endeavor to make you one still better," Smythe replied. "And you may have that in trade, if you prefer."

"Indeed?" Worley raised his eyebrows. "Those are rather bold words, young man. That is a Toledo blade."

" 'Tis a fine blade, milord," said Smythe, a bit hesitantly. "A good weapon, and very serviceable. But I would place its origin much closer, right here in England rather than in Spain."

"The devil you say! It so happens I was assured that blade was made by Sebastiani of Toledo. Do you dispute this? Explain yourself, sir."

Smythe cleared his throat. "Well, milord . . . 'tis true there is an *S* stamped on the ricasso of the blade, but I can assert with confidence that it stands for Somersby, a Sheffield cutler of some small repute. I know his makers' mark quite well; I have seen it many times at my uncle's shop, when we had occasion to sharpen or repair his blades for several of our customers. He is an able craftsman, but certainly not up to the standards of the masters of Toledo, something I am quite sure he would readily admit, as I am told he is an honest man. I . . . uh . . . would hope that whoever sold the weapon to you asked a price in keeping with its proper origin."

Worley cleared his throat. "Unfortunately, no. It would appear I have been cheated."

"Then perhaps you would like to take this back, milord, so

that you may seek proper recompense for the effrontery."

"No, no, you keep it. At least for the present. I shall let it serve as an object lesson to me to seek a more qualified opinion before I make a similar purchase in the future. You intrigue me, Mr. Smythe. For a number of reasons. You shall have your forge. Come to my estate at your convenience. Most anyone of consequence in London can direct you. We shall put your claim to the test. If you make good upon it, I can warrant that I shall have employment for you. If not, then you shall owe me the price of the materials and forging costs. If you lack the funds, then I shall take it out in labor. Fair enough?"

"More than fair, milord," Smythe said, with a small bow.

"Excellent. Marlowe, be so good as to find a likely lad to have my carriage brought around. The coachman doubtless prudently drove off when that riot began outside, and he'll be somewhere on a nearby side street, or I'll know the reason why. Oh, and Mr. Shakespeare, if you are even half as confident in your abilities as your friend seems to be in his, then perhaps there is a chance that you might find employment with the Queen's Men. They are keen to compete with Marlowe here, and Kyd, and as yet have found no resident poet who can measure up. That morose old stewpot, Greene, is lately drowning his rather mediocre talent in a bottle, and Lyly's shot his bolt, I think. They could do with some new blood."

"You will doubtless find the company disporting themselves at The Toad and Badger, in St. Helen's," Marlowe added. "Ask for one Dick Burbage and give him my compliments."

"Thank you," Shakespeare said. "I shall do that, Mr. Marlowe. I am in your debt."

"Well, now there's a switch," said Marlowe, with a grin. " 'Tis usually I who am in debt to others."

"My carriage, Kit," said Worley.

"Your word is my command, milord." Marlowe gave a sweeping bow, winked at Smythe, and left.

"I think he likes you," Worley said.

"And I like him, milord," Smythe said. "He seems a most amiable young man."

Worley raised an eyebrow and chuckled. "Amiable? Aye, well, that's one way of putting it, I suppose. 'Tis a good thing he has talent, else I should find his company insufferable. But one must make allowances for talent. 'Tis a rare commodity, and often does not come without some baggage."

"Your carriage awaits, milord," said Marlowe, sticking his head inside the door. " 'Twas standing by just around the corner."

"Well, at least my coachman does his job properly," said Worley. He turned to the tavernkeeper. "You may send me a bill for the damages, but see that you do not inflate it."

"Very good of you, milord," the tavernkeeper said.

"Oh, and add something for these two young chaps," said Worley. "They look as if they could use a meal and a drink. Good night, gentlemen. And good luck to you."

He followed Marlowe out the door.

"What a splendid gentleman!" said Shakespeare. "Tavernkeeper, two ordinaries and a couple of ales! Ah, yes, indeed! There, you see, Tuck? *That* is the sort of patron a poet truly needs! A cultured man! An educated man! A titled man! A . . ."

"A highwayman," murmured Smythe.

"What?"

"A highwayman," he repeated, keeping his voice low. "An outlaw. A road agent. A brigand."

"What in God's name are you talking about?"

"Do you recall when we met and I told you how I was accosted by a highwayman upon the road? And how instead of robbing me, because I had no money, he tossed a crown to me, instead?"

"Yes, I recall you told me that. A singular occurrence. But what of it?"

Smythe pointed toward the door. "That was the man."

"*Sir William?*"

"The very same."

Shakespeare stared at him with disbelief. "*Sir William Worley?* Are you mad?" He glanced around quickly and lowered his voice when he noticed he was attracting some attention. "Tuck . . . Sir William Worley is one of the richest men in London! And a knight of the realm, no less."

"Well, he is also a highwayman," said Smythe, softly.

"You must be joking."

"I am in earnest, I assure you."

"Then you have lost your senses. Why in God's name would one of the wealthiest and most prominent citizens of London, a man knighted by the queen herself, put on a mask and ride off to rob travelers out on a country road? 'Tis preposterous!"

"It does seem mad, I must admit," said Smythe. "And I cannot account for it. But I know what I know, Will."

"Wait! He wore a mask! You said the road agent wore a mask! So, of course, you never saw his face! How, then, could you possibly assert so firmly 'twas Sir William?"

"I saw his *eyes*," said Smythe. "And at first, I must admit, I did not recognize him, but when he inclined his head and touched his hat that way . . ." Smythe copied the way he did it, " 'twas the very same gesture I saw the brigand make. Exactly the same. And then I realized that his eyes were the very same eyes I had seen above the scarf he wore over the lower portion of his face. And then everything else about him suddenly seemed familiar. I noticed that his build was just the same, and his bearing, and his coloring, even to the color of his clothes."

"A chance resemblance," Shakespeare said. "Wasn't that what you had said yourself? I had no idea what you meant when you said it, but . . . this? 'Tis absolutely ludicrous. Surely you can see that!"

"Aye. Believe me, Will, I can appreciate just how mad it

sounds. But 'tis nevertheless the truth. I am quite certain of it. As I said, I cannot account for it, nor understand why, but I know he was the man. And what is more, Sir William knows I know."

Shakespeare leaned back against the wall, where they sat at a small plank table in the corner. The ales came and for a moment they did not speak as the tankards were set down before them. Then, when the serving maid had left to bring their dinners, Shakespeare leaned forward once again, putting his elbows on the table.

"Assuming for the moment that this ludicrous idea is true," he said, in a low voice, "even setting aside the whys and wherefores—which are certainly not lightly set aside, considering the circumstances . . ." he shook his head with disbelief. "Then if Sir William is indeed the man you think he is . . . an outlaw . . . and if he knows you know his secret, as you say . . . then you are in grave danger."

"No, I do not think so. I saw nothing threatening or intimidating in his manner," Smythe replied.

Shakespeare snorted. "Why should there be? He owns a fleet of ships, my friend, several of them privateers sailing under letters of marque from Her Majesty herself. He may not himself be a Sea Hawk, but he is unquestionably their falconer. His investments are many and varied, and all quite successful, I am told. He is one of the most admired and respected men in England. And one of the most powerful. All he needs to do is flick his little finger and you would be swept away like a cork upon the waves."

"Oh, I have no doubt of that," said Smythe. "Only why bother?" He shrugged. "What threat am I to him? Who would take *my* word over *his*, the word of a penniless commoner over that of a wealthy and influential peer?"

Shakespeare grunted. "Aye. There is that. No one would believe it."

"If I stop to think about it, I am not sure that I believe it, myself. There is no rhyme or reason to it, no sense at all. And yet . . ."

Shakespeare stared at him. "And yet . . . you are convinced of it. Beyond all doubt."

Smythe merely nodded.

"Aye, I can see that. Astonishing. And you think he knows?"

"Why else would he have loaned his sword to a complete stranger?"

Shakespeare shrugged. "With his money, it would seem an act of little consequence. The very rich are not like us, my friend. They are liable to do things on a whim that to us would seem incomprehensible."

"Such as becoming involved in a tavern brawl, say, or highway robbery?"

"Perhaps. Who is to say? There are more things in heaven and earth, Tuck, than are dreamt of in our philosophy. Things beyond the ken of the greatest thinkers of our time. What man truly knows himself and can plumb the depths of his own soul, much less those of other men?"

"He intends for me to return this sword to him," said Smythe.

"Or else embarrass yourself in attempting to make one better."

"Oh, that will not be very difficult. It will take some time, a bit of sweat, and honest effort, but my uncle taught me well. I do not pretend to be a master swordsmith, but then, neither is Cleve Somersby. The quality of his blades varies greatly, and while this one is entirely adequate, it is still not among the best examples of his craft. I could have bettered this in my third year of apprenticeship."

"Oh, so Sir William really was cheated, then," said Shakespeare.

"If he paid the going price for a Toledo blade, then he was not merely cheated; he was fleeced."

"If that is so, then I do not envy the man who fleeced him. He will wind up in prison before the week is out. Or worse still."

"Or else there is no such man at all," said Smythe. He ladled some meat out of the common bowl and put it on his trencher, then tore off a piece of bread and popped a piece of stewed mutton in his mouth.

Shakespeare gulped his ale and set the tankard down, frowning. "What?" His eyes grew wide. "Oh, I see! You are suggesting that Sir William knew all along the truth about the blade, and he merely said that it was from Toledo just to see if you would know the difference?"

"I suspect so," Smythe replied, washing down the bread and meat with some ale. He felt ravenous and grateful for the free meal.

"Well, I can see the sense in that, I suppose," said Shakespeare, filling his own trencher. "But then, why would a man of his position wear a merely ordinary blade? I should think that he would wish to purchase nothing but the best."

"Indeed. One would certainly think so."

"So then . . . why not the best? Why not a genuine Toledo?"

"Well, in all the commotion just now," Smythe said, "you most likely did not notice Marlowe's weapon, did you?"

"Marlowe's weapon? Tuck, my friend, I was much too busy staying out of the way of those blades to pay much mind to their quality of manufacture."

"Well, in all likelihood, most people would probably have failed to notice, too," said Smythe, "unless, that is, they were apprenticed for seven years to a master smith and farrier, who taught them everything he knew about the art of weaponscraft. Marlowe's rapier, as it happens, was an exquisite example of the finest Spanish craftsmanship. Its cup hilt was worked with gold and its scabbard was bejeweled in a manner I would not think a poet could normally afford."

"You think they had exchanged blades?" Shakespeare said.

"But why? It could not have been to test your knowledge, for Marlowe must have already had that blade in his possession before we had arrived."

"True. Perhaps Sir William gave it to him, either as a gift or perhaps as payment for some service rendered."

"An extravagant gift, indeed. Especially since Sir William seems not to like Marlowe very much. Or at the very least, he disapproves of him."

"He did make that rather strange remark," said Smythe. "About making allowances for talent or some such thing, because otherwise the man would be insufferable. I am not sure what he meant."

Shakespeare smiled. "He was alluding to Marlowe's tastes."

"His tastes?"

"When Sir William said that Marlowe seemed to like you, he meant he . . . *liked* you."

"What do you mean he . . . oh! Oh, God's wounds!"

Shakespeare chuckled. "That is why Sir William was so amused by your response. Amiable, indeed. But never fear, Tuck. I shall protect you from predatory poets. If you, in turn, protect me from murderous drunkards with rapiers."

"Done," said Smythe. "Now let's see about finding a place to sleep tonight, and then we shall seek out the Queen's Men."

5

THE BRIEF LETTER HAD ARRIVED by messenger. Had it not been sealed and delivered directly into her hand, Elizabeth was certain that her mother would have opened it and nosed through its contents first before she gave it to her. However, the messenger had insisted on delivering it to her in person, firmly stating that those had been his master's specific instructions, and that he was to wait for a reply. So now Elizabeth's mother hovered around her like an anxious hen, fluttering her hands and making clucking noises.

"Well? What is it? Who is from, Bess? What does it say?"

"Why, it is from Mr. Anthony Gresham," Elizabeth said with surprise, feeling a tightness in her stomach as she broke the seal and read the note. "He requests the honor and pleasure of my company in order to discuss a matter of mutual import."

"Oh, how splendid!" Edwina Darcie clapped her hands together like a small girl delighted with an unexpected present. Elizabeth rolled her eyes. It seemed as if her mother was liable to start jumping up and down with glee at any moment. "But this is wonderful news! A matter of mutual import! He means to discuss the wedding plans, no doubt. Upon what date does he invite you?"

"Tonight," Elizabeth said. "This evening."

"Tonight? *Tonight*! Why . . . why this is most irregular! Tonight! Such short notice! Barely even enough time to get dressed! Whatever could he have been thinking? Goodness, I . . . I haven't even the proper time to decide what I should wear!"

"I believe the invitation is for me alone, Mother," said Elizabeth.

"What? Oh, nonsense, don't be absurd. Why on earth would you think such a thing?"

"Because that is what the invitation says, Mother," Elizabeth replied. "It says, a matter of import that he must discuss with me *alone*."

"Let me see that!" Her mother snatched the letter from her hand. Her eyes grew wide with affronted dignity as she read it to herself. "Well! I have never heard of such a thing! To invite a young girl out without a proper chaperone . . . It is most irregular! Most irregular, indeed! We shall have none of this!"

"In truth, I am no longer a young girl, Mother," Elizabeth protested, politely. "I am a grown woman. And I do believe I should accept. Besides, it is not as if he had simply glimpsed me on the street and asked about in order to discover where I lived. There is, after all, an understanding, is there not? These are goods which have already been bartered."

"Honestly, Elizabeth!"

"Honestly, indeed, Mother," Elizabeth replied, matter of factly. "It is nothing but the truth, so why seem so affronted by it? I am merely being traded away to enhance Father's social position."

"Now what sort of talk is that? I simply cannot comprehend what makes you say such things! Perhaps your father was right that your tutor filled your head with all manner of nonsense. Lord knows, I certainly never raised you that way! Bartered goods, indeed! You speak as if we have never had your best interests in mind at all."

"Did you?" Elizabeth asked, softly.

Her mother's mouth simply opened and closed repeatedly,

like that of a fish out of water, as she struggled for an answer and couldn't seem to find one that was appropriate to the occasion. So Edwina Darcie did what she always did whenever her wits were not up to the task of formulating a suitable riposte. She raised her chin and sniffed contemptuously, then turned demonstratively and left the room in a flurry of skirts and umbrage.

Elizabeth sighed, then turned to the messenger, who still waited patiently for her response. "You may tell your master that I should be glad to accept his kind invitation."

"Thank you, milady," said the messenger, bowing slightly. "In that event, I am instructed to inform you that my master shall be sending his coach for you."

"You may thank him for me and tell him I am most grateful for his consideration," said Elizabeth, with a smile.

Mr. Anthony Gresham, it seemed, was nobody's fool. The betrothal may have already been arranged and, in the minds of both their parents, the marriage could well be a *fait accompli*, but he clearly wanted to see his intended for himself before he set off for the church. What other reason could there be for such an invitation? It was very nearly an imperious summons. It had been well and politely phrased, to be sure, but on such short notice, it was presumptuous and there was an air of arrogant expectation that it would be obeyed, right down to ordering the servant to deliver it directly into her hand and then await her response, which presumed that she would not even take any time to think it over. Her mother could not see the arrogance of it, because the subtleties escaped her. Her father certainly would, but then he would probably expect it from somebody like Gresham and excuse it, for wanting to attain a position where he could be as arrogant himself. Elizabeth sighed.

Well, she thought, with any luck, in their eagerness to see the matter settled, neither of them would think too much about what motives Mr. Gresham had behind this invitation. There was even a good chance that his coach would arrive to pick her up before her father came home for the evening. He often worked late. In that event, he wouldn't even have a chance to think about it and come up with some reason to postpone the meeting at the last moment, until such time as he would be in a position to exercise some more control over how and when it was conducted. For if he *did* have a chance to think about it, then he might realize that Fate had just handed his daughter the perfect opportunity to thwart his plans for her.

So, she thought, the high and mighty Mr. Anthony Gresham wanted to see the goods displayed before he bought them, did he? Elizabeth smiled, smugly. Well then, see them he would. And she would display herself in such a fashion as to make him blanch. It would be an evening that he would not soon forget. And then, she thought, chuckling to herself, we shall see if there shall be a wedding.

She hurried to get ready.

"When we came to seek employment with the Queen's Men, this was not the sort of position that I had in mind," said Shakespeare, wryly, as he held the horse while the gentleman dismounted.

Smythe came up beside him, leading a saddled bay by its reins. "Well, one has to start somewhere, I suppose. But I must admit that this was not quite my idea of working in the Theatre, either."

"Ostlers," said Shakespeare, with a grimace, as they led the patrons' horses to the stable. "We came to London to be players, and instead, we are mere ostlers. Stable boys! Odd's blood, I could have stayed in Stratford and done far better than this!"

"But you would not be in the Theatre," Smythe said, as they led the horses toward the stalls.

"And I would not have shit upon my boots, either."

"I thought you had previously arranged a position with the company when they had come through your Stratford whilst on tour," said Smythe.

Shakespeare grunted. "Well, I thought so, too. It seems, however, I was misled as to precisely what sort of position it was. 'Tis my own damned fault for listening to that pompous blowhard, Kemp."

"He was the one you made arrangements with? I thought you said he was an ass?"

"And I stand heartily by my first assessment, as you can see it proven out. But at the time, I thought he was in earnest. 'Oh, aye,' he says, 'you would be welcome to come with us when we leave Stratford to go out upon the road again. Or else, come and join us when you get to London! Always a place for likely lads in the Queen's Men! Always room for talent!' Talent, my damned buttocks!"

"Well, he did not specify what sort of talent, did he?"

"How much talent does it take to be a hotwalker?"

"It takes some. If you do not feel at ease and in control of the animal, 'twill shy, and then it may spook others, and then instead of walking mounts to cool them off, you've got them galloping wildly all over the place. You may not have secured the sort of position that you wanted, Will, but you did manage to get a job and you do have a way with horses."

They put up the animals and went back out again as several other ostlers met them coming in, each of them leading saddled mounts back to the stable. A few others hotwalked patrons' horses around in a circle at the edge of Finsbury field, where the theatre patrons who came to Shoreditch on horseback dismounted and turned their steeds over to the ostlers, either to put them up with some fresh hay in the stables or tie them up in the paddock during the performance, or else walk them around to cool them off if they were lathered from a run or a long trot.

Many of the patrons came by way of the Thames, ferried by the watermen in their small boats, but some of the wealthier ones came by coach or carriage. With those patrons, it was usually their coachmen who took charge of the equipage, either seeing to everything themselves or else directing an ostler or two in the unhitching and walking of the horses, if they needed it, or else watering and sometimes brushing and combing them, depending on what their masters had ordered. There were small fees for these services, of course, and an enterprising ostler who managed to attend a number of wealthy patrons could do reasonably well for himself if the company was putting on a popular play, but it was still a long way from being on the stage. And the Queen's Men seemed to have experienced better days. Dick Tarleton, their biggest draw, was ailing and the attendance was down from what they'd been accustomed to.

Nevertheless, thought Smythe, they had little to complain about, despite Shakespeare's disappointment. Within a day of coming to London, they had found employment, which was more than a lot of people could say, and a place to live, which in itself was something of an accomplishment.

Many people were arriving in London every day from the surrounding countryside, all in search of livelihoods they could not find in the towns and villages from whence they came. In many cases, those with little money had to share rooms with as many as six, eight, ten, or a dozen others, often leaving scarcely enough space for anything except a cramped place to sleep upon the floor. It made for a crowded and often pungent environment. He and Shakespeare had been much more fortunate.

They had found a room at The Toad and Badger, on the second floor over the tavern. It was small and sparsely furnished, a far cry even from the modest room Smythe had when he had apprenticed with his uncle, but it was a room they could afford, and did not have to share with others, thanks in part to Shakespeare's having set aside a little money to make the trip to London. It was also fortunate for them that their chance meeting with Sir William Worley and Kit Marlowe had resulted in a good word put in for them by Mr. Burbage, who had spoken with the land-lord and arranged for some consideration with the payments of the rent.

Smythe was under no illusion that Richard Burbage had done so purely out of the goodness of his heart. He was a pleasant enough young fellow, but he was also looking out for his own interests. The theatre that his father had built was dependent upon people attending its productions, and it certainly paid to remain in the good graces of one of the wealthiest men in London, who was known as a patron of the arts. And although Marlowe wrote for a rival company, the Admiral's Men, Burbage had every reason to maintain cordial relations with him, as well.

According to Shakespeare, Marlowe was the most promising young poet of the day and, with *Tamburlane,* he had served notice upon the players' world that a change was in the air. The pro-duction had shocked and thrilled audiences with its lyrical bom-bast and lurid violence, reminiscent of the Greek classics, and in contrast, the broad jests and prancing jigs and ribald songs per-formed by other companies seemed suddenly dated and low class. At least, this was the opinion Shakespeare held. Smythe had ac-tually *enjoyed* the ribald jests, the funny jigs, and the bawdy songs, and wasn't at all sure that something serious and weighty would be preferable. After all, despite Marlowe's education, university men did not constitute the bulk of the audience and the Theatre was not the Inns of Court, where productions were often staged in Latin by amateur barristers who would one day argue the law before the bench. Nevertheless, Shakespeare seemed convinced that Marlowe's work, as notorious as the man himself, heralded a new sort of drama, one that would cater more to the talents of serious actors such as Edward Alleyn and less to lowbrow jesters like Will Kemp. The days of the prancing clown, Shakespeare had insisted, were over. Of course, it was also possible that Shakespeare was exaggerating, just as he had exaggerated the nature of their relationship with Marlowe and Sir William, which was why Dick

Burbage had helped them with securing lodgings and given them both jobs.

"You know, one would think that friends of Sir William Worley and Kit Marlowe would deserve rather better than to be given jobs as ostlers," Shakespeare said, irritably.

"Well, for one thing, Will, we are not, in fact, *friends* of Sir William's and Mr. Marlowe's. We can only claim, at best, the briefest acquaintance with them. Quite aside from that, Mr. Burbage did not have to give us jobs at all, you know. And perhaps, under present circumstances, these were the only openings he had available. I am certain that, given an opportunity to demonstrate what we can do, we shall be able to advance ourselves in due course."

Shakespeare sighed. "I suppose you're right. There is a strongly practical streak about you, Tuck, which will doubtless serve you well. But I fear that I am not as patient as you are. I know what I am capable of doing, and I know where I wish to be, and on top of all that, I still have a family to support. And I am not going to be able to provide for them on an ostler's pay."

"I shall help you, Will. After all, you have helped me, from the moment we first met, and I would not now have the lodgings that we share if you did not advance the lion's share of the rent. I shall not forget that."

"You are a good soul, Tuck. And I, for my part, shall remember that, as well. Aha, look there . . ." He pointed toward the road that led across the field. "A coach and four approaches. Let's run and get that one, it positively drips with money. The owner must be a wealthy merchant or a nobleman. Pray for the nobleman, for merchants give miserly gratuities."

" 'Tis a nobleman, I think, or a proper gentleman, at least," said Smythe, as the coach drew nearer. "Methinks I see an escutcheon emblazoned on the door."

"Indeed," said Shakespeare. "But soft . . . I have seen those arms before, I think."

"As I have seen that team!" said Smythe. " 'Tis that same high-handed rogue who almost ran us down the other day! Well, I shall have a thing or two to say to him!"

"No, Tuck, wait!" Shakespeare reached out to grab his arm, but he was too late. Smythe was already running toward the coach. "Oh, God's bollocks! He's going to get himself killed." He started running after Smythe.

The driver found nothing at all unusual in the sight of two ostlers running toward his coach as he pulled up to the Theatre, so he reined the team in to a walk as he pulled up in front of the entrance. As the coach came rolling to a stop, Smythe ran up to it, with Shakespeare pursuing in a vain attempt to catch him. He reached out and yanked the door open.

"*Damn* it, sir! I'll have you know . . ."

Fully prepared to unload a torrent of enraged invective on the occupant, Smythe was suddenly brought up short. To his surprise, it was not the man he thought.

It was not even a man.

He stared, struck speechless, at the most beautiful woman he had ever seen.

She gazed back at him, then raised her eyebrows in an interrogative manner. "Do you always damn people so vehemently upon such short acquaintance?"

He flushed and looked down, sheepishly. "Forgive me, milady. I . . . I thought you were someone else."

"I see. And how, pray tell, did you happen to come to this conclusion?"

"I . . . well, 'tis of no consequence, milady. Forgive me. I did not mean to offend."

"You will offend me, sir, if you act as if my question were of no consequence. I would like an answer."

" 'Twas the coach, milady," said Shakespeare, from behind him. "This coach . . . or perhaps I should say, to be more precise, one very much like it . . . nearly ran us down the other day."

"And so your friend is justifiably incensed," she said. "I quite understand. But as this is not my coach, and I am only riding in it for the first time today at the invitation of Mr. Anthony Gresham, perhaps I could be spared your umbrage and assisted to step out?"

"Why, yes, of course, milady," Smythe said. He reached out to her and she took his hand as he helped her step down out of the coach. She squeezed his hand and, for a moment, their eyes met. Smythe felt a sudden, intense pressure in his chest and his mouth went dry. Was there meaning in that glance? He could have sworn that something passed between them, something pregnant with tension and desire. But surely, he thought, that could not be possible. Could it?

"Miss Elizabeth Darcie?"

They turned to see a liveried servant standing behind them, and Smythe at once recognized the man from the inn at the crossroads, the one who had come galloping ahead to announce that they'd been robbed. The other man, however, seemed not to recognize him. Indeed, Smythe thought, why should he? A mere ostler was beneath even the notice of a servant.

"I am Drummond, milady. Mr. Gresham's man. I am to escort you to his private box to join him for the performance."

"Certainly," she said. And then she paused and turned back to Smythe. "And thank you so much for you assistance, Mr . . . ?"

"Smythe, milady. Symington Smythe."

"He's just an ostler, milady," Drummond said, in a tone that clearly indicated she had no need to bother with anyone so insignificant.

"Aye, but a very handsome one," she said, with a wink at Smythe.

Drummond looked scandalized and did his best to rush her off through the theatre entrance before there could be any further exchange between them. Smythe stared after them for several moments before he finally realized that the coachman was giving him instructions for what he wanted done. The horses were to be un-hitched and given some hay in the paddock, then watered and brushed and hitched back up in their traces once again in time for Mr. Gresham and his guest to leave in a timely manner as soon as the production ended. Smythe knew what needed to be done and wasn't really paying very close attention. He could not get his mind off Miss Elizabeth Darcie, and how she had winked at him and said that he was handsome.

"Do not even think about it," Shakespeare said, as they were unhitching the team.

"Think about what?"

"Oh, please! Spare me the coy innocence. That Darcie woman, that's what. And pray do not tell me that you were not thinking about her. I could feel the heat coming off you from six feet away."

Smythe grinned, self-consciously. "She said that I was hand-some. Did you hear? And did you see the way she winked at me?"

"Aye, and so did Drummond. And you can be sure that he will report it to his master."

"Mr. Anthony Gresham," Smythe said.

"I believe that was the name she mentioned," said Shake-speare, wryly.

"You realize that she made a particular point of telling us whose coach it was?"

"I realize that she is trouble on the hoof," said Shakespeare. "I have seen her sort before. She is the type that likes to stir things up. She has a rich gentleman sending a fancy coach to bring her to the theatre, where she will enjoy the production from the in-timacy of a private box screened off from the remainder of the audience, and yet she takes the time to flirt with a mere ostler, and in so obvious a manner that the servant of the gentleman who squires her cannot help but notice. So, if you can stop being blinded by Miss Darcie's admittedly radiant charms long enough to think clearly for a moment, then what conclusion can you draw from this?"

"You believe that she was flirting with me in front of the servant on purpose, only to make this Gresham jealous?"

"Well, far be it from me to pretend I know a woman's motives for anything she does," said Shakespeare, wryly. "As for her doing it in front of Drummond on purpose, there can be, I think, no doubt of that. 'Twas clear to her you had a bone to pick with the owner of the coach that nearly ran you down. And so, as you observed, she made a point of telling you his name, when there was no need at all for her to do so. Especially after I had told her it could easily have been another coach that merely looked like this one. It seems clear to me she is intent on pointing you toward Gresham . . . and at the same time, giving Gresham ample reason to bear a grudge against you."

"But why? What reason could she have for causing trouble between the two of us?" said Smythe, as they led the horses to the paddock. "She does not even know me."

"Who is to say? She may have taken offence at your manner. Or else it had nothing to do with you at all. Perhaps she simply enjoys making Gresham jealous. Some women like to see men demonstrate their power, the more so if 'tis done on their behalf. In any event, the rhyme or reason of it really does not matter. The potential consequences do, for they represent nothing but trouble. Stay away from these people, Tuck. As I said before, they are not like us. And we mean less to them than the dirt clods they crush beneath their boots."

Smythe sighed. "I see the sense in what you say. You are right, of course. What possible interest could a lady such as that have in a lowly ostler?"

"Be of good cheer, Tuck. She was right in one respect at least; you are a handsome fellow, and this is London, after all, with opportunities at every corner. There shall be sweet young girls aplenty for you in good time. Just see to it that you are not incautious, and that you do not shoot your bolts at targets far beyond your reach."

"I defer to your superior wisdom, Father Shakespeare," Smythe said, with an elaborate, mocking bow.

Shakespeare threw a dirt clod at him.

An evening at the playhouse was not what Elizabeth had expected. However, she had not really been sure what to expect. A coach ride along the Strand? Supper or high tea at Gresham's home, or perhaps an outing in the park? The invitation had been mysteriously and frustratingly unspecific. Her mother had not been pleased about that, and she had been even less pleased about Elizabeth accepting it. Had it come from anyone else, there would have been no question about it, but Edwina Darcie knew how much her husband wanted this marriage to take place and, in his absence, had not been confident enough to stand upon her own authority.

She had found her daughter becoming much more willful of late and was not quite certain what to do about it. As a result, she had her own reasons for wanting the marriage to take place, and as soon as possible. Elizabeth was not a child anymore and her mother did not enjoy having another grown woman around the house to threaten, however indirectly, her domain. Aside from that, the social circles into which an alliance with the Gresham name would introduce them made her giddy with anticipation. Consequently, Elizabeth knew that her objections to the presumptive invitation were little more than posturing.

She, however, had her own reasons for accepting the invitation, and they had nothing at all to do with her regard for the proper way of doing things or for Mr. Anthony Gresham, for that matter. Indeed, he was falling lower in her estimation by the minute.

First, she thought, he sends a rather imperious invitation, on uncommonly short notice, which was both inconsiderate and rude in its presumption. Second, he had not even bothered to tell her where this assignation would take place, so that she could at least attempt to dress accordingly. As a result, she had chosen one of her best dresses, reasoning that it was better to be overdressed than underdressed for any occasion. And third, once she had arrived at the playhouse, he had not even bothered to meet her himself, instead sending a mere servant to escort her to his private box up in the galleries, where he waited like some potentate condescending to grant a common petitioner an audience. Mr. Gresham certainly seemed to think rather highly of himself. Well, she labored under no illusions that she was going to change that. Nor did she care to. But she could certainly do something about how he thought of her.

She had already decided that she was going to flirt in Mr. Gresham's presence with every man who caught her eye, but she had not yet even laid eyes upon her haughty host when she had started flirting with that handsome ostler who had so abruptly flung open the coach door and started shouting before he even knew who was within. Obviously, it had been a case of mistaken identity. But even so, that still said something about him, in that he did not hesitate to assert himself, and rather strongly, in the face of someone of superior social standing. It was, after all, clearly a gentleman's coach. For that matter, there was every possibility that he had *not* been mistaken, and that it *was* Anthony Gresham against whom he held a grudge. How could he have known that it was not Gresham in the coach? There had been such fire in his eyes! In all honesty, she had to admit to herself that her exchange with him had not been part of her original plan.

Drummond had witnessed it, of course, and he would surely report it to his master, for that was no more than his duty, and so it was just as well. It had worked out exactly as if that was the way she'd planned it. Save that she hadn't planned it and she hadn't known that Drummond would be there to see it. She would not make excuses to herself. There was no denying that the young man had an effect upon her. She had flirted with him because she wanted to.

What was his name? Smythe-something. No, Something-Smythe. Symington Smythe. That was it! It sound so euphonious. He certainly was handsome. And those shoulders! He seemed well-spoken, too, not at all thick, coarse, and rough-mannered, like so many of these common louts who worked around the Theatre, with their incomprehensible burrs and brogues and slurring speech and nose-wiping and forelock-tugging gruntings. She had, of course, been to the Theatre many times before, since her father was one of the investors whose money had helped build it, but this was the first time she had ever seen this rather striking young man. He must have been newly employed. Pity he was just an ostler. There could be no question, really, of her becoming more intimately acquainted with anyone like that. Her parents would both throw fits. Which, it occurred to her, was a tantalizing idea in itself.

The ensign hoisted in the turret an hour before the start of each performance was fluttering in the cool, late afternoon breeze as they went through the gate, past all the groundlings who had already arrived long since to jostle for the best positions in the rush-strewn yard. The hawkers were selling their refreshments and the trumpets were blowing the three blasts of the fanfare, signaling that the play was about to start as they mounted the stairs up to the expensive private boxes in the upper gallery, which were all screened off on the sides, blocking off all views except the one directly to the front. And therein, the much-lauded Mr. Anthony Gresham awaited her.

Having already formed a rather low opinion of him, Elizabeth had somehow expected his appearance to live down to it. She had imagined that he would be fat and unattractive, and probably with pockmarked skin. Instead, she was surprised to find that he was quite good looking, in a roguish sort of way, with well-formed, strongly defined features, a good complexion, a neatly trimmed black beard, and a full head of dark hair that he took some trouble to keep well groomed. He was also younger than she had expected, in his early to mid-twenties, and appeared to be quite fit.

"Miss Darcie," he said, rising to greet her. He bowed over her hand and brushed it with his lips. "How good of you to come on such short notice. 'Twas dreadfully rude of me, I know, to present the invitation in such a fashion, but under the circumstances, quite unavoidable, I fear. I hope you will find it in your heart to forgive me."

Taken aback a bit by his unexpected remarks and apparently sincere, apologetic tone, Elizabeth could think of nothing else to say or do but nod. He led her to her seat, which he had thoughtfully provided with several pillows, and offered to pour her some red wine. She accepted.

The play, in the meantime, had begun. As the first actor stepped out on stage to recite the prologue, Elizabeth recognized the play as one she'd seen before, *The Honorable Gentleman*, a rather tepid comedy of manners written by Greene or one of his many imitators, she could no longer remember which. The way these poets would often take older works and then adapt them to the stage, changing them around and frequently borrowing from other sources, as well as one another, it was sometimes difficult to tell who the original author was. And in the case of this play, it really didn't matter. The intent of the production was to lampoon the so-called, rising "middle class," the new merchant gentry who were often painted with a broad brush, in strokes that were anything but flattering, as bumbling, greedy, selfish, and duplicitous, often cuckolded fools. In other words, men just like her father. It was certainly a peculiar choice for Gresham to select.

However, as Will Kemp, the speaker of the prologue, delivered his lines with his usual leering and grimacing posturings to the audience, it became apparent that Anthony Gresham was not in the least bit interested in the play. He made a pretence of watching the stage, but spoke to her, instead.

"You are aware, of course, that our families intend that we should marry," he said, without preamble. It sounded more like a statement than a question, so Elizabeth made no attempt to answer. He glanced over at her briefly, saw that she was watching him silently, and raised an eyebrow in expectation.

"I have recently been made aware of it," she replied, in an unemotional tone.

He nodded and returned his attention to the stage, though it was clear that he had no real interest in the play. "Indeed, I was rather recently made aware of it myself. It was not, regrettably, a matter upon which I had ever been consulted. In fact, until only a short while ago, your name was not even known to me." He paused, as if choosing his words carefully. "And I would, perhaps, not be amiss in thinking that the prospect of marriage to a man whom you had never even met did not quite fill you with . . . eager anticipation?"

Elizabeth realized that things were not quite going the way she'd planned. What she had hoped for was an opportunity to create a bad impression and thereby discourage Mr. Gresham's interest. Instead, it was beginning to appear as if he had no interest. And she found that very interesting, indeed.

"I had always hoped," she said, "to fall in love with the man whom I would marry."

He glanced at her appraisingly and smiled faintly. "Ah. Love. Indeed. I quite understand. And as unfashionable as it may seem, I believe that there is a great deal to be said for love. Would you not agree?"

"I would."

"Good. Then in this one respect, at least, we are of like mind. You would prefer to love the man you were to marry, and I . . ."

He turned to look directly at her. "I would prefer to marry a woman that I loved."

Elizabeth abruptly realized what the purpose of this meeting was, and she caught her breath, scarcely able to believe in her good fortune. "And . . . is there such a woman?" she asked, meeting his gaze.

He nodded once again. "There is." When she did not respond immediately, he added, "And is there such a man in *your* life?"

She shook her head. "No. At least, not yet."

"Ah. Pity. Doubtless, there shall be before long."

"Let us understand one another, Mr. Gresham, and speak plainly," she said. "You do not want this marriage. Anymore than I do."

"No, Miss Darcie," he said. "I do not. And 'twas my hope that you would feel the same way. As, it would appear, you do."

"I do, indeed, Mr. Gresham. But I mean no offence toward you."

"Indeed, nor I toward you," Gresham replied, visibly more at ease now. "I was concerned that my desire to break off this betrothal might have been painful or distressing to you."

"The marriage was something that my father wanted," she said, "for reasons that had more to do with his ambitions than with mine."

Gresham nodded. "Aye. Our situations seem much alike. 'Twas my father who wanted this, as well." He smiled. "Apparently, the family fortune has been somewhat depleted by some unwise investments he had made."

"So he seeks to make a wiser one through you," Elizabeth replied, with a smile.

Now that she saw which way the wind blew, she felt a great deal more comfortable with Gresham. Her opinion of him had improved, somewhat, as well. She could now see why he had acted as he did. He could not very well have revealed the purpose of this meeting in his invitation. Not knowing how she felt, he had needed to be circumspect, and issue the invitation in such a manner that her family would have little or no time to prepare for it and interject themselves in any way. This was a matter that had needed to be discussed in confidence. Nor could she fault him for wanting to break off the betrothal. He was in love with someone else. What better reason could there be? She had wanted to find a way to break it off herself, because she was not in love with him.

Her sympathies became aroused toward him and she started to look upon him with more understanding. He was not a bad sort, after all. Without his cooperation, there could not have been a marriage. He had not needed to meet with her like this. He could have simply refused to go through with it. He would have raised the ire of his father and perhaps risked being disinherited, but he certainly had not needed to consider her feelings in the matter. And yet, he had done just that. He had wanted to speak with her, prepare her, make some explanation. In this respect, he had comported himself in every way like a true gentleman. Even an honorable one, she thought, smiling to herself at the irony, considering the play being acted below, to which neither of them was paying the least bit of attention anymore.

"I see that you have wit," said Gresham, with a smile. "Depending upon one's perspective, that will, in good time, either make some man very happy or else miserable beyond belief. More wine?"

Elizabeth laughed, both at his good-natured gibe and in relief that things had gone so well. "Please," she said, holding out her goblet and noticing that it was fine, engraved silver, not pewter. Out of the corner of her eye, she spotted the wicker basket Drummond must have brought, containing the goblets and the wine, as well as the trencher for the serving of the bread and cheese. Gresham clearly liked his comforts.

"So, here we are. The perfect pair," said Gresham, raising his goblet to her. "A son with a father in want of money, and a daughter with a father in want of position. A match made in heaven, one might say."

"Aye," she said, "if one father could but wed the other."

Gresham chuckled and they touched goblets. "I am glad we could achieve what the French call a 'rapprochement.' Now the question remains, how best to inform our families of this."

"Plainly, I should think, would seem the best course," Elizabeth replied. "I cannot imagine any way to tell them that would result in any sort of satisfaction on their part. So why not simply be plainspoken?"

"Well, for my part, that poses no great hardship," Gresham said, with a shrug. "Howsoever I may put it to him, I shall incur my father's anger and displeasure. 'Twould be neither the first time nor the last. If he wishes to improve his lot through marriage, then let *him* find himself some rich merchant's daughter who, unlike yourself, is concerned less with her heart's desire than with her comfort. I am sure my mother, rest her sweet soul, would understand. My father's ire is something I can bear without undue concern. But what of yourself, milady? Can we not devise some stratagem that will assuage or, at the very least, redirect your father's anger at the failure of this match?"

"My father's anger is something I have grown accustomed to as I have grown older, and become less the dutiful child and more the intemperate woman," Elizabeth replied, with a grimace. "But, to be honest, I did have a plan of my own to thwart this match."

Gresham raised his eyebrows. "Did you, indeed?" He looked amused. "Pray tell me what it was."

"I had intended, this very night, to prove myself a wanton hussy and a slattern in your eyes, by flirting coyly with every man in sight, so much so that you would have been outraged and sorely embarrassed at my boldness and utter lack of manners and discretion. And in conversation, I would have displayed a lazy intellect and a complete lack of interest in anything save my own indulgence. 'Twas my most earnest intent that by the time this night was ended, you would have found me *quite* unsuitable."

Gresham threw back his head and laughed, so loudly that it threw off the actors on the stage, who were not, at that particular moment, delivering any lines that were comedic. They looked up toward the gallery in dismay, but Gresham paid them no mind whatsoever and, with some annoyance, they continued from where they had left off.

"I almost wish that I had given you the opportunity to go through with it," he said, still chuckling over the idea. "But I much prefer that things have turned out as they did. 'Tis better that we are honest with each other. However, be that as it may, I think your plan has much merit in it. We shall agree, then, that I was an insufferable boor who found you quite unsuitable, as you put it. Though we shall not, I think, put it off to any failing of your own. You comported yourself with the very essence of feminine charm and grace, but I simply did not find you to my liking, being spoiled and petulant and impossible to please. You have never met a man so lacking in manners and discretion. I was a pig. You were appalled. I found you unbecoming and did not hesitate to tell you so. That, I think, would make a nice touch to raise your father's ire against me instead of you. And, with any luck, the next match that he proposes for you will be much more to your liking."

" 'Tis not that I find you dislikable," said Elizabeth. "At least, not anymore."

Gresham chuckled again. "Nor I you. A man could do far worse and not, I think, much better. We understand each other. It has been a rare pleasure not marrying you, Miss Darcie. And since you seem to have no more interest in this execrable play than I do, perhaps you would allow me the pleasure of taking you home?"

6

✳

THE MEMBERS OF THE COMPANY were not pleased with the play. The audience was restive, almost from the start, and a number of them had left before the second act. At the end, the applause had been indifferent, and there had been some boos and catcalls at the final bows. After the performance, they had repaired to The Toad and Badger to discuss what had gone wrong over bread and cheese and ale. Since they lived upstairs over the tavern, Smythe and Shakespeare had gone, too, as soon as they were finished with their duties at the stable. By the time they had arrived, tired, but looking forward to an evening's relaxation, the company were already arguing amongst themselves, trying to find something—or someone—to fault for the failure of that night's performance.

" 'Twas young Dick's fault, if you ask me," Will Kemp was saying as they came in. "He was much too heavy-handed with his part. It calls for lightness and expansiveness, like the tone I set in my speech during the prologue."

"If by expansiveness you mean leering and grimacing and capering like a randy drunken fawn, then indeed you set the tone," replied Richard Burbage, sourly.

"I'll have you know I played my part just as well as Dick Tarleton would have played it!" Kemp protested.

"Well, if Dick Tarleton had been drunk to near insensibility and trotting through an Irish peat bog, then I suppose he might have played it that way," Burbage said.

"The cheek! The impudence! Why, you young upstart . . ."

"Gentlemen, please . . ." John Fleming, one of the senior members of the company said, trying to make peace.

"Young upstart? I am just as much a member of this company as you are!" Burbage replied, hotly.

"Aye, because you rode in on your father's coattails," Kemp said, sneering. "If 'twasn't for the fact that he had built the the-atre—"

"Enough!" Edward Alleyn's stage voice at full volume cut through the air like a scythe, at once attracting the attention of all within the tavern. He put his hands upon the table and leaned forward, fixing them both with a glare worthy of an angry Zeus. "You bicker like a gaggle of small, annoying children! 'Tis enough to give one indigestion! Keep silent!"

"Damn it, Ned, I'll not have anyone accusing me of riding on my father's coattails," Burbage began, in an offended tone, but Alleyn didn't let him finish.

"You *did* ride in on your father's coattails, Dick," said Alleyn. " 'Tis not to say you have no merit on your own, for you have promise as an actor, but if it wasn't for your father, you'd still be playing girls or acting as the call boy."

"I told you so," said Kemp, smugly.

"And as for *you*, you gibbering ape, young Burbage here has more talent in his little finger than you possess in your entire, capering, bandy-legged, over-acting body!"

"Bandy-legged! *Bandy-legged?* Why, you insufferable stuffed ham, if not for *my* presence in this company, that playhouse would have been empty tonight by the end of the first act! 'Tis *me* they come to see, Will Kemp, who brings some joy and laughter to their lives, not some grave, overblown windbag who possesses all the lightness and charm of a descending axe!"

The entire company fell silent as Alleyn slowly rose from his seat, his eyes as hard and cold as anthracite. Kemp realized he had gone too far. He moistened his lips and swallowed hard, but held his ground, afraid to back down in front of everyone else. He stood stiffly, his chin raised in defiance, but a slight trembling betrayed him.

"I have had all that I am going to take from you, you ridiculous buffoon," said Alleyn. His normally commanding voice, legendary for his ability to project it like a javelin, had gone dangerously low. It was a tone no one in the company had heard from him before. He came around from behind the table, glaring at Kemp, his large hands balled into beefy fists.

"Ned," said Burbage, rising from his seat, but Alleyn shoved him back down so hard that the younger man's teeth clicked together as he was slammed back onto the bench.

Kemp's lower lip was trembling and his knees shook, but his pride would still not allow him to retreat. "Y-you d-do not f-f-frighten m-me!" he stammered.

"You had best be frightened, little man," said Alleyn, ominously, "for I am going to pound you into the ground like a tent peg!"

"You had best get out, Will," Shakespeare said, coming up beside him.

"Y-you stay out of this, you b-bumpkin!" Kemp said, vainly trying to maintain a pretence of being unafraid. "He cannot in-t-timidate m-me!"

He had gone completely white. Smythe frankly wasn't sure if he was simply stubbornly attempting to stand his ground or if fear had him frozen to the spot. But it was quite clear that Ned Alleyn meant precisely what he said. There was murder in his eyes. He stepped in front of the advancing actor.

"He is just a little man, Master Alleyn," he said. "If you strike him, you shall surely kill him."

"I fully intend to kill him," Alleyn said. "Now get out of my way!"

"I am sorry, sir, I cannot do that," Smythe replied, standing firmly between Alleyn and the trembling Kemp.

"You had best hold him back, for his own good!" said Kemp, his voice breaking to reveal his false bravado. "I'll take no nonsense from the likes of him, the intemperate boor!"

"That *does* it!" Alleyn said, through gritted teeth, and attempted to shove his way past Smythe. But for all his considerable size, he could not budge him. He grabbed him by the upper arms, to shove him away, but Smythe countered by putting his hands upon the actor's shoulders and squeezing. Alleyn's eyes grew wide and he turned red with exertion as he tried, without avail, to break Smythe's grip.

"Come on, Ned!" somebody yelled, shouting encouragement.

"No, hold him!" Burbage shouted, getting up and seizing the big actor from behind.

"Aye, hold him, else he shall face my wrath!" shouted Kemp, seeing now that Alleyn could not reach him.

"Will, get him out of here!" said Smythe, as he and Burbage wrestled with the powerful actor.

"Right, Kemp, off we go," said Shakespeare, grabbing the older man by the scruff of the neck and the seat of his breeches and frog-marching him out of the tavern.

"Let go of me, you lout! Let go, I said!" Kemp launched into a torrent of oaths that would have done a seaman proud, but Shakespeare relentlessly marched him out of the tavern and into the street to general laughter all around. Even Alleyn joined in, despite himself.

"You may let me go now, Burbage, and you too, young man," he said to Smythe. As they released him, the actor rubbed his shoulders. "I am going to be bruised, I fear," he said, looking at Smythe. "You have quite a grip there, fellow."

"Forgive me," Smythe said. "But you are a powerful man. It took all my strength to hold you."

Alleyn smiled. "I think not. I suspect you had a good bit more left in reserve. You are not even breathing hard. Remind me not to arm-wrestle you for drinks." He glanced at Burbage. "Are you all right, young Dick? I did not hurt you, did I?"

Burbage rubbed his jaw. "Good thing I had my tongue out of the way when my teeth clicked together as you sat me down, else I would now be speechless."

"And what a loss to the Theatre that would be, eh?" Alleyn said, with a grin. "Especially now that the Queen's Men shall need all the talent they can muster."

"What do you mean, Ned?" asked Robert Speed, one of the shareholding members of the company.

"I meant that I was going to kill that ludicrous popinjay, Kemp, and I shall do it," Alleyn replied, "but much more thoroughly than if I simply smashed his skull in like a wine keg. I am going to leave the company."

"Ned!" said Burbage, with shock. "You're not!"

"I am," said Alleyn. "I am going to join the Admiral's Men."

"What?" said Burbage. "Because of *him*?" He pointed at the door, where Kemp had been hustled out by Shakespeare. "You are going to let the whole company down because of *him*?"

"The company is already down, young Burbage, and not just because of him, although he certainly does not help the situation any," Alleyn replied. "The man plays the fool so well onstage because he is one offstage, as well. But the fact of the matter is that without poor old Dick Tarleton, who is on his last legs, I fear, there is no longer any reason for me to remain. I stayed this long only out of friendship for an old comrade. The Queen's Men have no decent repertory anymore. All the plays are all played out. The Admiral's Men have Marlowe and they have the Rose, which for my money is a better playhouse."

"And Henslowe, who owns the Rose, has a pretty daughter, as I hear," said Speed. "A comely, young, unmarried daughter. You've heard that, have you, Ned?"

Alleyn turned red. "I'll not dignify that with a response."

"You already have," said Speed, with a grin.

"Ned," said Burbage, with concern, "you are the finest actor in the company. The best in all of England. It is only fitting that the best be with the queen's own company of players!"

"Dickie, my lad, my mind is set," Alleyn replied. "And this company, sad to say, is no longer the best. That honor rests with the Admiral's Men. They have the best playhouse in the Rose; they have the finest resident poet in Kit Marlowe and the best and freshest repertory. Once I have joined them, they shall have the best actor, as well. And meaning no offence to your father, young Dick, but Philip Henslowe is by far the better manager."

"Ned, he runs a brothel," Burbage said, in exasperation.

"Among other investments, aye, and it turns a very handsome profit for him," Alleyn replied. "Besides, there is little enough difference between whores and actors, anyway. And a brothel is simply a playhouse with better furnishings."

"Ned, you cannot mean this!" Fleming said. "If you leave, 'twill sink us sure as Drake sank the Armada!"

"John, this ship is well and truly holed and sinking fast already," Alleyn said. "There shall be no saving it, I think."

"What sort of creature is it that leaves a sinking ship?" asked Speed, scratching his chin and staring at the ceiling as if in deep thought.

"Bobby, I shall ignore that because you are drunk," said Alleyn, with an edge to his voice.

"Truer words were never spoken," Speed replied, raising his tankard. "I shall now proceed to get much drunker. It has been a privilege working with you, Ned. Now go sod off." He drained the tankard in one gulp.

"Well, there is my exit cue, I think," said Alleyn, with a grimace. "Gentlemen, I wish you all the best. Except for that scoundrel Kemp, of course, but then, he is no gentleman. Good, sweet night to you."

"And a bleedin' good riddance to you," said Speed, with a prolonged belch, as Alleyn made his way toward the door.

Shakespeare came back in just as Alleyn was leaving. He sat on the bench beside Smythe and grinned. "Well, he swore and frothed and shouted up a storm, but did not resist me beyond a mere token show. Once he saw that Alleyn was not hard upon his heels, he blustered for a while out in the street, shook his fist, then headed home. And thus the storm blows over." He glanced around at everyone's expressions of gloom and doom. "On the other hand, maybe not. They all look as if someone has just died. What did I miss, Tuck?"

"Alleyn's exit," Smythe replied.

"No, I passed him going out as I came in," said Shakespeare.

"I meant his exit from the company."

"*What?* He quit the company?"

"Aye. That he did."

"An artistic show of temper, surely."

"I do not think so," Smythe said. "He is off to join the Admiral's Men and play the Rose. I had the impression that all of the arrangements had already been made."

"Oh, they were made, all right," said Burbage, miserably. "He would never have gone off like that unless the deal were done."

"What of his share?" asked Fleming, referring to his part ownership of the company as an investor.

"He shall sell it back to my father, I should imagine," Burbage said. "They will come to some agreement, I am sure. These things are all accounted for under the general terms of purchase. 'Tis no matter, either way. His leaving us is a devastating blow. Kemp remains a draw, because the groundlings like him, but without Tarleton and Ned Alleyn, we are crippled."

"Surely not," said Fleming. "Very well, so we have lost two of our company, valued members, true, but there are always other players that we could take on to fill the vacancies."

" 'Tis not so simple. We have not just lost two of our company," said Burbage, "but we lost our best comedic actor when Dick Tarleton quit the stage due to his failing health and now that Ned has left us, we have lost our best dramatic actor, too. 'Tis a crushing blow. I do not see how the Queen's Men can survive it." He shook his head. "This is the end."

"Nay, 'tis not the end until we say so!" Fleming insisted. "We are the Queen's Men, gentlemen! We shall fight on until the last man falls!"

Robert's Speed's forehead struck the table with a loud thump as he fell forward in a drunken swoon.

"Well, that's one," said Burbage, wryly.

"Perhaps the problem lies less with the quality of players than with the quality of plays," said Shakespeare.

"Eh?" said Burbage, as if noticing him for the first time. "And who might you be?"

"Shakespeare is the name. William Shakespeare."

"Oh. I remember you. The chap from Stratford, was it? You wanted work."

"My friend and I were hired as ostlers," Shakespeare said. "Admittedly, not quite what we had in mind when we applied to you, but 'twas the best, you said, that you could offer us at present. However, it would seem that present circumstances have undergone somewhat of a change."

Burbage grunted. He reached out to refill his tankard from the large clay pitcher. "Aye, 'twould seem so." He grimaced. "So what do you want, Shakespeare? To act?"

"Well, Tuck and I would both be pleased to help the company in whatever capacity 'twas deemed we best could serve," said Shakespeare. "For my part, acting is certainly within my compass, but more to the point, I also happen to be a poet. 'Tis there that my true vocation lies. And, if I may be so bold, perhaps 'tis in that capacity that I may best serve the company."

"A poet," Burbage said. He nodded. "I remember. Marlowe

sent you. But I also recall you said you had no formal academic training."

"True," said Shakespeare, nodding. "And yet, no amount of academic training can teach a man to write if he has not the talent. Marlowe and Greene are both university men who hold degrees as Masters of the Arts. But do both hold talent in equal degree? I am not a university man, 'tis true. But then, neither are most members of your audience. All I ask is a chance to show what I can do."

Burbage glanced at Fleming.

Fleming merely shrugged. "What do we have to lose?"

Burbage glanced at Speed, but Speed was unconscious. Burbage merely rolled his eyes. He sighed. "Very well, Shakespeare. You shall have your chance. Our next performance is tomorrow. The play is not working and we have just lost our leading player. We have some eighteen hours in which to salvage something of this mess. Let us see what you can do."

7

WHEN HE CAME HOME TO discover that his daughter had gone somewhere to meet with her intended, Henry Darcie was very much displeased. For one thing, he had no idea where she had gone, and he did not like not knowing things or not being in control. For another, he knew his daughter all too well, and knew she had inherited his willfulness and stubbornness, two qualities which had served him well in achieving his success, but which, he felt, were unfortunate and highly undesirable in women. And when Elizabeth came home later that night, delivered to her door by a coach that pulled away as soon as she stepped down, Henry Darcie became absolutely furious.

His worst fears were realized when he discovered that Elizabeth had done precisely what he had been afraid she'd try to do, given the opportunity. She had somehow managed to convince Anthony Gresham that she was utterly unsuitable. In just a matter of hours, Henry Darcie saw all the work that he had done in trying to arrange the match coming undone right before his eyes. The problem was, he was not sure what, if anything, he could do to remedy the situation.

"You are a miserable, ungrateful, spiteful little wench!" he shouted at his daughter, when she had told him how she spent her evening. "How could you do this? Do you have any idea what you have done? You have ruined your future!"

"I have done no such thing!" Elizabeth protested. "Anthony Gresham made his own decision."

"Made upon seeing your behavior, no doubt, which must have been disgraceful!"

"There was nothing wrong with my behavior, but a great deal wrong with his," she said, following the story they'd agreed upon. She kept her voice very calm, as if struggling to do so despite great inner turmoil. "I accepted his ill-timed and presumptuous invitation—much to Mother's dismay, I might add—because I believed you would have wished for me to do so. And having already displeased you, I did not wish to further anger you."

"That is true," her mother said, nodding emphatically. "I was very much against it, but believed you would have wanted Bess to go."

"Indeed? How good of you both to consider my feelings for a change," her father said, sarcastically. "And Bess had no feelings of her own in this regard, I take it?"

"I have told you before that I wish to love the man that I would marry," said Elizabeth, "but in Mr. Gresham's case, that would be utterly impossible. He is an ill-mannered, loutish boor who found me unsuitable in all respects, from the moment that he first laid eyes upon me. He had his mind made up before I even spoke a word." That much, she thought with some amusement, was actually true. "He found me unbecoming and had the lack of grace to say so."

"*What!* You mean he said so to your *face?*" her father replied, astonished.

"He said it plainly. I was not at all to his taste."

"He truly said so? Just like that?"

Elizabeth decided that there was no harm in embellishing a bit. After all, it was what they had agreed to, more or less, and since they would, in all likelihood, not be seeing Mr. Anthony Gresham again, there seemed to be no reason not to embroider a bit more, purely for effect.

"He said I was too skinny," she said, "and that my bosoms were too small."

"Good God!" Her father looked aghast.

"And he thought I was a bit too horse-faced for his liking."

"*Horse-faced!*" His jaw dropped.

Her mother gasped.

Elizabeth wondered if this was, perhaps, going a bit too far. She knew that she was pretty, and bore a strong resemblance to her mother. It would not be immodest to suppose that it would be a stretch in anyone's estimation to call her horse-faced, but the very idea of his daughter being so horribly insulted made her father apoplectic, especially since, given the resemblance between mother and daughter, it was an insult to his wife, as well. His face turned bright red and he sputtered with outrage. Her mother, meanwhile, had turned as pale as a ghost.

"*Horse-faced!*" he repeated, with stunned disbelief. "Elizabeth . . ." He reached out and took her by the shoulders, looking her straight in the eyes. "Elizabeth, are you quite certain you are telling me the truth?"

She had expected this and she was ready. She widened her eyes, as if with shock that he should question her veracity after what she had been through, and allowed her lower lip to quiver slightly. "Oh, Father!" she cried. "Oh! How *could* you?"

She pulled away from him and ran out of the room, sobbing.

She listened, afterward, from the other room, as her father shouted, paced and blustered, expressing his outrage and threatening to demand satisfaction, though Elizabeth was fairly certain that was nothing but a bluff, merely idle threats to soothe his injured pride. For of course, it was *his* pride that was injured and not hers. He cared less about her feelings than about the fact that it was *his* daughter who had been called horse-faced and unsuitable, thereby impugning not only his abilities to raise a daughter properly, but even his very humors, which had produced her. It was the seed of his loins that had been found defective and he took it as a personal insult. Elizabeth went to bed content and secure in the knowledge that there would be no marriage now. At least not with Anthony Gresham.

She was, therefore, caught completely unprepared when Gresham came calling the very next day, bringing with him a bottle of fine Portuguese wine for her father, a handsome gold brooch for her mother, and a lovely bouquet of red roses for her.

Her father was at work when Gresham arrived, but her mother was at home and when she summoned Elizabeth, sending one of the servants to tell her that she had a caller, Elizabeth had absolutely no idea who it might be. When she came in and saw that it was Gresham, she was absolutely stunned.

"Bess, dear, look who has come to see you!" said her mother, beaming. "Mr. Gresham, may I present my daughter, Elizabeth?"

For a moment, Elizabeth was simply too taken aback to speak. Her mother was introducing her to Gresham as if they had never even met. Gresham rose to his feet and came toward her, smiling charmingly.

"Miss Darcie," he said, holding his hand out to her. She gave him her hand, numbly and without even thinking. He bent over it and brushed it gently with his lips. "How delightful to meet you, at last. I was told that you were very beautiful, but in all honesty, I must confess that the reports I had received simply had not done you proper justice."

"Is he not utterly charming?" said her mother, with a smile Elizabeth could have sworn had a malicious touch. "So well spoken, and so handsome, too! Is he not everything you could have hoped for?"

Utterly confused, Elizabeth looked from her mother to Gresham and back again. "Mother, you speak as if Mr. Gresham and I had never met."

"Oh, do I?" her mother replied, innocently. "You mean to say you have?"

"I am quite certain I would have remembered, madame," Gresham said, with a smile.

Elizabeth frowned. This was not making any sense at all. She could not understand why her mother was acting as if the events of the previous day had never happened. Or why Gresham was acting that way, for that matter. She had no idea what he was up to, but she was not going to have any of it.

"Then you must have an exceedingly short memory, Mr. Gresham," she replied, stiffly.

Now Gresham frowned, infuriatingly. "I beg your pardon," he replied. "I am fairly certain that we have never met. Perhaps you have mistaken me for someone else?"

She stared at him with disbelief. "We were at the Theatre only yesterday," she said. "Could you have forgotten that already?"

Gresham stared at her with incomprehension. He glanced at her mother, as if seeking confirmation of Elizabeth's assertion.

"Elizabeth is having her little jest," Edwina Darcie said, with a smile.

"Ah," said Gresham, as if he understood, though clearly, he did not understand at all. He still looked faintly puzzled.

"Jest?" said Elizabeth. "Mother, whatever do you mean? There is no jest. You were right here when Mr. Gresham's invitation arrived yesterday by messenger!"

Now Gresham looked thoroughly confused. "Invitation? Messenger?" He shook his head, looking bewildered. "Am I missing something? I sent no messenger, nor invitation."

Elizabeth's mouth opened, but no sounds would come out. She was simply too stunned to speak.

"Now, you see, Elizabeth?" her mother said, with a smug tone. "This is what happens when you dissemble. You have been caught out. As the saying goes, oh, what a tangled web we weave when first we practice to deceive."

"I fear that I do not understand any of this at all," said Gresham, looking lost.

"Elizabeth concocted a bit of a tale for us yesterday," her mother said. "A drama, as it were. And a most complex little enterprise it was, too, even to the hiring of a messenger and coach! My goodness! Such an elaborate deception! Her father will be quite taken aback when he finds out. It seems he was completely taken in. As, indeed, was I. You see, she was having a bit of fun with her parents, Mr. Gresham. Her very gullible parents."

Elizabeth caught her breath. "Mother! You think that *I*...?" She could not even go on.

"You see, Mr. Gresham," her mother continued, "Elizabeth is quite a clever girl, with a most sprightly, irrepressible, and independent spirit." Her mother, to Elizabeth's chagrin, actually simpered. "She gets it from her mother, I suppose. Oh, the apple truly does not fall far from the tree, as they say. She had some foolish notion that she did not wish to subject herself to the most honorable and eminently sensible tradition of an arranged marriage, you see. In this regard, I must accept part of the blame, I fear, in that I . . . out of all the best intentions, you understand . . . had prevailed upon her father to engage for Elizabeth a tutor to instruct her in the finer points of appreciation of the arts. The young man we had engaged seemed most erudite and capable, but apparently he somewhat exceeded his commission and filled our daughter's head with all sorts of romantic nonsense from the sensualist poets . . . why, I blush even to say it!"

"I quite understand, madame," Gresham replied, nodding. "I know the sort of thing of which you speak. These poets are quite the fashion now amongst the glittering gentlemen at court. They all go about enraptured over their productions. 'Tis rubbish, really. Utter rubbish."

"I see that you are a discerning gentleman, Mr. Gresham," Edwina Darcie said. "So then, perhaps you will understand how, being young and impressionable, Elizabeth came away from her instruction with the notion that a proper marriage was not one in which the practical considerations of estate and family and mutual suitability prevailed, but one in which the woman was swept away by the passions of romantic love! And so, when she discovered that our families had agreed upon a match of eminent sensibility and benefit for all concerned, she devised, it seems, a little stratagem to make her father and myself believe that you, her prospective husband, did not desire the marriage to take place, because you had found her totally unsuitable! Can you imagine such a thing?"

"*Mother!*" Elizabeth said, with shock. "Are you accusing me of having made the whole thing up?"

"Well, now, Elizabeth, 'tis pointless to keep up the pretence," her mother said. "We have Mr. Gresham here to testify to what he did or did not do, and to what he did or did not say. I mean, really, Elizabeth, 'tis one thing to have a man see that his wife-to-be possesses wit, imagination, and resourcefulness, but 'tis quite another to have him believe that she is foolish, willful, and stubborn!"

Elizabeth was speechless. She stared at Gresham, who gazed back at her with seeming innocence, and she could not believe he had the nerve to stand there duplicitously and pretend that their meeting had never taken place. It was unconscionable! She did not know how to respond or even what to think. His presence was not only inexplicable, after everything that he had told her, but he was, by failing to admit the truth, essentially making her out to be a liar. And . . . to what end? What could his motives be?

"A beautiful young woman with her whole life before her certainly cannot be faulted for feeling some trepidation under such circumstances," Gresham said, in an oily, placating, condescending tone. "After all, we had never met. I could easily have been some monstrously appalling fellow, ill formed and of a hideous aspect, unschooled in the proper social graces, and intemperate by disposition. I trust, however, that I shall be able to dispel any such concerns and ease her mind on these accounts."

He smiled at Elizabeth and gave her a slight bow, and in that moment, she wanted nothing quite so much as to kill him. Except she could not, of course, and saw that any further insistence on her version of the story would be fruitless. Her own mother did not believe her and her father certainly would not. He would be furious beyond all reason at the thought that his own daughter had deceived him and had so very nearly upset all of his plans.

What was she going to do? It was unbelievable that such a thing could happen to her. Gresham was a monster. What in God's name did he intend by this? Now there would be no way she could convince her parents that it was he who was the liar and not she. She had no proof. Only her word against his.

And suddenly, it came to her.

"Drummond!" she said.

"I beg your pardon?" Gresham replied.

"Your servant, Drummond! You *do* have a servant named Drummond, do you not?" Elizabeth said. "Or was that also something I imagined?"

"Drummond," Gresham said. "Aye, he is my servant. What of it?"

"Ha! How could I have known that?" said Elizabeth, triumphantly.

"Elizabeth, really . . ." said her mother, with a sigh.

"I am not sure what you mean," said Gresham. " 'Tis no secret that Drummond is my man. I would be lost without him. I depend on him for a great deal. Everyone who knows me knows Drummond."

"I see," Elizabeth replied. "Well, 'twas Drummond who met me at the Theatre yesterday and escorted me up to your private box. He saw me there!"

Gresham frowned. He walked over to the door, opened it and called out, "*Drummond!* Come in here a moment, will you?"

His servant, who had been waiting with the carriage, came running in response. He bowed as he came in and took his hat off. "Aye, sir?"

"Drummond, do you see this lady here?" said Gresham, indicating Elizabeth.

"Aye, sir."

"Do you know who she is?"

"Mistress Elizabeth Darcie, sir."

"Aha!" Elizabeth said.

"And how do you know that, Drummond?" Gresham asked.

"Why . . . you told me so, sir. You said that you were coming here to see her."

"So I did. And what about last night?"

"Last night, sir?"

"Aye, last night. When you saw her."

"Sir?"

"Did you not see Miss Darcie last night?"

"Last night, sir?"

"Aye, are you deaf? Did you *see* her last night?"

Drummond, looking confused, shook his head emphatically. "Sir, I . . . No, sir. I never saw her before in my life, sir."

"You *liar!*" Elizabeth cried out.

"*Elizabeth!*" her mother exclaimed with shock. "Mr. Gresham, I am quite simply at a loss to explain my daughter's behavior! Honestly, I do not know *what* has gotten into her!"

"Mother, they are both lying!" said Elizabeth.

"Elizabeth, go to your room, this instant!"

"But, Mother . . ."

"I said go to your room! *Immediately!* We shall discuss this when your father returns home. Please forgive me, Mr. Gresham . . ."

Elizabeth ran out of the room in tears. She was furious with her mother, furious with Gresham and his servant, and furious with herself for crying. Drummond had lied, of course, because Gresham had told him to. That was the obvious explanation. The man was a servant; he simply did as he was told. She told herself that she should not really be angry with him. But Gresham . . .

She had never hated anyone so much in her entire life. The man was an utter villain! What possible reason could he have for making her out to be conniving and deceitful? Worse than that, a fool. He had seemed so earnest and sincere when he had said he loved somebody else. Was it all a lie? Apparently, it was. But why? She could make no sense of it.

Nobody would believe her. If her own mother did not credit her story, her father certainly would not. Especially after she had told him that Gresham said she was unsuitable. Too small bosomed and horse-faced. She never should have added that last part. But then, the whole thing had been his idea in the first place. Now, her father would know that she had made that up, and would, of course, believe that she had made all the rest of it up, as well.

Perhaps that was precisely what Gresham had intended, she thought, as she lay in bed and fought back tears of rage and helplessness. If he had wanted to create a rift between herself and her parents, he could not have succeeded more admirably. They already believed their daughter was too willful and too stubborn, now they would believe she was a liar, too. A spiteful, deceitful, and conniving shrew, she thought. That was what he had made her out to be. And now it would appear as if he were being magnanimous in taking her off her parents' hands. That might well allow him to turn the terms of the marriage more to his advantage, she thought. Much like a clever bargain hunter in the market, negotiating a cheaper price for a bolt of cloth because he had found a blemish in it. She gritted her teeth. What an utterly loathsome scoundrel he was!

And this, unless she could think of something absolutely brilliant to prevent it, would be the man to whom she would be married! It was unthinkable. It was simply monstrous. There had to be some way to escape this, to expose him. . . .

Surely, someone must have seen her at the Theatre. She had been there with her father dozens of times; he was one of the principal investors, people knew him there, and they knew her. . . . but no. She could not recall running into anyone she knew when she arrived. Most of the audience had already been seated in the galleries, and she would not know anyone among the groundlings, obviously, so nobody had seen her when Drummond had conducted her to Gresham's private box. And the box had been screened off, of course, so that no one could have seen her in there unless, perhaps, one of the actors on the stage had recognized her, though she did not really know any of them, had never spoken to them, so there was really no one who . . .

The ostler!

She sat bolt upright in bed. That handsome young ostler had seen her! They had exchanged words! More than words, they'd flirted. Surely, he would remember her! But who was he? *What was his name?*

Wait, he had told her. What was it? She racked her brain. Something rather common, and yet uncommon. It tripped rather fetchingly off the tongue, as she recalled. But what *was* it? Smythe! That was it! Something Smythe . . . Something Smythe . . . *Symington!* Symington Smythe!

She had a witness. A witness who could corroborate that she'd been at the Theatre that night. *And* that she had met Drummond! She had to find him. And as soon as possible. He was her only chance to prove that she had told the truth. She got up and quickly started to change her clothes.

8

G REEN OAKS, THE SPRAWLING ESTATE of Sir William Worley, was one of the most palatial homes that Smythe had ever seen. He had heard that the queen herself often visited Green Oaks, usually in late June or early July, when she would habitually leave London in procession with her entire court and make her summer excursions through the countryside, staying at various private residences. Green Oaks was where she usually began. Ostensibly, these excursions were a way for the queen to go out among her subjects every year and see some of the land she ruled. Coincidentally, they also got her out of London during the height of the plague season and allowed her to vacation in the country at the expense of her hosts. And these royal visits could apparently be quite expensive, as they required that the queen be entertained and could last anywhere from a month up to six weeks, or whenever the queen grew bored and decided to move on. It was not unusual for one of Her Majesty's hosts to shell out from two to three thousand pounds to pay for such a visit, but most considered the princely, indeed, the queenly sum well spent in exchange for the favor and influence they believed it could procure.

Obviously, if Sir William could afford to entertain the queen in such a fashion on an annual basis, he had to be fabulously wealthy, and his estate gave ample testimony to the size of his fortune. Located well outside the London city limits, on several hundred lushly wooded and meadowed acres, the house was a huge, rough-hewn, gray stone edifice laid out in the shape of the letter "H," with a windowed hallway as the cross-stroke separating two large interior courtyard gardens.

Smythe had ridden one of the stable post horses out to the estate and as he trotted up the road leading to the house, he wondered what would come of this visit. He had not yet made up his mind about Sir William, but more to the point, he wondered if Sir William had made up his mind about him. He knew that he could very easily disappear during this visit, never to be seen again, and no one would ever think that Sir William could possibly have had anything to do with it. Only Shakespeare would know, or at least suspect what might have happened, and who would listen to a penniless young poet? Especially when it was his word against that of one of the richest men in the land.

As Smythe turned his mount over to one of the servants who came out to meet him, he gazed up at the imposing residence and took a deep breath, marshaling his courage. Just the idea of a visit to such an opulent place would ordinarily have been enough to make him feel intimidated, much less visiting it under such peculiar and possibly even dangerous circumstances. The man who lived here was not only one of the richest and most influential men in the country, he was also a brigand who robbed travelers on the roads leading to London, a flamboyant highwayman who called himself Black Billy. It seemed absolutely insane. And yet, Smythe knew it to be true. And Sir William knew he knew.

What Smythe couldn't understand was *why*. The man seemingly had everything. Entering the house, he could see walls paneled in imported woods and hung with rich tapestries, ceilings patterned with delicate plaster ribs forming arabesques, geometrical forms and figures of birds and beasts, each room different from the other. There were ornate staircases, some straight, some spiraled, with solid oak block steps and massive handrailings and newel posts, all heavily and intricately carved by master artisans.

He was conducted to a great hall with a long gallery, just like in a castle throne room, from which people could look down on what was happening below or, alternatively, Smythe thought, from where archers could shoot down at anyone who was being a boorish guest.

He grimaced. The suits of armor standing at either side of the entrance to the chamber had given his mind an unpleasantly martial turn, as did the maces and the battleaxes and the morning stars hanging on the walls, alongside pikes and halberds and great swords and shields and bucklers. It looked like the armory at Tower of London, another place he was anxious to avoid.

I've made a mistake in coming here, he thought. There was nothing to be served in doing this. He did not belong here. Was assuaging his curiosity truly worth taking such a risk? He decided, despite his apprehensions, that it was. It could have been pure chance that he had happened on Black Billy on the road to London. Shakespeare had not run into him. The poet had not, in fact, run into any robbers at all on his way from Stratford, but perhaps that was because he had not been traveling alone. He had said that he had fallen in with a company of travelers for the sake of safety in numbers. It must have worked. Smythe had traveled alone and been accosted several times. So, perhaps it was mere chance. But then to run into him again in London, in that tavern—and in the company of Marlowe, when it just so happened that he, too, was in the company of a poet, albeit one who was not yet successful—it simply seemed as if there were some fateful influence at work here. And Sir William had invited him, after all. If he had wanted to dispose of him, he would certainly not have needed to invite him to his home. Assassins could be hired cheaply from among the men who loitered around Paul's, cheap even for men with far fewer resources than Sir William could command.

"Young Master Smythe, was it?"

Smythe turned to see Sir William entering the hall. He was dressed very plainly in black doublet and hose, and a pair of silver-buckled shoes. "Aye, sir," Smythe replied. "Though I cannot truthfully call myself a master of any art or craft. Did I come at an inconvenient time, milord? I could easily come back another day, if you prefer."

"Nonsense. Today is perfectly convenient. And you are welcome at Green Oaks. May I offer you some wine?"

"You are most kind, Sir William, but I would not wish to put you to any trouble on my account."

"Trouble? I have more wine in my cellars than I could possibly drink in a lifetime. Someone's going to have to help me drink it, you know. It can't all go down Her Royal Majesty's alabaster throat. And I would much rather it be an honest man who drank my wine than all those dissipated hangers-on at court."

Smythe smiled, despite his discomfort. "In that event, milord, it would be both an honor and a pleasure."

"Excellent. You should find a decanter of port and several glasses over on the sideboard there. Be a good fellow and pour us both a drink. I have given strict instructions that we are not to be disturbed."

Smythe glanced back at him as he made his way over to the heavy, carved mahogany sideboard. "That sounds rather ominous, milord."

Worley raised his eyebrows. "Does it? Are you afraid that I shall do away with you in here and secret your body underneath the floorboards? 'Twould eventually make the room smell rather piquant, don't you think?"

Smythe brought him a glass of port. No pewter or clay goblets here, he thought, but the very finest glassware. "To be sure, milord. In any event, 'twould be a far more elegant resting place than a man of my lowly station would deserve."

Worley raised his glass. "I see. Well, what shall we drink to, then? To . . . proper resting places? From each according to his ability to each according to his need? Hmm. In that event, paupers would be buried in Westminster and half the men at court would be thrown into Fleet Ditch."

Smythe chuckled. He was finding it impossible not to like the man. "Why not drink to chance encounters?" he said.

Worley grinned. "Splendid! To chance encounters, then."

They raised their glasses and drank.

"And 'twas, perhaps, our chance encounter that you wanted to discuss?" said Smythe.

"Which encounter?" asked Worley. "You mean the first or the second?"

"The first, milord. That day in the country, near the crossroads and the inn known as The Hawk and Mouse."

Worley smiled. "Ah. That encounter. Well, then. What of it?"

Smythe shook his head. "I . . . do not understand, milord," he said. *"Why?"*

Worley simply shrugged. "Why not?"

"But . . . you have everything, milord. Everything that it seems to me a man could conceivably want. Wealth, position, power, and influence . . . 'twould seem you lack for nothing. Why play at being some lowly highwayman?"

"I do it for the fun," Worley replied, bluntly.

"Fun?" said Smythe, with disbelief.

"Aye, fun," said Worley. "Is that so difficult to comprehend? That a man in my position might feel the need for some occasional stimulation? Some skylarking? A bit of fun? Besides, I am not just any highwayman, you know. I am the infamous Black Billy. Why, there are ballads and broadsheets written about me. You can pick them up in the stands down by St. Paul's. I have most of them here. I collect them. True, they exaggerate my exploits considerably, but I find them quite amusing."

"But . . . what of the risk, milord?"

"The risk?" Worley shrugged. "Oh, I suppose there is some slight risk, but that only makes it part of the fun, you see."

"Surely, you must realize that if they catch you, you shall hang."

"You think? Well . . . I may hang, I suppose. And then again, I may not. The queen is rather fond of me, you know. But she is a bit of a stickler for form. She might be moved toward clemency, or else she might just have me beheaded. Bit quicker that way. Or so they say. In any event, I should think the odds are greater that I might be killed during a robbery, rather than be apprehended."

"How can you discuss this with so little concern?" asked Smythe, amazed not only at the substance of their conversation, but at Worley's casual tone about it.

"Because it does not concern me," Worley replied.

"But . . . how can it *not*, milord?" Smythe asked, with exasperation.

"Look, sit down, Smythe, and stop standing there looking like some great self-righteous oak. If you will give me your attention for a few moments, I will endeavor to explain."

Smythe obediently sat.

"Good," said Worley, remaining on his feet, rather to Smythe's discomfort. He did not feel that he should be sitting in the presence of a knight, but then again, sitting in the presence of a brigand certainly seemed permissible. The protocol of the situation seemed rather confusing, not to say unsettling.

"Now then," Worley continued, pacing as he spoke, "as you have quite correctly pointed out, I am a very wealthy man. And I, indeed, have everything. Or so 'twould appear, at least, to anyone such as yourself. I could easily sit back and rest upon my laurels, like the rest of the slothful, parasitic fools who make up the larger part of our blue-blooded nobility, but then, such is not my nature.

"You see, Smythe, I did not inherit the fortune I now possess. I earned it. Or else stole it, depending upon one's perspective. Either way, I worked damned hard to get it. And I enjoyed getting it. Every damned bit of it. From my very first business venture, in which I risked every single penny I had earned since boyhood and parlayed it into my first ship, to the latest addition to my fleet, which is even now under construction in Bristol and promises to make Drake's *Golden Hind* look like a river barge, I have played the game of risk and won. Well, occasionally I lost, but losing is just part of the game. And the ones who play it best are those who are not afraid to lose.

"Look about you, Smythe," said Worley, indicating their surroundings with a sweeping gesture. "What do you see? Opulence. Grandeur. Elegance. Taste. . . . Well, I am not so sure about the taste part, for some of this monstrosity I call a home is rather overdone, I must confess, but the point is, it is the refined and genteel residence of a knight of the realm, soon, perhaps, to be a lord, as strange as that may seem. And yet . . . and yet . . . how did I *get* here? How did I achieve all of this?"

Smythe simply stared at him, uncertain as to whether the question was rhetorical or not. Worley was looking at him as if he expected an answer, but Smythe had none to give. Or else, all he could do was repeat back what Worley had just told him.

"Through hard work, milord?"

Worley snorted. "Through piracy, my lad. Through piracy. I worked hard at it, to be sure, but it was piracy, nevertheless."

"*Piracy*, milord?"

"Aye. Drake, Hawkins, Frobisher, the rest of them who either sail my ships or else have bought them from me . . . all pirates. A slightly better class of pirate, I will grant you, than your tarry-haired, rum-swilling, eyepatch-wearing, smelly buccaneer, but pirates, nonetheless. They attack ships and loot them, take them as prizes when they can and sink them when they cannot, and they are wined and dined as heroes here in England, instead of being strung up to dangle from the gallows. And why? Because they attack *Spanish* ships. And because the queen gets a share of all their booty. And that makes the queen no less a pirate than all the rest of them."

"I cannot believe that you would call the queen a pirate!" Smythe said, with astonishment.

" 'Tis the truth," said Worley, with a shrug. "And believe it or not, in private, she would even admit to it. Her Majesty is nothing if not practical. She always sees a thing for what it is, and not for what it should be or could be. And if she is not always honest with her ministers and courtiers and other heads of state, she is unfailingly honest with herself, which is why I rather like the old girl. She is a woman who has made her way in a man's world without ever once submitting to a man, and she has done so with courage and intelligence, duplicity and guile, good-heartedness and malice, trickery and effrontery, and pure, una-dulterated rapaciousness, God bless her great black heart, and I love her better than I loved my own sweet mother because I un-derstand that wondrous royal bitch. She, young Smythe, is every bit as much a thief as I am. And what is more, she revels in it!"

"As do you," said Smythe, as comprehension dawned. "Ex-cept that it sits ill with you to be so far removed from it as her. You cannot be a sea-going brigand, at least not anymore. It would ill suit a man of your position. But if you are going to be a thief, then you prefer to do the stealing with your own two hands, rather than have others do it for you. That way, at least, you own what you have done, and experience the thrill of it."

Worley pointed a finger at him and shook it slightly. "Ah, there, you see? I knew you were a smart lad from the moment I laid eyes upon you."

"You are most gracious, milord," said Smythe. "But the one question which puzzles me above all others is . . . why me? Why take *me* into your confidence? Merely because you know that I could never be a threat to you?"

"In part, that," admitted Worley. "But also because there was something about you that bespoke a difference from your usual, common sort of lout. 'This one has promise,' I said to myself. 'This one, given half a chance, is going to amount to something.'

I always recognize talent when I see it. 'Tis a gift. I felt the same sort of thing about young Marlowe when I met him."

"Have you taken him into your confidence, as well?"

"Marlowe? Perish the thought! He, unlike you, is dangerous. He is the most rash, impetuous, demented young fool that I have ever met, for all his brilliance."

"I should not think that he would be any more capable of being a threat to you than I could," Smythe said.

"On his own, perhaps not," Worley replied, "but Marlowe has some secret friends. Powerful friends. And he does not even realize how powerful and unscrupulous they are, more's the pity. More wine?"

"Uh . . . Aye. Please."

"Help yourself. Oh, hell, bring the whole decanter over. Are you hungry?"

"I could eat, milord."

"I have some of the queen's own venison being prepared. There is plenty. You shall stay for supper."

"You are most kind, milord. But you were speaking of Master Marlowe and his secret friends? Why secret?"

"Because they deal in secret things," said Worley. "Among them, murder."

"Murder?"

"Aye. Murder and intrigue. And at the highest levels."

"The highest levels of what, milord?"

"Of government, my lad, of government. Marlowe is a spy, the wretched soul."

"A *spy!*"

"Aye, he allowed himself to get drawn into it while he was pursuing his studies at Cambridge. A nasty, complicated business. Papist versus Protestant, Rome versus England, with dashing young Kit Marlowe all caught up in it and playing both ends against the middle."

"He told you all this?"

"Nay, I have other sources. Astonishingly enough, Marlowe *can* keep his mouth shut about some things. To a point, anyway. But he is irrepressible and, as his patron, I have been duly 'cautioned.' As an intimate of the queen, you see, I do receive some consideration. Especially since my ships have been so instrumental in helping line the pockets of the Privy Council. But enough about Marlowe. Believe me, the less you know about his intrigues, the better. You wanted to know why I am telling you all this, why I should take you into my confidence."

"Aye, milord. It seems . . . rather unusual. I mean, you do not know me, really. True, 'tis most unlikely that anyone in his right mind would take my word about anything over yours, but nevertheless, there is still the possibility that I might compromise you— or Master Marlowe—in some way. That is to say, I assure you that I would not, at least not intentionally, but how do you *know* that I would not?"

Worley chuckled. "Because you say such things, that is how I know. And because I do not know as little about you as you think. I have made inquiries. I know all about your father and his recent difficulties, for one thing, and I know about your uncle, for another. I was most especially interested in him, considering your claim that you could craft a sword superior to the one I loaned you. Was it merely arrogant boastfulness or simple honesty? As your uncle was the man who taught you, I was keen to learn what sort of work he did. Now, I believe you." Worley reached down to his side and drew a dagger from a sheath at his belt. He placed it on the table and slid it across to Smythe. "You will recognize the workmanship, of course, even without your uncle's maker's mark on the ricasso. The craftsmanship is among the best that I have ever seen."

Smythe picked up the dagger, already knowing it to be his uncle's work. He swallowed nervously. "I take your point, Sir William."

"I think you miss it," Worley replied, seeing the expression on his face. "I am not threatening your family, Smythe. I could, of course, but that was not my purpose. I wanted to find out more about you. That day on the road, I saw something in you that I do not see in men very often. I saw a remarkable forthrightness, and a complete lack of fear. Those are very admirable qualities. Admirable and rare. And they should be encouraged."

"I am not fearless, Sir William," Smythe said. "In all honesty, I was a bit afraid to come here."

Worley shook his head. "I do not believe you were, else you would not have come. I have no doubt you felt some apprehension, some uncertainty, to be sure . . . but fear? You are not the sort. You do not seem to have it in you. I sat astride my stallion with a pistol aimed straight at your chest and you did not blink an eye. You exercised the proper caution that the situation called for, yet you kept your head and even bantered with me. I admired that in you. It reminded me . . . of me. And you know, as enjoyably diverting as it may be to be Black Billy, the infamous highwayman that every schoolboy sings about, a large part of that joy is lost in not having anyone to *tell* about it. Well . . . now I have you." He smiled. "So, what say we take a quick look at that forge I promised you before sitting down to supper? You still owe me a sword, you know."

The play, thought Shakespeare, was appallingly inept. Its failure to draw a decent audience at the Theatre was not due to any particular failing of the actors, although from what he'd seen, the only really good performer in the company was Ned Alleyn, and he had just quit. Things were not looking very promising for the Queen's Men, but despite any flaws in the company's performance, the main fault lay in the play itself.

Part of the problem was that it was not a new play, but one that had been adapted from other sources and rewritten many times, so that he no longer had any idea who the original author was or precisely what had been intended. This particular version was credited to Greene, and it had his stamp all over it. *The Honorable Gentleman* was full of literary references and high-flown academic speech which suffered from the same pretensions that it aimed to satirize, and in those cases where these allusions did not go straight over the heads of most people in the audience, they were explained awkwardly by other characters, who were simply leaden in their coarseness and derision.

The honorable gentleman of the title was a prosperous merchant of the rising middle class, with pretensions to gentility, and throughout the play, he was held up as an object of cruel mockery and ridicule. His employees stole from him, his suppliers cheated him, his wife cuckolded him, and throughout, the main character remained blissfully unaware and foolishly convinced of his own genteel superiority. It was, thought Shakespeare bleakly, crass pandering to the groundlings and as unoriginal as sin.

The speeches were all grandiose and peppered with crude jokes, which seemed to be there for no other purpose than to break up the monotony of the declamation by allowing some character or other to play the fool and caper for the audience. At some point, perhaps, there was a cohesive story that somehow got lost along the way as a result of too many cooks pissing in the stew. And now, he was going to piss in it, as well. He was not at all convinced that his efforts would improve the flavor, either. Still, he had to try.

He had been up all night, working on it. At first, he had thought that he could simply polish a bit here and improve a little there, and tighten some things up a little overall, but it soon became apparent that nothing less than a complete rewrite would do. And that would not save the next performance, because there would simply be no time in which the members of the company could learn all their new lines. The task seemed utterly impossible, especially given the time constraints he had to work under. Had he begun from scratch, with a completely new, original play, it would have been much easier, but that was not what he had been asked to do. His job was to rescue *this* one. The trouble was, he could not generate any enthusiasm for the project, because he simply hated it.

Nevertheless, this was going to be his chance to show what he could do, and if he failed to deliver something much improved, he had little doubt that there would ever be another opportunity to prove himself, at least to this company. Somehow, before he could even entertain the notion of submitting his own plays for consideration, he had to make a start and convince them that he knew his business, that he could turn a phrase adroitly.

The main problem, aside from the awkward writing, which clearly, at least to his eyes, showed an author whose talents were well and truly on the wane, was that the characters were not very well delineated. They were stock characters, and nothing more. They had no complexity and were not drawn with any imagination. There was nothing to differentiate them from any number of similar characters in similar situations, which the audience had seen many times before. They were crude rather than subtle, snide rather than clever, bitter rather than ironic, and loud rather than brash. In short, every brushstroke throughout the play was broad and heavy-handed. And Shakespeare was not sure how to fix it short of simply tearing it all up and starting over. Unfortunately, that was not an option.

After agonizing over it for hours, he had finally decided on a course of action that might, perhaps, allow him not only the chance to prove he could improve this play, but gain more time to do so in the process, while still managing to meet the deadline. The trick, he thought, would be to improve the play in stages.

They had already committed to the next performance; the playbills had all been posted. The company could, if absolutely necessary, decide to put on another play at the last moment, but that might not sit well with the audience. Therefore, he decided to select certain scenes throughout the play where the alteration of a line or two, or even a short speech, would effect a slight improvement or produce a bigger laugh, so that the actors would not find themselves in the difficult position of having to learn too many new lines in only a few hours, at best. Then, he would spread the changes out in such a manner that they would gradually move the play along in a new and hopefully improved direction. But to do this, he would have to map out *all* the changes first, before deciding on the stages in which they would progress. He had spent most of the night and early morning doing so, and now he was exhausted.

He had been working by candlelight when Smythe went to sleep and he was still working in the morning when Smythe got up and went out to see Sir William. Shakespeare wondered how that was going. He felt a bit concerned for his friend, but reasoned that Smythe seemed to know what he was doing. Shakespeare still found it difficult to believe that Sir William was actually Black Billy, the legendary highwayman, but Smythe seemed certain of it and he had learned by now that his roommate was not given to idle flights of fancy. He was anxious for Smythe to return, so that he could hear all about their meeting. It would surely be a great deal more interesting, he thought, than working on this miserable play.

He put down his quill, removed his light, close-fitting, deer-skin writing glove, which had no mate for he had made it himself to keep the ink off his fingers, and rubbed his eyes, wearily. For a moment, his tired gaze focused on the quill, which he had laid flat on the table, and the well-worn, ink-stained writing glove beside it. The parchment, quill, ink pot, and glove looked rather like a still-life composition, the sort of thing that art students would practice at before they moved on to the more advanced techniques of portraiture. And, coincidentally, it also made, in a sense, for a portrait of his life . . . what it had been, and what it could yet be. The product of the glovemaker, next to the product of the poet. He could go in either one direction or the other. And this present task might well establish which direction that would be.

Perhaps it would not all come down to this, he thought. Even if he failed at this task of doctoring the play, there could yet be other opportunities to prove himself, though he did not know when or even if those opportunities would arise. The iron was, perhaps, not yet glowing hot, but it was warm, and it was up to him to strike just right, and in the proper time. He could not afford to dwell upon the play's deficiencies and bemoan Greene's clumsy unoriginality. To keep thinking about such things would make the task weigh even more heavily upon him, and he would start to work more and more slowly, taking more and more frequent breaks, and before he knew it, all momentum would be lost entirely. He needed to think of the play merely as a framework, a scaffolding upon which he would build a more solid and finished edifice. It was not the sort of beginning he had hoped for, but it was the beginning he would get . . . if he could properly begin it.

By the time midday was approaching, he had mapped out all the changes he would make to the whole play and finished the first and second stages. In all, there would be five stages of gradual changes to the play, each one adding new lines and new scenes for every part, and dropping others, until by the time the third stage was completed, it would be a play that was significantly different from the original version—or to be more precise, Greene's rewrite of whatever the original version may have been—and by the time the fifth version had been staged, it was a completely different play entirely. This way, Shakespeare thought, the actors would not be overwhelmed by having to learn too many different lines and scenes and cues, and the audience would have an unusual opportunity to see a work in progress, a play being performed even as it was being rewritten. It struck him as a novel experience, and anything new could only help the Queen's Men at this point. They certainly needed help of some sort after that last performance.

Now all that remained was to get the play to Burbage and,

unless it was deemed completely unacceptable, a frenzy of activity would begin down at the Theatre. It would be necessary to make a clean and legible "fair copy" of the play for submission to the Master of the Revels, for which purpose a scribe was usually employed. Poets . . . or playwrights, as some thought poets who wrote plays should be called, though this made it seem more like a craft rather than an art . . . were not generally known for their calligraphic skills. Their first drafts were usually covered with ink blottings and crossed-out lines and changes written in the margins and between the lines and, not infrequently, food and ale or wine stains. Hence, the term "foul papers" for the manuscript initially submitted.

The company scribe who made the fair copy was often the bookkeeper, and he needed to be especially trustworthy, for no acting company wanted to see any of its plays fall out of their hands or, worse yet, be published. That would mean that rival acting companies could get their hands on them and thereby stage rival productions. Of course, there was really nothing to prevent a rival company from sending people in to mingle with the audience at a popular play staged by the competition and thus try to copy down the lines, but this was a rather more difficult and time consuming enterprise, not to mention potentially risky if the offending copyist was caught in the act.

In this case, Shakespeare knew that there would not be time enough to produce a fair copy of the play before the next performance, which entailed several potential problems. The first order of business would have to be producing new scrolls for each actor, detailing the alterations in each part. Fortunately, his handwriting was reasonably legible, for given that only a few hours remained until the next performance, everyone in the company would be enlisted in this task, which was usually the province of the bookkeeper. The remainder of the time would be spent in learning the new lines and blocking out any necessary changes in the action on the stage. It would not be easy, but Shakespeare had anticipated this and allowed for it by the expedient device of altering the play in stages. And that was both a solution to the problem and a potential problem in itself.

The fair copy that would be produced would most likely be of the finished fifth stage of the rewritten play. In the meantime, the actors would participate in having their individual changes written out. Under ordinary circumstances, this would be the province of the bookkeeper, who would take the edited and marked-up manuscript that came back from the Office of the Revels and write out each part separately on scrolls, which would then be handed out to the actors who would play each part. Except that in this case, there would be no time to submit a fair copy to the Office of the Revels, and consequently, no time to have it reviewed and stamped.

The role of the Master of the Revels, to whom every new play had to be submitted for review, was to scrutinize each manuscript and look for any criticism, real or implied, of government policies or of the Church of England. If any such offending lines or scenes were found, the Master of the Revels would then strike them out, or else demand that the company strike out the seditious or offending lines or scenes before the play could be produced. Once that was done, the play would then officially be stamped for approval, at which point it could be staged. Except that with the next performance only hours away, there would be no time for that.

This could, thought Shakespeare, involve a certain element of risk. As the play stood when he first came to it, it had already been approved. But by the time the fifth stage of changes was completed, it would be in essence a completely different play. At that point, obviously, a fair copy could easily be submitted to the Master of the Revels and there would be ample time for it to go through the approval process. The question was, what about the earlier changes?

It was not at all unusual for actors to make ongoing changes to a play as it was being performed without the Office of the Revels demanding that each and every little change require a separate stamp of approval. But at what point would the Master of the Revels feel that *The Honorable Gentleman* had become a brand new play?

Shakespeare felt reasonably certain that they could get away with at least the first and second sets of changes, and possibly the third, especially if they did not change the title. But by the time the fourth set of changes was incorporated, it would really be a different play. By then, he reasoned, they would be ready to submit the fair copy for review. There would have been more than enough time for it to be prepared, and in the meantime, the company could easily stage other plays in its repertoire. But would the very next performance be safe from censure?

In all likelihood, he thought, it would. It was, however, up to the company to make that determination, because the Master of the Revels could not only fine a company for violations, he could stop a performance, close down the playhouse if he chose, or even send the author and the members of the company to prison. Still, the chance of anything like that occurring would be very slim, thought Shakespeare, considering that his rewrite of the play was aimed solely at making it more amusing, without including any controversial content of either a political or religious nature. He had no axe to grind, after all; he merely wanted to prove his ability so he could get a better job.

The final step, which would take place just prior to the performance, would be the hanging of the "plot," a large sheet of paper pasted on wood or cardboard that the bookkeeper would write out and hang upon a nail in the tiring room. Here would be written out the cast, the props, the cues for entrances and exits, what sound effects were needed and when, and other incidental stage business. This would be consulted throughout the performance to ensure that things ran smoothly. And if all went well, thought Shakespeare, there should be time enough. . . . perhaps just barely . . . for everything to come together for the next performance.

He sat back, rubbed his eyes wearily and stretched his stiff muscles. He had done the best job he could, considering what they gave him, but he had managed to improve it, and that improvement would be evident with the very next performance. He took a sip of wine, then pushed back his bench and rose to gather up the manuscript. At the same moment, someone started frantically knocking at the door.

"Never fear, Burbage, I have finished it!" he called, going to the door and opening it. He blinked. Instead of Richard Burbage, a beautiful young woman stood there, clasping her hands and gazing at him anxiously.

"Mr. Smythe," she said, looking past him into the room. "I must speak with Mr. Smythe at once!"

9

MYTHE HAD NOT INTENDED TO spend most of the day at
Green Oaks, but Sir William was a genial and gracious host
who had seemed genuinely pleased to have his company. And after
a few hours with him, Smythe began to understand why. Sir William's success had introduced him into elegant society, and eventually, into a life at court. He had risen from the most humble
beginnings to become one of the wealthiest men in the country,
one who could even claim the queen as an acquaintance. He was
the living embodiment of the new age in England, where a man
could rise above the station of his birth through industry and
perseverance—and a little luck—and through success in trade
achieve entry into the upper ranks of society. Even, possibly, attain
a peerage and become a member of the aristocracy.

It was, Smythe realized, precisely what his father's dream had
been, only his father had overreached himself. Like Icarus, whose
wings had melted from the sun, his father had tried to fly too high
too quickly and his hopes had melted as his dreams came crashing
down around him. Now he was a bitter old man, confronting the
specter of his own mortality and fallibility, and Smythe found it
impossible even to speak with him. It was a source of some discomfort to him, even a little shame, for he felt he owed his father
more than that, but he could not give more than would be accepted. And his father, at least for the present, could not bring

himself to accept anything from him. Not even his sympathy.

By contrast, Sir William had achieved success far beyond what Symington Smythe the elder could have dreamed, but while he outwardly seemed to enjoy the fruits of it, inwardly, he was frustrated and displeased. The society in which he moved now had its own rewards and privileges, and they were not inconsequential, but in many ways, it was a society that felt alien to him. These were not people like himself, who had pulled themselves up by their own bootstraps, but people who had been born to wealth and privilege—"born to the blood," as the saying went—and he did not feel any kinship with them. He found them indolent and decadent, sycophantic and fawning, especially toward the queen and the members of her inner circle, and most of all, he found them detestably superficial.

"In the queen's court," he had said, sarcastically, "a 'friend' is one who stabs you in the *chest*. I know them all, every last one of the treacherous leeches, and there is not a one who has not, at one time or another, asked a favor of me—most of which I granted—and to be fair, on occasion, I have asked favors in return. Yet, for all that, I would still not turn my back on any of them."

"Not even the queen?" Smythe had asked.

"Oh, especially not the queen. But in her case—and I suppose Walsingham's, as well—that is understandable. They do not live by the same rules as all the rest of us. They cannot afford to. Those two *are* England, and they must think of England first and foremost, above all else. The true statesman cannot afford a conscience. And if the queen has one, she has hidden it well away and has shown it to no one. I neither think ill of her for that nor fault her in any way. She is, after all, Henry's daughter, and she has seen firsthand what the caprices of statesmanship and the vicissitudes of politics can do. And Walsingham, her chief minister— some would say her headsman—is merely a creature spawned by such a world, a man who stands forthrightly at her side even as he moves among the shadows like a ghost. Every monarch needs a Walsingham, and every country could benefit from a monarch like our queen. But as for all the rest of them . . ."

His voice had trailed off in disgust and he simply shook his head. And so, as Smythe rode home at an easy pace, he thought he understood Sir William, perhaps better than any of his elegant friends at court could ever understand him. He knew now not only why Sir William pursued a secret life as a brigand called Black Billy, but why he was a patron to a man like Marlowe, an immoral young rooster of a poet who seemed to thrive on danger and sensual overindulgence. It explained why, instead of eagerly attending the masques and balls at court, which he felt forced to do upon occasion, he much preferred the raucous company of a rowdy Cheapside tavern. And why, instead of sitting stultified with boredom while some court musician played effetely on the virginals, he preferred a lusty, bawdy songfest at a roadside inn where no one knew his name. Sir William was a charming and rakish eccentric, to be sure, but more than that, he was a man out of his element and that often made him feel lonely.

The forge at the smithy on his estate was first rate, as could be expected, and more than large enough for any project. It did not receive much use and Sir William had said that he could help himself to it anytime he pleased.

"I shall hold you to that debt that you incurred. I want to see what you can do," he had said. "And if your skill with forging steel is anywhere near that of your uncle, then you could have a brilliant future as a swordsmith and forget all about this acting nonsense."

"But 'tis what I yearn most of all to do, milord," Smythe had replied.

"Well, then by all means, go and do it. Perhaps you will work it out of your system. But if you ask me, a life as a player is no fit occupation for man. Still, if acting is your dream, then you should certainly pursue it. Far be it from me to tell a man what he should or should not do, for as much as I have done that which I should, I have done even more that I should not, and have enjoyed the latter far more greatly than the former."

"I thank you for your sentiment, milord, and for your hospitality. But I fear that I may no longer have a job when I return, for it is getting late and now I shall never make it back in time for the next performance."

"Never fear," Sir William said. "I am not without some influence, you know. I shall write out a message to James Burbage, the owner of the Theatre, that you were doing me a service at my bidding and should therefore be excused your absence. Your job shall be safe when you return."

Smythe had thanked him and departed, feeling in a curious way that he had made a friend, and yet, he knew that true friends truly needed to be equal, and he could never be the equal of Sir William. And perhaps that was what he needed to remember most of all about his fascinating new acquaintance. He could be on equal terms with a brigand, but never with a knight.

As he entered London, his thoughts turned toward his roommate. He knew that Will had worked all night, trying to rewrite the play, and he hoped that he had been successful. But it had seemed to him a monumental task. Almost impossible. How could an entire play be thoroughly rewritten in one night? Burbage had been monstrously unfair in laying such a task on Shakespeare. But then again, Smythe remembered, Shakespeare had volunteered for it himself. It took nerve, but he had been desperate to show what he could do and he had struck when he saw his opportunity. The question was, had he struck too soon?

Another chance might have arisen later, but now, if he failed at this task, a second chance might never come. It was a risky wager and Shakespeare was betting all upon himself. It took considerable faith in one's own abilities to gamble in this way, but Will had dutifully and purposefully applied himself to the rather daunting task.

Though the poet had tried hard not to disturb him, before

he went to sleep, Smythe had heard him mumbling and muttering to himself as he sat hunched over at the table, holding his quill in a gloved hand. On occasion, Will had moaned over some clumsily rendered line, and once, he had straightened on his bench, arching his neck back and gazing at the ceiling, groaning from either muscles sorely tested or sorely tested wits. And he was still hunched over the table and working feverishly when Smythe had left for Green Oaks early in the morning, saying nothing so as not to disturb his concentration.

By now, he thought, all would have been decided, one way or another. It was late in the afternoon and drawing into evening. The performance had long since started and by the time Smythe reached their lodgings, it would have been nearly finished. Had Will managed to deliver the doctored play in time? And had there been time enough for the actors to prepare it, incorporating whatever changes he had made? Or else had Shakespeare failed in his task or, worse yet, finished only to learn that the result had been found wanting? Smythe knew that he would not have very long to wait before he would find out. The company would repair to the tavern downstairs immediately after the performance and he would meet them there.

In the meantime, he would shake the dust out of his clothes, and use the washbasin, and perhaps lie down for a short while to mull over the remarkable events of the day. But when he opened the door to their room, there was yet another remarkable event confronting him. The bed was occupied by a young woman.

Awakened by the creaking door and the weight of his tread upon the squeaky floorboards, she gasped and sat bolt upright in the bed, alarm clearly written on her features. But when she saw him, she seemed at once relieved.

"Oh! 'Tis you, at last!"

For a moment, Smythe thought he had intruded upon a serving wench from the tavern who had been bedded by his roommate in celebration of the completion of his task, but then he saw that she was fully dressed and suddenly realized why she looked familiar. She was not one of the serving wenches from the tavern, but the young woman who had arrived at the Theatre in that coach . . . Anthony Gresham's coach. He had made a point of remembering the name. She was not wearing the same elegant dress she had worn then, and had garbed herself most plainly, but he recognized her nonetheless. And she, apparently, remembered him. Indeed, it sounded as if she had come specifically to see him, which seemed even more remarkable.

"Milady?" Smythe said, taken aback. "Forgive me my impertinence, but am I to understand you have been waiting for me?"

"Oh, for hours!" she said, in exasperation, swinging her legs down to the floor. Smythe caught a tantalizing glimpse of bare calves and ankles nearly to the knee and discreetly looked away. "I had begun to think that you would never come!"

"But . . . how did you get in here?"

"Your friend, Master Shakespeare, let me in. He told me you would soon return and that if I cared to wait, then I should make myself at home."

"Master Shakespeare, is it? Well, we shall see. But I must admit that I am mystified, milady. To what do I owe this unexpected pleasure?"

She smiled, and seemed to look a bit more calm. "You are very well spoken for an ostler."

"I always try to be well spoken to beautiful women I find lying in my bed," he replied.

She chuckled. "You *are* impertinent, but I do believe it suits you. Your name is Smythe, if I recall aright. Symington Smythe. Is that not so?"

"It is, milady. But friends such as Master Shakespeare call me Tuck."

"Tuck," she repeated, as if trying it on him for size. "I like it. It suits you, too. I am Elizabeth Darcie."

"How do you do, Mistress Darcie?" he bowed slightly from

the waist. "You must have come here on an urgent errand, indeed, to risk your reputation upon an unchaperoned visit to an ostler's lodgings. Perhaps, all things considered, it would be better if we spoke downstairs, in the tavern?"

She waved him off. "I have slept up here for hours," she said. "If there is any damage to be done to my reputation, then 'tis already done and doubtless past repair. What is more, I do not care about that in the least. I have a pressing concern that is far greater."

"Perhaps you should care," Smythe replied. "However, be that as it may, I am at your service." He pulled the bench over and sat down.

"I had hoped you would be," she replied. "You have a kind and honest face. And right now, I need a kindness from you, and some honesty."

"If it lies at all within my capability, milady, then consider it done," he said.

She smiled. "Thank you. You are very gallant. What I need from you should not greatly tax your efforts, nor inconvenience you to any great degree. At least, that is my hope. Allow me to explain. . . ."

Smythe nodded, indicating that she should go on.

She took a deep breath and began. "Such is my unhappy situation: Unwillingly, I had been betrothed to Anthony Gresham by my father, who seeks to improve his social standing through the marriage. In turn, my dowry would help the Greshams to recover from some poor investments they had made. And so 'twould seem the match would be of benefit to everyone concerned . . . save for the unfortunate, reluctant bride, who wants to have no part of it."

"I see," Smythe said. "Your situation sounds indeed unfortunate, though not at all unusual, I fear. Marriage these days, especially among the upper classes, is far more often a matter of convenience and expediency for the families involved than a fortuitous result of love between the bride and groom. Tenanted estates and lands hang in the balance, as do mercantile interests and position in society."

She sniffed. "You sound like my father. And so love matters not at all?"

"I did not say that," Smythe replied. "As it happens, 'twould matter a great deal to me. But then, my opinion on such matters carries little weight, and these days, few outside the working classes even expect love to play a part in the arrangement of a marriage. My own father's thoughts along these lines were quite similar to those of yours, save that mine squandered the family fortune and thereby spared me the advantages of an inheritance and an arranged match. So now that I am common as the dirt beneath your feet, unlike the socially superior, I can afford to indulge common emotions such as love."

Elizabeth sighed. "Truly, it does seem common to them. It is beyond the compass of my comprehension. The wisdom of our elders holds that in a proper marriage, love would follow on the heels of marriage, and not necessarily hard upon. If, indeed, it ever came, 'twould come in time. Contentment and security, amiability and civility are virtues seemingly far more valued in a marriage than romantic love. Those qualities are said to make for marriages that are more sensible and stable than one based upon an emotion as common and ephemeral as love. At least, such are the prevailing, conventional beliefs. Unfortunately, they are not beliefs I share. And as my beliefs were not conventional, it did not seem I would prevail. That is, until just yesterday, when I received an invitation to the Theatre, an invitation from the very man I was to marry."

"Ah," said Smythe. " 'Twas the reason you arrived in Gresham's coach."

"Just so. And 'twas you who met that coach, mere moments

before Gresham's servant, Drummond, came to escort me to the box up in the gallery, where Anthony Gresham awaited with the most unexpected news."

"And what news was this?"

"That he no more desired to marry me than I desired to marry him!"

"Indeed? Well, there is no accounting for taste."

Elizabeth smiled. "You are most kind. However, this was very welcome news to me, as you might well imagine. He told me that he was in love with someone else. He did not say with whom, but 'twas of no consequence. I was elated and relieved to hear it. And I confessed to him that it had been my intention to behave in such a manner on that night as to convince him I was quite unsuitable, a wanton hussy. And I must now confess to you that 'twas in that spirit I had flirted with you shamelessly, especially once Drummond had arrived."

"So that of course he would report this to his master," Smythe said, nodding. "I understand. And was this the reason that you wished to speak with me? So that I would not speak of how you had behaved that night?"

"Oh, no, not at all!" Elizabeth replied. "In truth, it did not even occur to me that you might do so. On the contrary, it is of utmost import that you *do* speak of it!"

Smythe frowned. "I fear I do not understand."

She made a downward motion with the palms of her hands, as if to forestall his questions and settle herself at the same time. " 'Tis my fault. I have not made it clear. Allow me to continue."

"I wish you would."

"Thus: Anthony Gresham and I had a long talk. And we agreed that the proposed marriage was in neither of our best interests. We also agreed that I would tell my parents he had found me totally unsuitable and had so forcibly and rudely expressed himself in this regard that any attempt to pursue the match would be unthinkable."

" 'Twould seem like a sound plan," said Smythe, wondering where this was leading.

"And so I thought," Elizabeth replied. "And so I went home and followed through with it exactly as we had agreed. My father was outraged. My mother was appalled. And it seemed as if the whole problem had been solved until the very morning, when who should arrive to pay a call but the same Anthony Gresham, only behaving like a completely different man! He denied that he had ever sent the coach for me, or even made the invitation, and what is more, he denied that we had ever even met before!"

"You mean to say that on the very day after this Gresham fellow made it plain to you that he did not desire this marriage any more than you did, he came to your home and acted as if none of the events of the previous day had even happened?" Smythe said, with a frown.

"Precisely so," Elizabeth said. "You may imagine how mortified I felt! There, in my mother's presence, I was made to appear an abject liar and prevaricator! And my own mother believed that I had made up the whole story in some foolish attempt to foil the marriage! I have never been so humiliated in my life! And that . . . that . . . that *insufferable . . . arrogant . . . pernicious . . . gentleman*—" she spat the last word out as if it were the vilest poison, "—stood there smiling all the while . . . *smiling*! Ohhhh, if I were a man, I would have wiped that insolent, smug smile straight off his face!"

"And . . ." Smythe proceeded cautiously, "was *this* the service that you wished me to perform?"

She looked startled. "Oh! Oh, heaven forfend! What must you think of me? I would never ask for such a thing!"

"Then what . . . ?" It dawned on him abruptly. "Ah! I see! I am to witness that you came to the Theatre on that night, since 'twas I who met the coach that brought you. And 'twas Gresham's coach, at that, blazoned with his family crest."

"Indeed," she said, with relief. "And I also need you to affirm that I was met by Gresham's servant, Drummond, who denied ever having seen me in his life, the despicable cur! Would you be willing to give testimony to these facts?" She hesitated. "I . . . I could pay you for your trouble. Perhaps not very much, but . . ."

"I would be happy to vouch for the truth of what you said, milady," Smythe replied, holding up his hand to forestall her, "and no payment would be necessary. I would not take it in such an event, in any case, much as I appreciate your offer. But then, your offer is precisely to the point here. You *could* pay me. To lie on your behalf."

"To *lie*?" She frowned. "Why, whatever do you mean? I asked for no such thing!"

"Of course not. But consider this, milady. Why would your father, an eminent tradesman in the community, accept the word of a mere ostler, a man who could have easily been paid to bear false witness? You could go down to Paul's Walk right now and within the hour, for not much more than a few crowns, you could employ half a dozen men to bear false witness for you and testify to anything you wished."

Her eyes widened. "This sort of thing is done?" She seemed astonished at the very idea.

"Done and done quite commonly, it seems," said Smythe. "I was told that one could always make some extra money selling his integrity in such a fashion. Not, I hasten to add, that I would find such dubious employment tempting, but there are others who have no such scruples. I fear your father, already disposed to disbelieve you for your reluctance to accept his plans for you, would readily assume that I was precisely such a man."

For a moment, she simply stared at him with disbelief, shaking her head repeatedly, as if not wishing to accept what he had told her, but then the logic of his reasoning became apparent to her and as Smythe saw it sink in, he prepared himself for tears. Instead, she bunched her slender fingers into fists and raised them, as if taking a pugilistic stance, trembling with barely repressed fury.

Fearing that she might swoon from such overpowering emotion, Smythe raised his hands, palms toward her, and said, "Strike my hands, milady. 'Twill help to vent your anger."

He did not expect such an immediate and spirited response. With a cry of pure rage, she came off the bed like a tigress leaping on its prey, swinging at his hands, and he caught one blow on his outstretched right palm and then the next one on his left, surprised at the vigor with which they were delivered, and then her momentum carried her forward and the bench went crashing to the floor as they both fell backward and landed in a heap, with Elizabeth on top of him.

Momentarily stunned, Smythe could only gaze up at her with complete astonishment as the shock of the fall broke through her rage and she stared down at him, herself amazed at what she'd done, and then her gaze intensified, becoming soft and dreamy, and Smythe was pulled into that gaze as he kissed her full upon the lips.

"*Success! Victory!*" shouted Shakespeare, throwing open the door and startling them both. His eyes widened as he saw them on the floor. "Odd's blood! Victory on two fronts, it would appear!"

They both scrambled to their feet. Elizabeth's face turned red and Smythe had a feeling that his own was flushing deeply. He certainly felt warm. "Damn it, Will! You could at least knock!"

"At the door of my own room? How the hell was I to know you would be entertaining company?"

" 'Twas you who let her in, you twit!"

"Ah. Well, so I did. In all the excitement, I had quite forgotten." He bowed. "My abject and sincerest apologies to you both. I shall withdraw to a pint of ale downstairs. I beg you to forgive the interruption. Carry on. . . ."

"Will! Wait. . . ."

But he had already stepped out of the room and closed the door behind him.

Smythe shook his head and sighed, then turned to Elizabeth. "I am sorry," he said.

"For what?" she countered, archly. "For the kiss or for the interruption?"

He felt himself blushing. "To be quite honest, I am not sure. And perhaps, under the circumstances, you had best be on your way back home. 'Twould not help your reputation, nor my credibility as witness for you, should people think that anything had passed between us other than a perfectly innocent conversation."

"You are a gentleman," she said.

"No, milady. Merely an ostler, and one whose word, I fear, shall carry very little weight. But you shall have it just the same."

"Well, I trust the lady has been honorably served," said Shakespeare, coming up to him and handing him a pot of ale as he came into the tavern. "Here am I, rushing home to share the tale of my first theatrical success, and you chase me out of my own room while you entertain a lady. Odd's blood, but you are a cold-hearted fellow."

"Forgive me, Will, I . . ." Smythe cleared his throat, uneasily. " 'Twas all perfectly innocent. I came home and simply found her there, sleeping on the bed. She said that you had let her in to wait for me. I was quite taken by surprise, you know."

"I would call that being very pleasantly surprised, indeed. It looked to me as if she took you like Drake took the Armada. Heave to, young Tuck, and prepare for boarding."

Smythe grimaced. "The poet, it seems, can turn a phrase not only at Robert Greene's expense, but mine, as well."

"Oh, well said!" Shakespeare replied, with a grin. "An excellent riposte. There may be hope for you yet. Some of me must be rubbing off on you."

"Then I must remember to scrub harder."

Some of the other players were still engaged in drinking and sharing bread and cheese. The actors waved them over and they engaged in some good-natured bantering for a while, discussing the performance of that night, which had apparently been quite a success. For the first time, Smythe felt as if they were being treated as members of the company, rather than outsiders, and this seemed largely due to Shakespeare's efforts. The first stage of his rewrite of Greene's play had improved greatly on some of the jokes and puns and physically amusing scenes, and now they would immediately begin preparing to add the second round of changes to the first. Everyone had been quite pleased with the job that he had done, even the normally petulant Kemp, who had benefited greatly from new lines and bits of foolery that gave him bigger laughs.

Burbage had been quite impressed and had spoken with his father, with the result that Shakespeare would be given the opportunity to look over some of the other plays within their repertoire to see if he could effect similar improvements. Moreover, they had paid him two pounds for the job he'd done, and would pay more if he could do the same for other plays. It was not yet an offer of regular employment, but it was a good beginning and Shakespeare was justifiably excited. After they had spent some time drinking with the other players, Shakespeare took his leave of them and led Smythe to a nearby table.

The poet chuckled and clapped him on the back as they sat down together in a corner, dimly lit by the candle on the tabletop. He was clearly in high spirits. "All in all, a good night for us both, it seems. See, I told you there would be opportunities for you aplenty once we got to London. I must admit, though, I did not expect them to come knocking directly at our door. You must have really charmed her that night when you met her coach."

"In all honesty, Will, 'twas not why she came to see me," Smythe said. "She came to ask a favor."

"I see. She had lost her virtue and you were helping her to look for it upon the floor?"

"We were not doing anything upon the floor! She merely came to speak with me!"

"It must have been an exhausting conversation," said Shakespeare. "When I came in, I saw you resting from it. But do go on. I am curious to hear what happened."

Over more ale, Smythe recounted the story she had told him and Shakespeare listened with interest. When Smythe was done, the poet simply sat there for a moment, stroking his wispy beard and thinking.

"So, seriously now, what do you make of it all?" asked Smythe, after a few moments.

"Well . . . to be honest, I am not quite sure," Shakespeare replied, slowly. His mood seemed to have shifted as he had listened to Smythe's tale. The euphoria of his success, having already been indulged in the company of the Queen's Men, now gave way to a contemplative puzzlement. "There seems to be much here we do not know," he continued. "Or at the very least, we have only the lady's word that certain events transpired as she claims they had. Mind you, I do not say she has lied to you, merely that 'tis only people's nature to describe things in a manner favorable to their own predispositions. Someone else, observing these same events, might see them rather differently. And then, of course, not to cast aspersions, but merely to recognize a possibility, there *is* always the chance that she has lied."

"Do you believe she has?"

Shakespeare shrugged. "I do not know. I have had too little contact with the lady to form a reliable impression of her character. However, all jesting aside, in the short time that we did speak, she struck me as sincere. And as someone who was greatly agitated. I certainly believe she is sincere when she tells you that she does not want this marriage to take place. I cannot imagine any reason why she would lie about that. I cannot see anything that she would have to gain. Indeed, 'twould seem she would stand to gain much more if she went along with it. So I conclude we can accept her at her word there and safely assume there are no hidden reasons why she would play at intrigue in this matter."

"So that leaves us with Gresham," Smythe said.

"It does, indeed. On the face of it, Miss Darcie's actions seem quite clear and understandable. At least, to me. She does not wish to marry a man she does not love, his social standing notwithstanding, so to speak, and thus far, her comportment in this matter seems consistent. Mr. Gresham, on the other hand, if we are to accept Miss Darcie's version of events, is something of a puzzle."

"And we have reasons of our own to dislike Mr. Gresham," added Smythe, with a sour grimace.

"True. All the more reason to make sure those reasons do not interfere with reason," Shakespeare said, holding up an admonishing forefinger.

"That does it. Enough ale for you. We had better cut you off before you start tripping over your own tongue."

Shakespeare chuckled. "For all your considerable bulk, my friend, the day I cannot drink three of you under the table is the day I go back to lapping mother's milk. Meanwhile, I shall have another pot as we contemplate this matter further." He waved over the serving wench for a refill. "Now then . . . as to our friend, Mr. Gresham . . ." He frowned. "Have you seen the fellow?"

"He was the one at the inn that night, remember? He took the last available rooms. And the next day nearly ran us down."

"Ah, quite so, but I caught merely a glimpse of him as he came in. I remember a tall man, dark hair, wide-brimmed hat, and traveling cloak and not much else."

"I am surprised you remember that much, considering how much you drank that night," said Smythe, with a grin.

Shakespeare grunted. "You had a better look at him, in any case. He was well spoken, as I recall, but then one would expect that from a gentleman."

"He does not strike me as much of a gentleman if he makes a woman out to be a liar," Smythe said.

"A woman who has just allowed you to kiss her, and therefore raised herself considerably in your esteem," Shakespeare replied.

"You think a pretty face would make all of my sound judgement take sudden flight?" Smythe countered, irritably.

"Perhaps not. But add to the face an ample bosom, a saucy waist, and a pretty pair of legs wrapped around your middle and I suspect you could become quite addle-pated."

Smythe shook his head. "You do the lady a disservice, Will. You make her out to be a strumpet, and she is most assuredly not that."

"Of course not," Shakespeare replied. "Look, Tuck, I am not trying to disparage the lady or upset you. But you are my friend, and I feel it is my duty to play the Devil's advocate and point out some things you may have failed to consider. To wit, what do you suppose would happen if Gresham were to learn what just transpired upstairs?"

Smythe stifled his initial response, which was to protest once again that nothing happened. He had been alone with her in a room that had a bed in it, and he had kissed her. To a man like Gresham, that would have been enough. "Well, I should think he would surely call the marriage off. At the very least. I suppose that he might also choose to engage me in a duel."

"Oh, nonsense," Shakespeare said, with a dismissive wave. "One can only duel with equals and a gentleman would not duel with an ostler. 'Tis much more likely that Gresham would simply have you killed. You have placed yourself in a precarious position by promising to help her."

"What would you have me do, turn her away?" asked Smythe.

" 'Twould be a practical consideration," Shakespeare said, "but then if we were practical, we would not have joined a company of players." He took a drink, pondered for a moment, and then nodded. "I am inclined to take the lady at her word, I think, and accept what passed between you as a brief and innocent romantic interlude with no ulterior motives on her part, except perhaps a reaching out to form a bond and gain some sympathy. 'Tis even possible that, upon reflection, she now regrets what she has done. Either way, you seem to have become involved now. If she no longer wants your help, why then, she will doubtless say so."

"But until she does, I am inclined to help her, if I can," said Smythe.

"Which brings us back to Gresham once again," said Shakespeare.

Smythe nodded. "What motive could he have for lying?"

"Difficult to say. If, as the lady claims, he truly did tell her that he does not desire the marriage any more than she does, then his actions seem a mystery."

"She believes his purpose in dissembling with her mother was to make it seem as if she had lied about their meeting at the Theatre, made up the whole story in an effort to get out of the marriage."

"That seems rather foolish," Shakespeare said. "I mean, 'twould seem a foolish thing for her to do. If one is going to tell a lie, then it behooves one to tell it in a manner that prevents one from being easily found out. And in this case, 'twould have been a very simple matter for her to have been found out. All her parents would have had to do was ask Gresham if they had ever met."

"Which was precisely what he had denied."

"Except that we know that she was here," said Shakespeare. "We both saw her."

"But we both could have been paid to bear false witness in her favor, and that is what Gresham will doubtless claim," said Smythe. "No one would take the word of a couple of ostlers over that of a gentleman."

"Quite so. An excellent point. In all likelihood, our testimony would not resolve the problem, especially if her parents are predisposed to disbelieve her because they want the marriage to take place. But the important thing is that we *know* that she is telling the truth, at least insofar as having met Gresham at the Theatre goes. I suppose 'tis possible he might not have told her that he does not want the marriage, but then, if that were so, then why not simply deny that? Why deny meeting her at all?"

Smythe nodded. "I think the more we look at it, the more it becomes self-evident that Mr. Gresham is a liar."

"And I do not like him, anyway," said Shakespeare. "I can still remember having my arse turned into a pincushion from diving into those thorn bushes when he nearly ran us down." He winced. "I am still sore from that, damn his eyes. Arrogant bastard."

"Fine. We are agreed then that he is a liar and a worthless bastard," Smythe said. "The question is, what do we do about it?"

"Well, we try to find a way to prove he is a liar," Shakespeare said. "Or, failing that, 'twould serve your lady's purposes as well if we could devise some way to thwart the marriage."

"Agreed. But we have yet to determine what his motives may be. If we knew that, it might help us to devise a plan of action."

"Perhaps. You say the lady's parents are well off?"

"Her father is a wealthy merchant who desires to advance himself socially."

"Hmmm. A lot of that going around these days. 'Tis all rubbish if you ask me. If you have a lot of money, society eventually comes to you. There is no need to go fawning upon them."

"That is what Sir William said, though not in so many words," Smythe agreed. "In the old days, he said, a man won his spurs upon the battlefield. Nowadays, he simply buys them."

"Which is what Elizabeth Darcie's father hopes to do," said Shakespeare. "She is the bait with which he hopes to snare a gentleman of rank. And, of course, the bait is made more tempting with a dowry, which as a wealthy merchant, he can

easily afford. But suppose our Mr. Gresham happens to be particularly greedy?"

"What do you mean?"

"We were talking earlier about how Miss Darcie seemed dis-
tressed, but not unbalanced," Shakespeare said. "But what if she
did seem to be unbalanced?"

"She certainly did not strike me that way."

"No, no, of course not. But *suppose* she was. Not completely
out of her mind, you know, but nevertheless, a little touched."
The poet tapped his temple with his forefinger. "Or if she were
one of those shrewish women who tend to lie and shout and
throw tantrums whenever they are not given their way. 'Twould
make her far less desirable as a wife, I should think. Especially if
she had a reputation for such behavior."

"I see!" said Smythe, realizing where the poet was going.
"And if her father were a very wealthy man, then he might well
be moved to increase the size of her dowry considerably, as an
incentive for a prospective husband to take her off his hands!"

"You get my drift," said Shakespeare.

"I do, indeed. Gresham makes her out to be touched in the
head, or else failing that, a shrewish maid who would be nothing
but a trial to her husband. He plays at following through with the
arrangement, but at the last moment, seems to hesitate, as if
having second thoughts as a result of Elizabeth's behavior. And
her father, desperate to see them married so that he can make use
of Gresham's social stature, offers him more money to recompense
him for the inconvenience he shall experience in trying to tame
this shrew. The result: Gresham gets himself a pretty wife *and* a
pretty windfall!"

"Perhaps even a piece of Darcie's business, if he plays his cards
right," said Shakespeare. "You know, in a perverse sort of way,
there is a kind of symmetry to all this. Darcie wants to marry off
his daughter to a gentleman so that he can take advantage of the

connection to advance himself, and Gresham wants to marry money. Each gets what he wants."

"Except Elizabeth," said Smythe, "who only gets used by both."

"True, true," said Shakespeare, nodding. "It really is too bad that you are not a gentleman. You think you could get Sir William to adopt you? If you could manage that, then you might just displace Gresham and the two of you could live happily ever after, even with her father's blessing."

"Were you planning on drinking that pot of ale or wearing it?" asked Smythe.

"Now you see how you are?" Shakespeare replied. "I do my utmost to help you with your lady's problem, and arrange for your debut as a player, too, and you threaten to upend a pot of ale over my head. There's gratitude for you."

"I am grateful, Will," said Smythe. "Truly. But . . . wait. What did you say just now? My debut as a player?"

"Well, 'tis a walk-on, really, and only one line, but everyone has to start somewhere," Shakespeare said.

"You got me a part in a play?" Smythe said, with disbelief.

"A very small part," Shakespeare said, holding his thumb and forefinger about an inch apart.

"Will! An actual part in a play? However did you do it?"

"No need to get carried away now," Shakespeare said. "They were very pleased with the job I did for them, as you just saw. And I wrote in a small part for you and asked if you could play it. They were dubious until I said that 'twas only a small part in the second act, and they would not need to add another hired man. You could perform your duties as an ostler before the play begins, have plenty of time to come inside and change, come on-stage, do your part, and then go back outside and help with the horses at the close. They were quite amenable, especially when they saw that you are a great, hulking, handsome chap who will doubtless make the ladies in the audience go all aflutter. And not only ladies. There is always a place in the theatre for tall, strapping fellows. With Alleyn gone, they need someone for the audience to gawk at, and while young Burbage is a decent looking sort, he is not the manly brute that you are."

"I never know if you are serious or if you are teasing me," said Smythe, with a grimace.

"I do both," said Shakespeare, with a smile. He lifted his pot of ale. "Here's to your debut."

10

ELIZABETH DID NOT KNOW FROM whence came this sudden, exhilarating boldness, and it both alarmed and pleased her at the same time. As she made her way home, she thought about what she had done and it seemed difficult to believe that she had really done it. She wondered what her father would do if he discovered that she had been at an inn, alone with a man, and a lowly ostler, no less. She could just imagine his reaction.

If he called her a slut, beat her bloody, and drove her out of the house, no one would question his right to do so. By any decent person's standards of morality, she had disgraced herself and she had disgraced her family. But she did not feel disgraceful and she did not feel like a slut. She felt like a woman who had suddenly seized control of her own destiny and made her own choice about something. For far too long, all her choices had been made for her. For once, she had chosen for herself. And whether it had been a wise choice or not, it made her feel marvelously free.

She did not feel very close to either of her parents. Like many other children, she had been sent to live with another family when she was very young and did not return until she was nearly thirteen. This was considered a sound practice, for it kept parents from forming too close a bond with their children and thereby suffering from too much grief in the event those children should not thrive. And a great many children did not survive the first few years of infancy. Even adulthood was not without its risks, as the Plague demonstrated all too grimly every summer, so emotional attachments within families were best kept within reasonable bounds.

Still, though she had grown to know and understand all this, when she finally came home again, Elizabeth felt as if she had come home to strangers. She had seen the family resemblance, particularly with her mother, but the similarities between them seemed to go no further. And as Elizabeth grew older, she and her mother had continued to grow even farther apart. When she considered her mother now, she saw a vapid, vain, and foolish creature, a woman with whom she felt no real kinship, who cared much more about appearances than the way things truly were. And when her mother looked at her, Elizabeth knew she saw a daughter she could not even begin to understand.

Elizabeth wondered if there had ever been a time when her mother had felt the same way about things as she did. Had there *ever* been a time when she was young? There must have been, but it seemed difficult to credit. Sometimes, when she was looking at her mother, Elizabeth tried to imagine what she must have been like when she was young. She must have been a great deal like me, Elizabeth often thought, at least in her outer aspect. But inside, Elizabeth could not believe that they were anything alike. If she were to accept that her mother could have ever been anything like her, then it would have also meant accepting that something must have happened to change her into the woman she had now become. And that was a disturbing, even a frightening thought, because it implied that she might wind up the same way.

Elizabeth could not imagine being married to a man like her father. Although her father had never mistreated her in any way, and had provided a good home for her and seen to all of her material needs, neither had he shown her any affection. He seemed to care more for his sports, his fighting dogs, than he did for either her or for her mother. He was hardly ever home, tend-ing to business during most of each day, and at night he went out socializing, ostensibly also to increase his business and make new contacts and connections with people who might help him advance himself. On those nights when he came home at a reasonable hour, all he did was issue orders to her mother and herself. And he was always finding fault and never seemed to have any shortage of complaints.

Elizabeth had never heard him exchange a tender word with her mother. She had never seen any sign of physical affection pass between them. She had never seen them kiss, or caress, or hold hands, or even hug. And yet, for all that, her mother seemed to consider it a good marriage. Well, Elizabeth thought, if theirs was a good marriage, she would hate to see a bad one! Whatever became of love? Beyond romantic poetry, it seemed to have no currency. From what Elizabeth could see, a good marriage was really nothing more than a sound business transaction. And Elizabeth was not interested in going into business.

As she walked through the cobbled London streets, all around her, she saw people whose lives were a constant, desperate struggle merely to survive. These were the honest, working class people of London, skinners and saddlers, cutlers and tanners, ropemakers and weavers, coopers and costermongers, and cobblers and simple unskilled laborers mingling with beggars and trollops and cutpurses and alleymen . . . all of whom people like her father and Anthony Gresham never even deigned to notice as they drove through the city streets in their fancy, curtained coaches. These people were the lifeblood of the city, and yet, they did not impinge upon the world of her father and of the upper classes, which gave them no more thought than a carter would give his dray horse. And even there, she thought, the dray horse would fare better, because the carter knew his livelihood depended on the animal and thus he cared for it, whilst the prosperous middle and upper classes cared nothing for the lowly worker, save for how they could use him most profitably, and with the least amount of inconvenience to themselves.

Her tutor had been right, she thought. We have forgotten how to *feel*. The poets were the only ones who knew the true depth of the human soul. There was no honor in the upper classes, but only avarice and selfishness and sloth. The true beauty of the human struggle was to be found within the breast of the working man, those tireless toilers all around her who would wither and grow old before their time, assuming they survived the next Plague season. Elizabeth sighed. Her father had discovered what sort of things her tutor had been teaching her—doubtless, one of the servants had been directed to report to him—and the man had been dismissed. She missed him. He was the only one who had ever truly understood her.

"Elizabeth!"

She glanced up at the sound of her name and saw the open carriage that had just passed her stopped in the middle of the street. And standing up in it was Anthony Gresham!

"Elizabeth? It *is* you! What are you doing there, walking through the streets unescorted?"

"And pray tell what business would that be of yours?" she asked, as she approached the carriage.

"Well, quite aside from looking out for a lady's welfare, as any gentleman should do, I could say that as your intended, it is very much my business, since it would appear that I *am* still your intended. And this despite the agreement we had made."

" 'Twas not *I* who did not honor *my* agreement," Elizabeth replied, tersely. She resumed walking, holding her head high.

"Indeed? Well, 'twas certainly not I." He stepped down from the coach and caught up to her. "As it happens, I was just on my way to see you to demand an explanation."

"Demand?" She could feel the color rushing to her face. She wanted to throw herself upon him and pummel him to the ground

for the insufferable way that he had treated her, but she was not going to give him the satisfaction of seeing her lose her temper and act like the very shrew that he was trying to make her out to be. "*Demand* an explanation? You dare, sir, to take such a tone with me after the dishonorable way that you have acted?"

"My dear lady, if anyone has acted dishonorably in this matter, then 'twas certainly not I!"

"Oh, indeed? Are you implying then that *I* am the one who has acted dishonorably?" She simply could not believe the sheer gall of the man! She was so angry, it was all that she could do to hold herself in check.

"Well, what do *you* call it when someone makes an agreement with you and you break it?"

"*I*? 'Twas *I* who broke the agreement?" She stared at him with disbelief. "You astonish me, sir. You truly do. Your arrogant effrontery seems to know no bounds!"

The carriage, driven by the despicable Drummond, followed them slowly down the street. Within moments, however, a carter and a coach had come up behind them, both drivers shouting angrily at being blocked. Drummond immediately started shouting back at them and a furious argument ensued.

"Drive *on*, Andrew!" Gresham waved Drummond on before a fight could erupt. "I shall escort Miss Darcie home and meet you there!"

"I may not *wish* to be escorted by the likes of you, sir!"

"Be that as it may, I shall escort you nonetheless," Gresham replied, taking her by the arm as Drummond used his whip and the carriage passed them, pursued by the oaths of the following drivers. " 'Tis neither safe nor proper for a young woman to be abroad all by herself."

"Please let go of me, Mr. Gresham," she said, twisting her arm out of his grasp. "You are entirely too familiar for a man who impugns my integrity."

"As you wish," he said, holding up his hands as if in a gesture of surrender. "However, if my familiarity offends you so, I must admit to being somewhat puzzled as to why you would wish to marry me."

"*Marry* you!" She stopped, staring at him wide-eyed. For a moment, her mouth simply worked as if of its own accord as she struggled vainly to find speech.

"Aye, marry me. The very thing you had told me that you wanted to avoid, if you will recall our discussion at the playhouse."

"Indeed, I do recall it very well, Mr. Gresham! Good day!" She turned and walked away from him, forcing him to run several steps to catch up to her again.

"It would be good evening," he replied, "and the hour grows much too late for you to be walking home alone, howsoever undesirable my company may seem to you."

"Rest assured that it is as undesirable as it is possible for it to be."

"So you say. Nevertheless, I fear that I must inflict my company upon you for a while longer, long enough, at least, to see you safely home and perhaps receive the explanation that I came for."

"An explanation? You ask *me* for an explanation?" Elizabeth replied, in a tone of outrage. She felt so furious she was trembling.

"You think that an unreasonable request?"

"Unreasonable, unwarranted, and utterly unfathomable!" she replied.

"Understood," he replied. "Which is to say, I understand that you feel that way. What I do *not* understand is why."

"*Why?*" She rounded on him with astonishment, startling him so that he almost tripped. Involuntarily, he stepped back away from her, apparently genuinely puzzled by the intensity of her response.

"Indeed," he replied, looking confused. "*Why?*"

"You *dare* to ask me why?"

"Apparently, I do," he said, wryly. "I wonder if you dare to answer."

She shook her head and took a deep breath, then lit into him like an alley cat pouncing on a rat. "Oh, this is intolerable! This is simply not to be borne! You make me out to be a liar, come to my home and utterly humiliate me, deny the agreement you have made, and pretend that we had never even met, so that even my own mother is convinced that I have made the whole thing up, and then you have the unmitigated gall to act as if *I* were the one who broke faith with *you*! How in God's name can you stand there and look me in the eye and pretend to be an innocent when 'twas you all along who set out to undermine my honor and my reputation, to make me out to be some shrewish liar and manipulative prevaricator whom no man in his right mind would wish to marry, so that my father, fearing to see all his efforts come to naught, would then increase the size of my dowry, paying you a small fortune to take me off his hands!"

As she railed at him, she kept advancing, backing the astonished man away from her, until they had approached a narrow alleyway. She didn't even notice. She simply could not hold her temper anymore and she kept at him relentlessly.

"But, milady . . . but . . . Elizabeth!" he kept saying, over and over, vainly trying to get a word in edgewise as he kept backing away from the unexpected onslaught.

"You *knave*! You *worm*! You miserable cur dog! You lying . . . faithless . . . dishonorable . . . misbegotten . . . loathsome gutter-snipe! If there were any justice in the world, then by God, you would be struck down where you stand this very instant!"

Gresham gave a sudden, sharp grunt and his eyes went very wide. He gasped and fell forward into her arms, dragging her down. She cried out with alarmed surprise and fell to her knees, unsuccessfully trying to support his weight. Then she noticed the dagger sticking up out of his back, the blade buried to the hilt between his shoulder blades. Shocked, she released him and he dropped lifeless to the ground.

Elizabeth screamed.

The insistent hammering on the door and the shouting woke them both from a sound sleep they had only recently fallen into, aided by copious celebratory pints of ale. Shakespeare was the first to rouse himself, though he could not quite manage to raise his body off the bed. It seemed to take a supreme effort just to raise his eyelids.

"*God's wounds,*" he moaned, "what *is* that horrifying row? Tuck? *Tuck!*"

There was no response from the inert form beside him in the bed.

"*Tuck, roast your gizzard! Wake up! Wake up!*" He elbowed his roommate fiercely. Just outside their door, the noise was increasing.

"Wha'? Whadizit?" came the slurred and querulous response.

"There is a woman shrieking at the door," said Shakespeare.

"Tell her we don' want any," Smythe said, thickly, without even opening his eyes.

"*What?*"

Smythe grunted and rolled over. "Tell her t' go 'way."

"*You* damn well tell her!"

"Wha'? Why the hell should *I* tell her?"

"Because she is screeching *your* damned name!"

"Wha'?"

"*Get out of bed, you great, lumbering oaf!*"

It began to penetrate through Smythe's consciousness that he was being beaten with something. It took a moment or so longer for him to realize that it was Shakespeare's shoe, which the poet was bringing down upon his head repeatedly.

"All right, all right, damn you! *Stop* it!"

He lashed out defensively and felt the satisfying impact of his fist against something soft. There was a sharp wheezing sound, like the whistling of a perforated bellows, followed by a thud.

"Will?"

There was no response. At least, there was no response from Shakespeare. From without, there was all sorts of cacophony. Smythe could hear frenzied hammering on the door, voices, both male and female now, raised in angry shouts, running footsteps, doors slamming open . . .

"Will?"

He sat up in bed and the room seemed to tilt strangely to one side. *"Ohhhhh . . ."* He shut his eyes and brought his hand up to the bridge of his nose. Somewhere right there, between his eyes, someone seemed to have hammered in a spike while he'd been sleeping.

"Tuck! Tuck! Oh, wake *up*, Tuck, *please!"*

He recognized the voice. It was Elizabeth Darcie. And she sounded absolutely terrified. He shook off the pain in his head, not entirely successfully, and lurched out of bed.

"I'm coming!" he called out.

"Ruaghhhh!" The growling sound from the floor on the opposite side of the bed scarcely seemed human.

"Be quiet, Will! And get up off the floor!"

"Oh, bollocks! I shall stay right here. 'Tis safer."

Smythe unbolted the door and opened it. Elizabeth came rushing into his arms. "Oh, Tuck! You must help me! 'Twas terrible! Terrible!"

There was a crowd gathered just outside his door. Several members of the company were there, or what little was left of the original company since Alleyn had departed. Dick Burbage was not present, for he did not lodge at The Toad and Badger, but stayed at his father's house. Will Kemp, however, was there in his nightshirt, as were Robert Speed and several of the hired men who had rooms at the inn.

"What the devil is going on?" asked Kemp, in an affronted tone. "What is all this tumult?"

Elizabeth was sobbing against Smythe's chest and clutching at him desperately.

"What is this?" demanded the inn's proprietor, the ursine Courtney Stackpole, elbowing his way through the onlookers. "What is the cause of all this noise?"

"I do not know . . . yet," Smythe replied, holding Elizabeth protectively.

"He's *dead*!" Elizabeth sobbed. "Oh, Tuck! He's dead! Murdered!"

"Who is dead?" asked Speed. "Who was murdered?"

"*Murdered?*" Kemp drew back. "Good Lord! Who? Where? *Here?*"

Everyone started talking at once.

"*Silence!*" Stackpole bellowed. "Go on and get back to your rooms, all of you! We shall determine what has happened here." He turned to Smythe. "Who is this lady?"

"Her name is Elizabeth Darcie," Smythe replied. "And I am going to take her inside where she may sit for a moment and compose herself."

"We still have some wine, I think," said Shakespeare, from behind him. "A drink might do her good."

"Darcie?" Speed said. "Not Henry Darcie's daughter?" He took a closer look. "Good Lord, it is! God save us!"

"Who is Henry Darcie?" Stackpole asked, as Smythe led the distraught Elizabeth back inside the room and shut the door.

"Only one of the principal investors," Speed replied.

"What, in the company?" said Shakespeare.

"In the playhouse itself," Speed replied. "Henry Darcie is one of the principal investors in the Burbage Theatre."

Shakespeare groaned. "Oh, no."

"Wait a moment," said Kemp. "I remember now! That was

the same girl who was here before. She was the one with Smythe in . . . oh, *no!*"

"Will," said Speed, "Sweet Will, pray tell us he did *not* bed the daughter of one of the Theatre's principal investors."

"He did not bed the daughter of one of the Theatre's principal investors," Shakespeare replied.

"Oh, no," said Speed, shutting his eyes. "And now he's got her mixed up in some murder?"

"Oh, for God's sake, Speed!" Shakespeare replied. "She was here earlier this evening and left calmly, with her virtue intact, I am assured, without any talk of death or murder, and since then, Smythe has been in our presence all night long! Use your head, man! This is something that has happened only since she left!"

"But who is it that's been murdered?" Kemp asked. "And where? And how? And what has she to do with it? More to the point, what have *we* to do with it?"

"I imagine Tuck is attempting to ascertain those very things even as we speak," said Shakespeare. "In any event, we are not going to learn anything by congregating in the corridor. I suggest we all repair downstairs until Tuck can speak with her and then tell us what has transpired."

They all trooped downstairs, where Stackpole opened up the bar and, behind shuttered windows, they sat anxiously, drinking ale by candlelight and discussing what to do. They decided that Dick Burbage should be informed as soon as possible, and John Fleming, too, since both were shareholders of the company and Dick's father was in business with Henry Darcie. A couple of the hired men were at once dispatched to their homes. Otherwise, they did not yet know anything about the murder that Elizabeth had spoken of, such as who has been killed or how or where, but foremost in all their minds was the singular fact that one of their ostlers, and to all intents and purposes, one of their company, for Shakespeare had arranged a part for Smythe as a hired man, had

become involved with the daughter of one of the principal investors in the Burbage Theatre.

Save for Smythe and Shakespeare, who were still new with the
company, Hency Darcie was well known to them all. A wealthy
merchant who, along with James Burbage's in-laws, had invested
heavily in the construction of the playhouse, he received as a shareholder of the Theatre, as opposed to of the company, a portion
of the profits. Before any of them got paid, Hency Darcie got paid
and as such, he was a very important person in all of their lives.
James Burbage, Richard's father and the owner of the playhouse,
owed a great deal to Henry Darcie, and if—as it certainly appeared
to all—Smythe had indeed ruined his daughter, who was, as Speed
seemed to recall, betrothed to some nobleman, there would certainly be hell to pay.

"Oh, of all the bloody wenches he could have pronged, why
in God's name did he have to choose Henry Darcie's daughter?"
Kemp moaned, putting his head in his hands and overacting, as
usual. "We are undone! We are all undone!"

"Well, for one thing, 'tis not so certain that 'twas Smythe who
did the choosing," Shakespeare said. "Remember, I was there
when she arrived. 'Twas *she* who came knocking on our door in
search of *him*, and insisted upon waiting for him to return while
I went to deliver my rewrite of the play."

"And you let her *stay*?" Kemp said, in a tone of outrage.
"*Alone* in an inn, in a room shared by two men, *unchaperoned*?"

"Well, if she were alone, then she *would* be unchaperoned,
wouldn't she?" Shakespeare replied.

"You can save your poet's word games, you know damned
well what I mean!" said Kemp, angrily. " 'Twas *your* fault, then,
that this whole miserable event happened in the first place!"

"How exactly do you arrive at that ridiculous conclusion?"
Shakespeare countered. "How was I supposed to know whose
daughter she was? I had never even heard of Henry Darcie. On

the other hand, when she first arrived here and went up to our room, every single one of you was right here, wassailing and gorging yourselves on bread and cheese and meat pasties, toasting the success of the last performance. Which, I might add, would have been a miserable failure had I not doctored up your play for you."

"Oh, I see! So now 'tis *you* who are the savior of the company, is that it?" replied Kemp. "Why, you insolent young puppy—"

"Be quiet, Kemp, for Heaven's sake!" interrupted Speed. "This is getting us nowhere. For one thing, the play was *not* working, and he fixed it. And I, for one, did not hear anyone disputing that fact after the performance. For another, our friend, Shakespeare, is absolutely right. We *were* all here, Dick and John included, when the girl arrived and asked for Smythe and none of us paid her any mind. 'Twas not as if Elizabeth Darcie had never attended the Theatre before. She had been to many of our performances together with her father and she had met us all. We simply were not paying attention. We all *saw* her, but we did not *notice* her, because we were all much too busy celebrating."

Kemp snorted. "Well, I cannot go paying attention to every wench who happens to pass by!"

"You pay no attention to any of them," Speed replied, wryly, "and we all know why."

"The question is, what are you lot going to do now?" asked Stackpole. "The girl's parents are going to be concerned that she is missing. The sheriff's men may be called out."

"Oh, that is all we need!" wailed Kemp. "We shall all wind up in the Marshalsea!"

"No one is going to prison," Shakespeare said. "None of us has done anything wrong. Smythe, admittedly, looks to be somewhat at risk, but the rest of us have not broken any laws."

"It makes no difference," Kemp said. "Henry Darcie has influential friends. Powerful friends. He shall have the playhouse shut down and we shall all be out of work!"

"As a principal investor, if he has the Theatre shut down, then he only ends up taking money out of his own pocket," Shakespeare said. "And I have never known a merchant willing to do that."

Before long, Fleming and young Burbage both arrived. When they'd heard what happened and whose daughter was involved, they had wasted no time in getting there. They were quickly informed of what had transpired in their absence. By that time, Smythe rejoined them. He was alone. No sooner had he come into the tavern than they all surrounded him, peppering him with questions and accusations.

"Enough!" Stackpole shouted at them all. "Leave the lad alone! Give him a chance to speak!"

Smythe glanced at the burly innkeeper gratefully and thanked him.

"First things first," said Shakespeare. "How is she?"

"She has calmed down a bit and is resting," Smythe replied. "I gave her some wine. She will sleep now, I think. She has had quite a fright, indeed."

Stackpole brought him an ale. "There ya go, lad. On the house."

"Thanks, Court."

"What happened?" Speed asked.

Smythe related everything Elizabeth had told him, from the time they first met when she came to the Theatre in Gresham's coach to her report of Gresham's murder.

"Oh, God!" said Kemp, running his fingers through his hair. "Now we have a murdered nobleman! This just keeps getting worse and worse!"

"Be quiet, Will," said Burbage, with an annoyed glance at Kemp. "Did she see who did it, Tuck?"

Smythe shook his head. "She does not recall seeing or hearing anyone or anything. They were engaged in an argument, it seems, and she was furious with Gresham for the way he'd treated her and wished that he would be struck down. The very next moment, he was."

"Good Lord!" said Fleming.

"She said he gave a sort of grunt and fell against her. She almost went down herself, trying to support his weight, and then noticed a dagger protruding from between his shoulder blades. She quite understandably panicked and took to her heels. She ran straight back here."

"The poor girl!" said Fleming.

"I do not understand," said Burbage, frowning. "How could he have been stabbed and she not have seen who did it?"

"I was a bit confused about that, too," said Smythe. "It took a while to calm her down and she does not seem to remember what happened very clearly. But she does recall that there was an alleyway behind them, so my conjecture is that someone threw the dagger from within the alleyway."

"Threw it!" Fleming said. "Lord! It might have hit the girl!"

Smythe shook his head. "I doubt it. She said it had gone in up to the hilt. That much, she remembers vividly. Whoever threw that dagger knew what he was about."

"What do you mean?" asked Burbage.

"He means the man was an assassin," Shakespeare said.

"What!"

"An assassin!"

"But how could you know that?" asked Burbage.

"It only stands to reason," Shakespeare replied. "There seems to have been no attempt at robbery. And Gresham's clothes alone would have fetched a tidy sum, to say nothing of his jewelry and what he must have had in his purse. Elizabeth certainly would not have deterred a robber who was willing to kill to get what he wanted. So, if the man was not killed for what he had, then he was killed for who he was. Somebody wanted Anthony Gresham dead."

"But there is no way you can know any of this for certain," Kemp said.

"No, not yet, anyway," Smythe replied. "But for the moment, I can think of no other explanation."

"So then she simply left the body lying in the street?" asked Kemp.

"What did you expect her to do, pick it up and carry it back here?" said Speed, with a grimace.

"Well, I merely meant that someone would certainly have discovered it by now," said Kemp.

"That would be a reasonable assumption," agreed Burbage. "Men are killed on the streets of London every night, but they are not often noblemen. The sheriff's men will surely be asking questions."

"But not necessarily of us," said Speed.

"And why not?" asked Fleming.

"Well, Gresham was killed a considerable distance from here," Speed replied. "And none of us had anything to do with it. We were all right here, in the tavern. All night long. So why, then, would the sheriff's men want to question any of us about anything?"

"But the girl came here," said Fleming. "She came here straight afterward."

"And she was here before," said Kemp.

"And the less said about that, the better," Speed replied. "If she knows what's good for her, then she will keep her mouth shut about the whole thing."

Smythe frowned. "What are you saying?"

"Just this, my lad," Speed replied, "that she should not have been here with you in the first place, and in the second place, if everything she told you about this Gresham chap was true, then this neatly solves her problem for her, does it not? Gresham's dead." He shrugged. "His body will be found, if it has not been found already, and the sheriff's men will ask their questions, and it shall turn out, as it always does, that no one has seen anything or heard anything. And even if anyone did, why then, they heard no more than a woman screaming and they saw no more than a woman running. It is highly unlikely that anyone will ever connect her with any of this."

"You are forgetting the servant, Drummond," Smythe said. "He was driving Gresham in the carriage. And he saw Elizabeth."

"What of it?" Speed replied. "You said she told you that Gresham told him to drive off. So he was not there when it happened. Elizabeth will simply say they spoke on the street and then they parted and he must have been killed afterward. The point is, there is no reason to drag any of us into this. And if she does, then it shall only make things worse for her. If it comes out that she has been with you, then her reputation will be ruined and Henry Darcie will certainly hold you to blame, if not all of us. There is simply nothing to be served in her being honest here. 'Twill certainly not bring Gresham back. 'Twill only bring disaster down on one and all."

For a moment, nobody spoke. Then Stackpole broke the silence. "He has a point, you know."

"Aye, he does," agreed Burbage, nodding. "I cannot say that I like it, but it does make sense."

"Makes sense to me," said Kemp.

Smythe looked from one to the other of them. Finally, his gaze fell on Shakespeare. "Will?" he said.

The poet pursed his lips thoughtfully. "I hate to admit it," he said, "but Speed does have a point. I cannot see where honesty in this case would be the best policy at all. Quite the contrary, 'twould only hurt everyone concerned. Especially the two of you."

"The question is," said Burbage, gazing at Smythe intently, "can you make *her* see that?"

Smythe exhaled heavily. "I suppose that I shall have to try. For her sake, and for all of yours, if not for my own."

"Then we are all agreed?" said Burbage, glancing around at

his comrades. "Elizabeth Darcie was never here at all. Not to-night, not earlier today . . . not at all. We never saw her. None of us. We do not know anything about this. Is that quite clearly understood?"

Everyone agreed.

"But what shall she tell her parents she was doing tonight?" Shakespeare asked. "If she does not have a good story for them, one that they would easily accept, then if they pressed her for the truth, she would probably break down and tell them."

"Is there not some friend she could say she was visiting?" asked Speed.

"Perhaps," said Smythe. "But whereas a friend might lie for her, the others in the household probably would not. Parents, servants, any of them could give her away."

"True," said Shakespeare. "We would need a rather more convincing fiction, I should think."

Burbage glanced at Stackpole. "Granny Meg?" he said.

The innkeeper grinned and nodded. "Granny Meg," he agreed.

11

WHO *IS* GRANNY MEG?" ASKED Elizabeth, as they rode through the nearly deserted streets together in the small carriage Burbage had arrived in.

"She is what some people call a 'cunning woman,' " Burbage replied.

"In other words, she is what other people would call a witch," Shakespeare said, wryly.

"A *witch*!" Elizabeth's eyes grew wide. "You are not taking me to see a *witch*?"

"My dear Mistress Darcie," Burbage said, "you have just, by your own account, witnessed a murder. Surely you are not going to quail before the notion of visiting a harmless old woman?"

"But a witch!" Elizabeth replied. "They are said to be in league with the Devil!"

"They are no such thing at all," Burbage said, calmly. "Cunning women such as Granny Meg have been around long before your doctors and apothecaries. For hundreds of years, in fact. They are folk healers and charmers and diviners whose knowledge is passed on from mother to daughter throughout the generations."

"But they practice sorcery and black magic, do they not?" Elizabeth asked, apparently not quite reassured.

"There are some who would say that sorcery and black magic

were one and the same thing," Burbage replied. "And there are others who would differentiate between sorcerers and witches. Yet still others who would claim that magic is simply magic, neither white nor black, just as intent can be either good or evil. If you ask me, most of the talk one hears about magic, white or black, is all a lot of arrant nonsense. But call it what you will, I can attest that there is something to be said for the skills of cunning women."

"As can I," added Smythe. "We had a cunning woman in our village, an old and well-respected woman named Mother Mary McGee. If a farm animal fell ill, or if someone were to have need of a poultice to help cure an injury or else an infusion to quell a fever, why, old Mother Mary was the one they went to, always. And no one ever thought that Mother Mary had any dealings with the Devil, to be sure. She was a kindly old soul who would never hurt a fly."

"As is Granny Meg," said Burbage, nodding.

Elizabeth looked dubious. "And why must I go to see this Granny Meg? You have still not made that clear."

"Well, in this particular case, 'tis to save your reputation," Burbage replied. " 'Tis not the sort of request that Granny Meg would ordinarily receive, but we are old friends and she will do me the kindness of helping you, I have no doubt."

"What will she do?" asked Elizabeth, with an uncertain, worried look.

"We shall merely ask her to vouch for you," said Burbage. "Specifically, we shall ask her to vouch for your whereabouts today. We do not wish it known that you were *ever* at The Toad and Badger. That is not at all the sort of place a young woman of your standing should go to, unescorted. And I might add that there are many who would call it an unsuitable environment for a proper young woman even if she *were* escorted. 'Tis a place known to be frequented by actors and bear wards and jugglers and minstrels and the like, and 'twould cast a certain pall upon your character if 'twere known that you had been there, especially alone."

"I have nothing to be ashamed of," Elizabeth protested, with a sidelong glance at Smythe.

"And I, for one, would be inclined to agree with you," Burbage replied. "However, I am quite certain that your parents would not. You have spoken of concerns that you have had about this proposed union with the late and apparently unlamented Mr. Gresham. Well, you went to Granny Meg with those concerns, upon someone's recommendation, we shall refine the details of our story later, and then you were with Granny Meg for most of the afternoon and evening, in an attempt to learn your future and what it held in store."

"And what of the servant, Drummond, whom Gresham had sent on ahead?" asked Smythe. "He saw her in the street."

"Well, he may present a minor problem," Burbage said, "but I have been thinking about that. With Gresham dead, the servant is the only one who can place Miss Darcie at the scene of the murder. And he had been sent on to drive ahead, so he was not there when it occurred. When Gresham never came to meet him, what would he have done?"

"I imagine he would have doubled back to see what happened," Smythe said. "Perhaps he even found the body and called the sheriff's men."

"Perhaps. Or perhaps it had been found already. In any case, we have only his word—the word of a servant—that Miss Darcie was even there. She could either claim he was mistaken and the time was later or else deny that she was ever there at all."

"And this Granny Meg can be relied upon not to change her story should the sheriff's men come calling upon her to make inquiries?" Smythe asked.

"She is an old friend of the family," said Burbage, nodding

emphatically. "She can be relied upon. We shall take Miss Darcie there, then drive her home and let her out close to her house, so that she shall not be seen with us."

"You are all most gallant," Elizabeth said.

"Thank you. However, much as we appreciate the compliment," said Burbage, "in truth, I should point out that our motives are not entirely unselfish. Your father and mine are partnered in a business venture that affects all of our lives. Our very livelihoods depend upon it."

"Nevertheless, you have all been very kind," Elizabeth said. "And I shall not forget that."

The carriage pulled up in front of a small apothecary shop on a dark and narrow, winding side street. The small wooden sign that hung out over the street was painted with a mortar and a pestle.

"Granny Meg has an apothecary shop?" Shakespeare asked.

"What did you expect to find in the middle of London?" Burbage asked, with a smile. "Some dotty, wild-haired old woman living in an overgrown and tumbledown, ramshackle cottage hidden in a stand of trees?"

The poet grimaced. "But the apothecaries have a guild, do they not?" he said. "And I have never heard of any guild that would admit a woman."

"Nor have I," Burbage replied. "But I never said that Granny Meg was the apothecary, did I?"

They rang the bell and, a moment later, a small eyehole appeared in the heavy, planked front door. Elizabeth gasped slightly as an eye filled it briefly, then the plug was reinserted and the door was opened slowly with a long, protracted creaking sound. Elizabeth convulsively seized hold of Smythe's arm. He patted her hand reassuringly and they entered.

What struck them first was the heady fragrance of the place, for they could see next to nothing in the darkness. It seemed to be composed of a cacophony of smells all wafting through the air and mixing together, subtly changing from moment to moment, depending upon where they moved.

"What *is* that smell?" Elizabeth asked.

"Herbs," said Smythe. "Drying herbs, hanging from the beams up in the ceiling."

The door behind them creaked shut slowly and now there was almost total darkness in the shop, save for the glow coming from a brass candle holder that looked like a little saucer with a ring attached. The tallow candle stuck in it was nearly burnt down to a stub, with lots of melted wax caked upon it and the holder.

As the man holding the candle came away from the door and moved toward them, his candle brought illumination and they could see in the dim light the bunched, drying herbs hanging from the ceiling. It looked almost like a thatch roof turned inside out. There was vervain and rosemary and thyme, bay and basil and chive, elder, fennel, lemon balm and marjoram and hyssop and many, many more. Earthenware jars of various sizes filled the wooden shelves on all four walls. In front of one row of shelves there was a long wooden counter, laden with mixing bowls and mortars and pestles and scales with weights and measures and cutting boards and knives and scoops and funnels and all the other common tools of the apothecary.

"Good evening, Master Richard," the old man said as he approached them, in a voice that sounded surprisingly strong and resonant.

If he was the apothecary, as Smythe surmised, then he certainly looked the part. Tall and gaunt, he had an almost sepulchral aspect with his deeply set dark eyes, prominent cheekbones and high forehead. He wore a long black robe and wisps of long and very fine white hair escaped from under the matching, woven skullcap. His beard was also white and wispy, reaching down to the middle of his chest. Smythe felt Elizabeth squeeze his arm and huddle close to him. In the dim candlelight, in the dark and heavily herb-scented shop, the old man seemed the very image of a sorcerer.

"Good evening, Freddy," said Burbage, dispelling the illusion with the entirely prosaic name. "The hour is growing late, I know, but we have come to see your wife, if we may."

Freddy, for all the amiability of his name, appeared to have an expression that was perpetually grim and somber. He nodded gravely and replied, "Meg is always pleased to see you, Master Richard. Allow me to light your way."

They went to the back of the small shop and passed through a narrow doorway covered with an embroidered hanging cloth, the poor man's tapestry. Freddy had to bend over as he pushed aside the cloth and went through the doorway to lead them up a narrow flight of wooden stairs against the back wall. They climbed single-file behind him as he lit their way. Smythe noticed that Elizabeth was looking more and more apprehensive. Her nerves were already frayed from the day's events and Freddy's appearance had unsettled her. The cadaverous apothecary towered over her, as he towered over all of them save Smythe, and Elizabeth was doubtless thinking that if this was Granny Meg's husband, then what must Granny Meg herself be like?

At the top of the stairs, they came to the private living quarters just above the shop. It was a small, narrow, one-room apartment longer than it was wide, with whitewashed walls and a planked wood floor that was, unusually, not strewn with sweet-smelling rushes, as in the shop below, but swept clean. The straw bed was back near the front window, the only window in the place, and partially hidden by a freestanding wooden shelf that also functioned as a divider and a screen. The furnishings were simple and rough-hewn. There were a couple of plain and sturdy chairs, several three-legged wooden stools and a number of large chests, a wood planked table and a fireplace in which hung several black cauldrons of various sizes on iron hooks over the flames.

Smythe was a bit taken aback by this. He had never before

seen a fireplace on a second floor. In a nobleman's house, perhaps, it would not have been surprising, though he had only been in one such house, Sir William's, and then only on the first floor. However, he recalled seeing numerous chimney tops sticking up out of the roof. Perhaps Sir William had fireplaces upstairs, too. But in a thatch-roofed house such as the one Smythe had grown up in, a fireplace on a second floor would have been an invitation to disaster. With no wood between the interior and the thickly piled thatch, the fire hazard would have been extreme. When it was dry, bits of thatch—along with bugs and sometimes mice—would often fall upon the occupants, for which reason cloth canopies were usually put up on posts over the beds. And when it rained, domestic animals who often slept upon the soft thatch roof would occasionally slip through and fall into the house, giving rise to the expression that it was "raining cats and dogs."

The overwhelming impression of the place, though it was very clean, was one of nearly incomprehensible clutter. As below, wooden shelving lined all four walls and each shelf was filled to overflowing with books, earthenware jars, and other bric-a-brac. There were little pieces of statuary on the shelves such as Smythe had never seen, little figures carved from stone, some having shapes vaguely reminiscent of pregnant women and others resembling birds and animals, though of a type that Smythe had never seen. There were little tiny clay pots and great big ones, holding God only knew what, and there were beaded necklaces and amulets and little leather pouches suspended from thongs, apparently meant to be worn around the neck. No matter where one looked, there were a hundred things to draw the eye. Smythe's gaze was drawn by a strange-looking dagger lying on a shelf in front of a row of jars. Curious, he reached out for it.

"Please do not touch that, young man."

The voice was unmistakably feminine, soft and low, yet with a melodious richness that at the same time somehow managed to soothe and command authority. Startled, Smythe jerked back his hand. He felt a bit embarrassed. He, of all people, should have known better. His uncle had taught him the significance of having respect for other people's property, especially their blades.

"Forgive me," he said, uncomfortably. "I did not mean to offend. I . . . that is, I was . . ."

"Drawn to it?" She came into the firelight.

"Aye," Smythe said, softly. He blinked. He was not even entirely certain where she had come from. He had not noticed anyone come from behind the shelves dividing the main portion of the room from the sleeping area, but neither had he seen her in the room before. Yet, suddenly, there she was, as if she had somehow suddenly appeared from out of nowhere. Smythe felt Elizabeth shrink behind him, as if trying to conceal herself.

Yet, as he beheld Granny Meg, Smythe realized that she did not look anything like what he might have expected. She was of average height, with long, thick, silvery gray hair that fell in waves down past her shoulders to her waist. Her eyes were large and luminous, the sort of eyes that it was difficult to look away from. They were a pale shade of blue-gray, like cracked ice on a pond in early winter. Her features were sharp and elfin, bringing to mind some nocturnal forest creature. Her chin came almost to a point, her cheekbones were high and pronounced, and her nose had a delicate, almost birdlike sharpness. Her pale, flawless skin was practically translucent. It almost seemed to glow with vibrancy. Smythe could not begin to guess her age.

Clearly, she was no longer young, but her skin, while faintly lined in places, had no wrinkles and there were no liver spots upon her hands, neither moles or blemishes upon her face. She was slim, girlishly so, and willowy, with a figure most young women would have envied. She wore a simple homespun gown of dark blue cloth with some vine-like embroidery around the low-cut neck. The skin at her throat also belied her age. Smythe would have put Freddy's age at around sixty-five or even seventy or more. In any case, he was obviously a man well advanced in years. Granny Meg, however, did not truly live up—or perhaps down—to her name. She could have been in her fifties, or her sixties, or her seventies . . . it was impossible to tell. She was certainly not young. But she was the most singularly beautiful older woman Smythe had ever seen.

"Good evening, Granny Meg," said Burbage.

"And a good evening to you, Master Richard. It is good to see you again. How is your father?"

"Well, thank you, mum."

"*You* are Granny Meg?" said Shakespeare, as if giving voice to Smythe's thoughts. "The name does you an injustice. You scarcely look old enough to be beyond your middle years."

She turned toward him and smiled. "I am old enough to be *your* grandmother, young man."

"If, indeed, you do speak truly," Shakespeare replied, "then never in all my days have I seen a woman who wore time so lightly."

"How prettily you speak," she said. "Yet, as you are a poet, I think that you shall write more prettily still. About time . . . and other things."

"Odd's blood! How could you possibly know I am a poet?" Shakespeare asked, taken aback. "However did you divine it?"

" 'Tis true," Elizabeth whispered in Smythe's ear, "she *is* a witch!"

" 'Tis no great feat of divination," Granny Meg replied, with a graceful shrug. "Your pretty speech betrays you. And there are little ink spatters low upon your doublet, such as would occur when one sits and dips a pen too quickly and, in a rush to set words down, fails to shake off the excess ink. Together with the fact that you came with Master Richard, who keeps company mainly with his fellow actors and with disreputable poets, and it was no great leap of intuition to deduce your calling."

Smythe grinned. " 'Twould seem, Will, that even a disreputable poet can learn a thing or two about detailed observation."

Shakespeare gave him a wry look.

Granny Meg then turned toward Smythe. "You, however, do not strike me as an actor."

"And yet, I soon shall be," said Smythe.

Granny Meg pursed her lips. "Well, perhaps. But methinks I see another role for you. Perhaps no less dramatic. And as for you . . ." Her gaze fell upon Elizabeth. "Come here, girl."

Elizabeth now went to her without fear or apprehension. Indeed, thought Smythe, it would be difficult to feel any such emotion in this woman's presence. She seemed to radiate a peaceful calmness, a grace and serenity that spoke of wisdom and experience. And . . . something else. But what it was, Smythe did not know.

As Elizabeth came up to Granny Meg, the older woman gently touched her underneath her chin and lifted her head slightly, to gaze straight into her eyes. "I sense a great turmoil within you, girl. A most profound disquiet. Perhaps even desperation . . . You have recently seen death."

Elizabeth gasped and pulled away. "You had no ink stains from which to deduce that!"

"Some signs are merely more subtle than others," Granny Meg replied. "Give me your hand." She reached out to her. Elizabeth hesitated briefly, then held out her right hand. Granny Meg took it and turned it palm up, then traced several lines upon it with her long and graceful forefinger. "You shall have a long life," she said. She smiled then. "And many lovers."

Elizabeth snatched her hand back.

"Come, all of you, sit at the table," Granny Meg said. "Freddy, could we have some tea, please?"

"Are you going to read the tea leaves?" Shakespeare asked.

"No, we are going to have some tea," Granny Meg replied.

Burbage chuckled. "Granny Meg, we have come to ask a favor. . . ."

"This much I had surmised," she replied, "but it can wait. There is something else I must do first." Seemingly from out of nowhere, she produced a deck of cards and began to shuffle them. She stopped at one point and selected one, the Queen of Pentacles, and placed it face up in the center of the table, then continued to shuffle. After a moment or two, she handed the deck to Elizabeth. "Take these, girl, and shuffle them, as I did."

"I am afraid that I shall not be able to do it near as quickly," Elizabeth replied, watching her dubiously.

"Do it as slowly as you like then. The point is just to mix them up."

Elizabeth took the deck and started to shuffle the cards awkwardly. "I have never seen cards such as these," she said. "They are quite beautiful. What sort of game are they for?"

"They are called tarot cards," Granny Meg replied. "And they are not used in any sort of game." She shrugged. "Well, some people might call this sort of thing a game, I suppose. And their results would, of course, come out accordingly."

"How long should I do this?" Elizabeth asked.

"Until you feel that you have done it enough. There is no set time or number."

Elizabeth glanced at her uncertainly and promptly dropped some of the cards on the table.

" 'Tis all right," Granny Meg said. "Just pick them up and put them back into the deck, however you like."

Elizabeth did so, and after a moment more, said, "I think I have mixed these well enough."

Granny Meg nodded. "So be it. Put them down here, upon the table. Now, I shall cut them three times, and then you do likewise."

When each of them was done, Granny Meg picked up the deck. "Now," she said, "this spread is called the Celtic cross. This card here," she pointed to the Queen of Pentacles, "signifies you. And this," she pulled one card off the top of the deck and covered the Queen of Pentacles with it. ". . . this covers you. The Six of Cups. It depicts children playing in a garden, as you see. Behind the garden is a manor, with servants, all signifying wealth, happiness, contentment, childhood . . . but these things have largely passed now. This next card signifies your obstacles, those things which now oppose you. . . ."

As she gracefully drew the next card from the deck and turned it over, they could see it was reversed, or upside down. Granny Meg laid it crosswise over the first two cards. "The Knight of Cups, reversed. A messenger, or a new arrival, an invitation or a proposition. Reversed, however, it implies treachery and deceit. Duplicity and fraud oppressing you."

"That would be Gresham," Smythe said, grimly.

"Please," said Granny Meg. "She is the one who must interpret these things for herself."

Smythe merely nodded and kept silent.

Granny Meg drew another card and placed it face up on the table, in a position directly above the others. "This is the crowning influence," she said, looking at Elizabeth. "It represents what you hope to achieve, but have not, as yet. And it is the Lovers." She smiled. Elizabeth blushed at the frank depiction of a nude young man and woman on the card, surmounted by the sun and a godly or angelic presence. "You long for simple things, for what any young girl longs for. Attraction, beauty, true love, contentment and security, trials overcome. . . ."

She drew another card and laid it down below the others. "This is beneath you," she said. "It signifies your past, what is yours, what you must work with in order to achieve that which you desire. The Eight of Swords."

Elizabeth drew in her breath sharply at the depiction on the card. A woman, bound and blindfolded, surrounded by eight swords stuck into the ground.

"You are in a crisis," Granny Meg said, looking at her. "There is conflict, bad tidings, and censure. And your ability to act is limited, if indeed, you have any ability to act at all in this current situation."

Elizabeth glanced at Smythe, alarmed at the accuracy, so far, of the reading. Granny Meg continued, drawing yet another card. "This is behind you, that which has passed or is passing even as we speak." She turned up the Death card and Elizabeth cried out and brought her hands up to her face, getting a sharp glance from Granny Meg. "The Death card does not always mean literal death, although it could," she said. "It could also signify mortality, corruption, destruction or a decisive end, a discovery, or an event which shall change the direction of the querent's life."

She dealt another card and put it in the opposite position, completing the formation of the cross. "This is before you, that which is coming into action, or about to come to pass. The High Priestess. Interesting. This signifies secrets, mysteries . . . the unrevealed future. There is much intrigue surrounding you, girl. Much that has yet to be revealed and resolved."

She dealt the next four cards in quick succession, placing them face up on the table to the right of the cross formation, one above the other. She pointed to the lowest card. "This card represents yourself," she said to Elizabeth, "and your attitude in relation to your current circumstances. It is the Tower."

"It is a frightening card," Elizabeth said, softly. "Even more so, 'twould seem, than the Death card."

"It frightens you because it represents your emotions and your current state," Granny Meg replied. "A tower struck by lightning, flames bursting forth, a man and woman, apparently a king and queen, plunging to their destruction . . . it all signifies catastrophic transformation, ruin, disgrace, adversity, a fall from grace, deception, sudden change. All most unsettling, of course. And this card," she pointed to the one immediately above it, "signifies your house or your environment, the influence of people and events around you. The Seven of Wands. A young man armed with a staff, or wand, in a belligerent attitude as he stands upon a height, confronting six staves that are raised against him. His opponents are unseen. This signifies bravery and valor, for he battles against superior numbers, and yet has the advantage of position."

Elizabeth glanced at Smythe and smiled wanly. She looked a little pale and she was breathing shallowly, through slightly parted lips.

"This card," Granny Meg pointed to the second to the last card, "represents your hopes and fears. It signifies how you would like things to turn out, or else how you fear they may turn out. 'Tis the Emperor. A father figure. The representation of power and stability and protection. A great man, one with the qualities of reason and conviction."

She pointed to the final card. "This is your final outcome. It represents how your current situation shall be resolved. And here we have the Wheel of Fortune. The card of destiny."

"What does it signify?" Elizabeth asked, anxiously.

"The end of troubles," Granny Meg replied. "Fortune, change, a moving ahead, either for better or for worse."

"It sounds like a good outcome," Smythe said. "I would say 'tis most encouraging."

Elizabeth seemed somewhat relieved, but still, she was uncertain. "You are sure 'twill all turn out well in the end?"

"These things are never certain, girl," Granny Meg replied. "Conditions could change at any moment. As things stand right now, this is what your situation portends. But there is much around you that is uncertain. A roiling, turgid cloud of intrigue. I sense that it does not truly have anything to do with you, but that you are caught up in the middle of it."

"What sort of intrigue?" Shakespeare asked.

"That I cannot say," Granny Meg replied. "But I sense great powers at work behind it all. As if great winds were gathering from far off to produce a fearsome storm. And somehow, for some reason, she has found herself at the center of it all, trapped within the tempest."

*   *   *

All throughout rehearsal the next day, Smythe kept thinking about Elizabeth, wondering how things had gone for her after they had taken her home. Had the story they had concocted for her been believed? It had been Burbage's idea on their way to the Darcie residence to have Elizabeth tell her parents that Granny Meg had seen favorable omens for the marriage and that Elizabeth had therefore changed her mind about it and was now willing and even eager to proceed. This would, of course, mean absolutely nothing in that Gresham had been killed, but as Burbage pointed out, her parents would probably not know that yet and it would allow Elizabeth to tell them something that they both wanted to hear.

Burbage had explained that this ploy would predispose them to accept the story, because people always tended to believe what they wanted to believe, regardless of any facts to the contrary. On the face of it, his reasoning had seemed to make sense at the time, but Smythe somehow could not shake the feeling that something somewhere had gone wrong. And it affected his performance. Not that there was much performance to affect. He had only one entrance and one line, but he couldn't even seem to get that right. Here was his dramatic stage debut, about to occur in the very next performance, and he was making a horrid mess of it.

"*No, no, no!*" Shakespeare said, standing in front of the stage and holding the book as Smythe missed his entrance cue for the fifth time in a row. "The cue is, 'I would give a king's ransom for a horse!' And *then* you enter from stage left, come to the center of the stage, and say your line. You do not enter *before* the cue has been given, nor do you enter *while* the cue is being given. You enter *after* the cue has been given. God's wounds, is that so difficult?"

Smythe sighed. "No, 'tis not difficult at all. I am sorry, Will. Truly, I am."

"Aye, you certainly *are* sorry," Will Kemp said, as if the comment had been addressed to him rather than the other Will. "You are the sorriest excuse for a player that I have ever seen."

"Oh, come on now, Kemp," said Speed, from stage right. "Give the lad a chance."

"Aye, 'tis only his first time," said Fleming. "I am quite sure that *you* were not perfect your first time on the stage, either."

"Perfection is one thing," Kemp replied. "And doubtless 'tis entirely unreasonable to expect perfection from a novice player. But with this one, even bare adequacy seems utterly beyond him!"

There were times, thought Smythe, when he wanted nothing quite so much as to hammer Will Kemp into the ground like a tent peg. Instead, he held his temper, took a deep breath, and said, "You are quite right. I have been making a thoroughgoing mess of it. I shall try once more. And I shall keep trying until I get it right."

Will Kemp sighed dramatically. "Send out for victuals," he said. "We may be here all night."

"All right, everyone, I think a break would be in order at this time," said Shakespeare. "We shall resume from this point in a few moments. But let us take a little time to clear our heads."

"With some of us, that will take less time than with others," Kemp said, wryly. He turned and stalked offstage.

Smythe stared daggers at his back.

"Tuck," said Shakespeare, coming up to the edge of the stage and gazing up at him. "What the devil is wrong with you? Are you unwell?"

"No, no, nothing of the sort," said Smythe, sitting down on the edge of the stage. He sighed. "I just keep thinking about Elizabeth."

"What you *need* to be thinking about is the *play*," said Shakespeare, irritably. "The way you have been acting—or perhaps I should say *not* acting—you have already convinced Will Kemp that you have no ability as a player whatsoever. The rest of the company is disposed to be somewhat more lenient, since this is only your first time upon the stage, but if you keep this up, their patience will wear thin, as well."

"I know, I know."

"After all," said Shakespeare, " 'tis just *one* line! How difficult can it be to remember just *one* entrance cue and just *one* line? You come in on your cue . . . you walk to center stage . . . you say your line . . . and then you leave the stage. I do not see how I could possibly have made it any simpler for you!"

"You are quite right, Will. 'Tis really very simple. Just that I cannot seem to get it right. I do not know why. My head is all muddled."

"See here, Elizabeth will be fine," said Shakespeare, placatingly. "Her troubles, for the most part, are now over. All the portents were quite favorable. What you need to do now is get her out of your mind completely. Move on. She is much too far above your station. So stop mooning over the wench. 'Twill only drive you to drink."

"You speak from experience, do you?"

"Oh, sod off! Just learn your one damned line, come on at the right time, and say it right; 'tis all I ask."

"I know. And I am grateful, Will. I truly am. I greatly appreciate this chance."

"Then stop cocking it up, for God's sake!"

"I shall, Will. That is, I shall get it right, I promise."

"You had damn well better, or you will be back to holding horses at the gate."

"Well, I shall have to do that anyway, both before and after I complete my scene."

"Oh, *your* scene, is it? One line, and now 'tis an entire scene. Tell you what, I shall settle for *one line*, and then we shall see about a scene, all right?"

"You needn't be so peevish about it!"

"No, *Kemp* is peevish. *I*, on the other hand, am exasperated! I am trying my best to help you, Tuck. I am trying to help *us*. We have a chance here, both of us. We must not muck it up. All you need to do is walk onstage and say, 'Milord, the post horses have arrived.' And Kemp shall say his line and then you shall walk off with him. And that is really all you need to do! Is it not simple?"

Smythe exhaled heavily and nodded his head. "I know. 'Tis very simple, truly. I do not know why I cannot get it right."

"Because you have got your mind fixed upon that damned girl! Forget about her, will you please? She is not for you and never shall be. The odds are you shall not even be seeing her again."

"I say, Smythe," said Fleming, from the entrance to the tiring room, "is that not your lady from last night?"

They both looked in the direction he was indicating and, sure enough, there was Elizabeth Darcie, standing at the entrance to the playhouse, together with Dick Burbage and his father, James, along with another older gentleman and a younger, well-dressed man who looked vaguely familiar. Smythe frowned. And suddenly, it came to him.

"Good God! *Gresham!*"

"What, the man Elizabeth said was murdered?" Shakespeare said.

"Aye!"

"Are you quite certain?"

"Aye, we both saw him at the inn the night we met, remember?"

"In truth, I remember very little of that night," said Shakespeare. "I do seem to recall a gentleman arriving, but I do not believe I'd know him if I laid eyes on him again. And you are saying this is he?"

Smythe nodded, dumbstruck.

"How curious," said Shakespeare, turning back to look at the group. "I have heard it said that ghosts walk at the witching hour, but I have never heard of one who went abroad in daylight."

Smythe jumped down off the stage to the ground. "I do not understand this. Elizabeth said she saw him killed last night!"

Shakespeare shrugged. "Well, he seems to have recovered nicely."

Elizabeth spotted them and glanced in their direction. She did not say anything, nor did she gesture, but Smythe saw a look of desperate panic on her face. Gresham appeared hale and hearty, but she was the one who looked white as a ghost.

"I shall soon get to the bottom of this!" Smythe said.

Shakespeare grabbed him by the arm. "Hold off a moment," he said, in a level tone, "before you go making a complete fool of yourself."

At the same time, Dick Burbage saw them and quickly detached himself from the group and hurried toward them, gesturing to Smythe to stay where he was.

"What the hell is going on here?" Smythe muttered.

"I suspect we are about to find that out," Shakespeare replied.

12

 OU ARE, 'TWOULD SEEM, AS surprised by this turn of events as I was," Burbage said, as he approached them. He shook his head and beckoned to one of the hired men, who came running up to the edge of the stage. "Miles, tell the others that we are sticking to our story about last night. And to betray no surprise, whatever they may hear. I shall explain all in due course."

As Miles ran to pass the word, Smythe turned to Burbage and said, in a low voice, "Dick, what the devil is going on? That man with Elizabeth is Anthony Gresham, is he not?"

"Indeed, he is," said Burbage, with a wry expression. "And you may well imagine my surprise when my father introduced me to him. Fortunately, my training as a player stood me in good stead. I think I managed to conceal my astonishment, for the most part. I clearly saw yours written on your face when we came in."

"But . . . how does he come to be alive?" Smythe asked, utterly perplexed.

"By the simple expedient of not having died yet," Shakespeare said, dryly. He put his hand on Smythe's shoulder. " 'Tis painfully self-evident, my friend. The wench has lied to you."

Smythe shook his head. "No. No, I cannot believe it. She was in earnest. You were there, you heard!"

"The proof stands yonder," Burbage said. "Together with her father, who has brought Mr. Gresham here to meet with my own father about investing in the playhouse. Mr. Gresham, 'twould seem, is most interested in the arts. In plays, especially."

"But . . . but I simply cannot believe she lied to me!" said Smythe, shaking his head as he stared at the group talking by the entrance to the playhouse. He saw Elizabeth looking toward him, desperately trying to catch his eye without seeming too obvious about it. Their gazes met and she shook her head, very slightly, but emphatically.

"Tuck, my friend, you would not be the first man lied to by a woman," Shakespeare said, gently.

"You do her an injustice, Will," said Smythe. "Look at her. She looks absolutely terrified."

"Aye, she had much the same look when she saw me," said Burbage. "The look of a surprised deer. She is afraid, all right. Afraid that we shall give her game away."

"What game?" asked Smythe, frowning.

"Her lie about the supposed murder of her intended, who now stands before us. Aye, she played us for a bunch of fools. She had her fun sporting with you and then we kindly provided her with the perfect alibi to avoid any suspicion of wrongdoing or impropriety." He snorted with derision. "All she had to do was ask our help and we would have done it anyway. Lord, the last thing Henry Darcie needs to know is that one of our players bedded his daughter. His *very much betrothed* daughter."

"But I did not . . ." Smythe broke off in exasperation and took a deep breath, trying to calm himself. The other players would never believe he had not bedded the girl and all his protestations would only serve to make them more convinced. "Look, how was I to have any way of knowing who her father was?" he asked. "I had never even heard of Henry Darcie."

"Nevertheless, you still should have known well enough to realize that she was well beyond your station," Burbage said, in a tone of reproof. "And therefore, liable to be trouble. If Gresham ever found out about you, he could easily have you killed, you know. The whole thing is a bad business all around. If you ask me, the woman's touched, and I do not envy Gresham if he marries her. But then again, Henry Darcie has a lot of money, and money can buy no small amount of solace. Do yourself and all the rest of us a favor, Tuck, and keep well away from her. She will only bring you trouble. And that may bring *us* trouble, and I would prefer to avoid trouble, if at all possible. Now, Will, would you do me the courtesy of coming to see Sir Anthony? He would very much like to meet you."

Shakespeare frowned. "Why on earth would he want to meet me?"

"As I said, he is interested in plays," Burbage replied. "And I have told him that we have found a bright young poet who is just about to make his mark as one of England's greatest playwrights. A bit of an exaggeration, perhaps, but when dealing with investors, it never hurts to oversell."

"I'd like to make my mark, all right," said Shakespeare, in a surly tone. "Right on his damned jaw. I still remember all those thorns in my bum from when his coach ran us off the road that day!"

"Now don't *you* be giving me any trouble," Burbage said, sharply. "The man has come with money to invest. And we could *all* benefit from that. Aside from that, if you play your cards right, you never know, you might even get yourself a wealthy patron. 'Twould be well worth taking a few stickers up the arse, I should think. Now come on, put on your best fawning, servile manner and make a decent leg. This is business, my friend, business."

Smythe stood there and watched them head off toward the others. Dick waved to them and his father gave a jaunty wave back. Henry Darcie stood there with his arms folded, looking pompous, as if he owned the place—which, to some degree, he did—and Sir Anthony had his hands upon his hips and stood looking about like the cock of the walk. Elizabeth, however, looked on the verge of tears. She looked at Smythe and once again shook her head slightly, in jerky little motions, back and forth, like a tremor going through her.

No, thought Smythe, something here was decidedly not right. All the evidence of his senses pointed toward the explanation that Dick Burbage gave as being the only logical answer, but in his gut, Smythe could not accept it.

He did not delude himself that Elizabeth Darcie loved him or that they could ever have any sort of future together. That wasn't how he thought of her in any case, and he knew it certainly wasn't how she thought of him. But he recalled how terrified she had been and could not believe it was a lie, as both Shakespeare and Burbage thought.

Clearly, she had *not* seen Gresham killed, for here he was, in the too, too solid flesh, not even remotely ghostlike and very much alive. So then, if he was to assume she had not lied, what *had* she seen? She was not a girl given to the vapors. She had been apprehensive last night at Granny Meg's, even frightened at first, and yet, she had gone through with it, with neither fainting nor faint-heartedness. And when she came to him and told him what she'd seen, she had seemed very much in earnest. Not even the great Ned Alleyn, he thought, could act a part so well. Therefore, assuming that she had been telling him the truth, she must have seen what she had only *thought* was Gresham being murdered.

Could she have been mistaken? He thought back to her words. They had been most definite. She had said that Gresham fell against her, so heavily that he had dragged her down with him, as if he were dead weight. Dead weight, indeed. With a dagger plunged to the hilt between his shoulder blades. Which meant it had been thrown with considerable force, and by someone who knew what he was doing. She had left him then, a corpse upon the ground. Except here he was, alive. So if Elizabeth had told the truth, then it must have been a trick, an elaborate deception. And if that was the case, then Gresham must have been behind it.

But why?

What could be his motive? Elizabeth had said that Gresham had already been toying with her, making her out to be a liar and a shrew, the better to seem undesirable for wedlock, even in her parents' eyes. With the arrangement already made, a daughter who suddenly began to act erratically, to the point of lying or having flights of fancy she could not control, could certainly induce a wealthy father to increase the dowry, thereby making the prospective husband more eager for the marriage and perhaps more likely to overlook the daughter's faults.

According to Elizabeth, Gresham had even gone to the extent of using his servant, Drummond, to lie for him. Smythe remembered Drummond from that night back at the inn, and again the day that he had met Elizabeth for the first time, outside the Theatre. An officious, unpleasant, arrogantly boorish man. Smythe had disliked him from the start. And according to Elizabeth, Drummond had denied that he had even been there.

Elizabeth had said that Drummond had been driving the carriage when she had met Gresham on the street, and that Gresham had sent him on ahead, supposedly because by following them slowly in the carriage, he had blocked the way. A convenient ruse, perhaps? If he had slowed the carriage to the pace of two people walking, he would have blocked the street, of course. There were more and more carriages and coaches on the streets of London every day, so much so that they were causing blockages all over. So Gresham could have had Drummond follow until someone came up behind him and started to cause a commotion about it, then Gresham would wave him on ahead. . . . Meet me at the Darcie residence. And Drummond drives on, out of sight, then has ample time to leave the carriage somewhere and double back on foot . . . so that the two of them could stage a little drama of their own?

As if he could feel Smythe's gaze upon him, Gresham turned and glanced toward him. For a moment, their eyes met. Smythe did not look away. Gresham arched an eyebrow, frowned faintly, and then turned back to the others in the group. "No," Smythe said softly, to himself, "by God, Elizabeth is not the liar here."

He met her gaze again and nodded. She saw it. And she understood.

The remainder of the rehearsal was no improvement over his previous performance. If anything, it was even worse. He kept forgetting his one line, or else he came in on the wrong cue and stepped on Kemp's line, or else missed the cue entirely, or came in on cue only to miss his mark and move too far downstage, thereby unintentionally upstaging Kemp, which only served to further infuriate the irritable comedian. Nor did it do very much to improve Shakespeare's disposition. Since Shakespeare had punched up the old play with a new rewrite, he was, naturally enough, the logical person to function as the bookholder and prompter during the production, and therefore, the responsibility of the production running smoothly from start to finish had settled largely on his shoulders. It was an important job, and Shakespeare knew it represented an equally important opportunity for him in the company. Consequently, he was less than pleased with Smythe's performance.

Smythe knew the only reason he had his small role was because Shakespeare had recommended him for it. By botching it thoroughly, he was making his roommate look bad. He hated that, but he couldn't seem to help it. He just couldn't get it right, no matter how hard he tried. It was almost as if he were under some sort of a curse.

They finally decided to abandon the scene altogether and move on, though Kemp had kept demanding that Smythe be replaced with someone who had more intelligence, such as one of the mules from the stable. Smythe held his temper in check in the face of Kemp's relentless and abusive sarcasm, in large part because he knew that in the present circumstance, Kemp's remarks were thoroughly well deserved. For almost as long as he could remember, Smythe had dreamed of being a player, and now that he had his opportunity at last, he was making a complete mess of it.

He kept telling himself that it was because he could not get his mind off the situation with Elizabeth, but deep down inside, he was beginning to wonder if that truly was the reason. Perhaps the truth was that he was never meant to be a player. He pushed that thought aside. It was his dream. This was what he'd always wanted. He would get the hang of it. He was still new to it and he was nervous, overanxious, and . . . preoccupied. He could not do justice even to his one miserable little line so long as he kept thinking of Elizabeth.

It certainly did not help that she had been right above him, looking down from the gallery seats, where James Burbage had taken them to watch the company rehearse and give them a good overview of the entire theatre. And every time they had run through his scene . . . well, his line, in any case . . . and he had bungled it, he had heard their laughter from the upper gallery. Gresham's laughter, in particular. The miraculously resurrected Sir Anthony had one of those throw-your-head-back, arch-your-back, and roar-out-to-the-heavens laughs that rang throughout the Theatre. It was booming and infectious, and Henry Darcie and James Burbage both joined in, as did many of the players. Each time, Smythe could feel his ears burning . . . and each time, he could feel the burning gaze of Will Kemp searing scorn into him like a branding iron.

When they became exasperated and decided to stop working on that scene and move on, Smythe left the playhouse quickly, before anyone could have a chance to speak to him. In part, it was his embarrassment and anger with himself that made him seek escape, but at the same time, it was his overwhelming desire to learn the truth about what truly had transpired the previous day. The only problem was, he was not quite sure just how he was going to go about it.

His first instinct was to follow Gresham and the Darcies when they left the Theatre, and then observe them from a distance until he could have a chance to speak with Elizabeth alone. Unlike Shakespeare and Burbage, he could not accept that she had lied to them. Her terror had been all too real. She had truly believed that she had seen Sir Anthony Gresham murdered. So what must she be thinking now? To see a man slain right before your eyes, to be convinced beyond any shadow of a doubt that he was dead, only to have him apparently come back to life and act as if nothing had happened . . . to someone already driven to distraction by people questioning her motives and veracity, it had to seem as if she were descending into madness.

A chill ran through Smythe at the thought, as if someone had walked over his grave. Here was yet another frightening possibility. If Elizabeth could be convinced that she were going mad, or more significantly, if everyone around her, including even her parents, could be convinced of that, then once the marriage had taken place and the dowry was safely in Gresham's hands, she could be confined to what had once been the priory of St. Mary of Bethlehem, now better known as St. Mary's Hospital, or Bedlam, an asylum for lunatics.

Compared to that, thought Smythe, even death would be a preferable fate. And if that was Gresham's plan, then the man was much worse than an unprincipled scoundrel. He was absolutely diabolical. But the more Smythe thought about it, the more the details seemed to fit. He could not allow something like that to happen. He had to stop it somehow. He would follow Gresham and, one way or another, he would find out for certain what the man was up to.

He did not have very long to wait. They did not bother to stay for the entire rehearsal. James Burbage walked them to the front gate of the Theatre, where they got into their coach—the same coach as the one that nearly ran them down that day not long ago, when Smythe and Shakespeare were on the road to London. By the time they left the playhouse, Smythe had already saddled one of the post horses from the stable, a privilege he was abusing, since it was not an ostler's due to borrow horses anytime he chose, but he had promised old Ian Banks, the stablemaster, that he would make it up to him somehow. When Gresham, Henry Darcie, and Elizabeth drove off, with Drummond at the reins, Smythe was right behind them, keeping far enough back that he could keep the coach in sight without alerting them that they were being followed.

He needn't have worried. From inside the coach, they could not see who was behind them, and Drummond had no reason to suspect that anyone would follow, so he never turned around. When they reached the congested streets of the city, Smythe closed the distance between them so as not to lose them. He followed the coach back to the Darcie residence, then reined in, keeping back out of sight around a bend as Gresham dropped off Henry Darcie and Elizabeth. When the coach drove on, Smythe hesitated only for a moment and then followed. He decided he could double back and try to see Elizabeth later, if he had the chance, but for now, there was a more important task at hand. He wanted to find out where Gresham lived and see what sort of opportunities, if any, might present themselves.

Curiously, instead of going home, Gresham drove from the Darcie residence straight to Bishopsgate Street, where he stopped at the inn known as The Strutting Gamecock. The large, painted wooden sign outside the inn depicted a pair of fighting birds within a ring. It was one of the inns in London where sporting games were held and plays were often staged, and like The Toad and Badger, it was frequented by actors, musicians, bards, balladeers, and artists, along with other somewhat less reputable types. Smythe was unaware of any productions being staged here at the moment, so perhaps Sir Anthony had decided to take in an evening of some sport and wagering. But it was still a little early for that sort of thing and Smythe could not imagine what other business a gentleman like Gresham would have in such a place. On the other hand, he thought again, perhaps he could.

Gresham went inside the inn, but Drummond remained waiting for him with the coach, rather than driving in to stable it. It seemed that Gresham would not be staying very long. A brief assignation with some strumpet, perhaps? The corners of Smythe's mouth turned down. If that were so, then he could not say much for Gresham's taste. The sort of women he would find in there would certainly be of the more common, coarser sort. Sir Anthony had not struck him as the type who would consort with harlots, but then appearances could often be deceiving. Sir William was certainly a case in point.

Smythe wondered if he could presume on his acquaintance with Sir William to ask some pointed questions about Gresham. They moved in the same circles and doubtless knew each other. But then, what exactly would he ask? He could not very well ask Sir William if Gresham was the sort of man who would stage his own murder to take advantage of an innocent girl for personal gain. Or could he? No, he thought, not really. On the face of it, the notion seemed quite daft. And suppose the two of them were friends? He needed something more. But he was not yet sure what that could be.

He waited, debating with himself whether or not to risk stabling the horse and going in to see what he could learn. What if Gresham spotted him? For that matter, would Gresham even recognize him?

He thought back to the times they'd seen each other. The first time had been at that roadside inn outside of London, The Hawk and Mouse. When Gresham had come in, he hadn't even glanced at him. There had been no reason for him to have noticed him. He was, after all, just another poor, common traveler sitting at a table with a friend and Gresham had been intent on getting rooms. The only time they had actually confronted one another, if indeed it could be called a confrontation, had been a short while later, when Smythe had carried a nearly insensible Will Shakespeare up the stairs and, paralyzed with drink, the poet had directed him to the wrong room. There had been that moment when Smythe had opened the door and briefly seen Gresham standing in his room, in conversation with a young woman, and Gresham and the woman turned and glanced toward him, then Drummond had quickly stepped up and closed the door right in his face.

Aside from that, the only other time he had actually seen Gresham had been just a short while ago, back at the Theatre. And though their gazes had met briefly across the playhouse yard, Gresham had shown no sign of having recognized him. Might his memory be jogged if he saw him yet again? Or did he simply not remember him at all from that night at the inn? And what of Drummond? The servant had seen him close up, at least once, the night he had met Elizabeth at the Theatre. And Andrew Drummond had, of course, been there at The Hawk and Mouse that night, as well. But Smythe felt fairly certain that neither Gresham nor Drummond had noticed him that night.

He decided to take the chance. He rode up to the inn, right past Drummond waiting with the coach. The servant did not even glance toward him. Smythe turned his mount over to a burly ostler at the inn and went inside. Inside the tavern, he looked around. The place was reasonably full, with men drinking and eating and, in some cases, consorting with the women. The atmosphere was fairly noisy and pipe smoke filled the air from the long, clay churchwardens that were all the rage. Someone was playing on a cithern, brushing the wire strings with a plectrum and singing some new ballad that was making the rounds. Some of the other patrons joined in on the chorus and Smythe suddenly realized that the ballad was about none other than Black Billy the brigand, whom he knew better as Sir William Worley. He wondered what these good, working class tradesmen, artists, and apprentices might think if they knew that the bold outlaw who had captured their imaginations was, in reality, one of England's wealthiest noblemen. In all likelihood, he thought, they never would believe it.

There was no sign of Gresham. He went up to the bar and bought a pint of ale. He drank it slowly, not wishing to become tipsy when he needed to have his wits about him. If Gresham was not in the tavern, then he had to be in one of the rooms. He had obviously come to see someone here. But if he had not come to sport with some strumpet in one of the rooms upstairs, then for what purpose had he come?

A moment later, he spotted Gresham coming down the stairs near the entrance to the tavern. And there was someone with him, someone in a black, full-length, hooded cloak. The hood was up, covering the entire head and face, so Smythe could not see who it was. They headed outside. Smythe followed.

They walked out to Gresham's coach and stood there talking for a few moments. Smythe had to keep far enough back so as not to be noticed, so unfortunately, he could not hear what was said. After a moment or two, Gresham got back into the coach, alone.

Smythe had a quick decision to make. Follow Gresham, or try to find out who the mysterious stranger in the hooded cloak was? He hesitated, then decided just as Drummond whipped up the horses and the coach drove away. He could find out where Gresham lived easily enough. The ominous-looking stranger in the hooded cloak was the greater mystery for the moment.

The stranger turned and headed not back toward the tavern, but the stables. Smythe followed at a distance. From the courtyard of the inn, he could observe the entrance to the stables, where he saw three big, rough-looking men approach the stranger from inside. One of them was the very ostler to whom Smythe had given his horse. They spoke briefly, then Smythe frowned as he saw the black-cloaked stranger take out a purse and shake it out into a gloved hand. He saw the glint of the gold. The money exchanged hands.

Clearly, these tough-looking men were being paid for something. And whatever it was, Smythe had the feeling it was not for the care and feeding of some horses. Smythe tried to move in closer, to see if he could hear what they were saying. But at the same time, the three men and the stranger went inside the stables. Smythe moved quickly toward the entrance. The men were back inside, in the stalls. He could hear movement, the clinking of tack, the whickering of horses, and the creak of saddle leather. He tried to listen over the sounds.

". . . so then it makes no difference to you how we do it, eh? Right, then. We are your men. Consider it as good as done. This Will Shakespeare fellow is a dead man."

The words fell upon Smythe's ears like hammer blows. Thunderstruck, he leaned back against the wall, eyes wide with disbelief. *Shakespeare!* What in God's name had Will to do with any of this? And why in heaven would Gresham want him dead? For it was clearly Gresham who had to be behind it all for some reason he simply could not fathom.

But Gresham had only met Shakespeare that very morning! Burbage had introduced them merely hours earlier! And yet, after pausing only long enough to drop off the Darcies at their home, Gresham came straight here to meet with the dark-cloaked stranger and, apparently, to give him money. Money which had now been used to hire these blackguards to help kill his friend! Smythe knew he had to get back to the Theatre as quickly as possible and warn Will of the danger. But his horse was in the very stable where the men were standing even now.

In the next instant, he heard the sound of hooves on the hard-packed dirt floor in the stable and he just had time to duck back out of the way as four riders came trotting out, led by the dark-cloaked stranger. They spurred up to a canter and headed off down the street . . . in the direction of the Burbage Theatre.

Smythe bolted into the stable and ran to get his horse. He did not even know which stall the murderous ostler had put his horse in. Desperately, he started checking all the ones that weren't empty. The fourth one he checked held his mount, still saddled, fortunately. The ostler had merely loosened up the girth to let the animal breathe more easily. As Smythe quickly cinched up the girth, he felt a hand upon his shoulder. Startled, he spun around, raising his fist . . . and came face-to-face with a masked man, holding a dagger to his throat.

"Easy there, Tuck," he said, pulling down the black scarf covering the lower portion of his face. "You wouldn't want to hit your old friend, Black Billy, would you?"

"Sir William! Good Lord! What the devil are *you* doing here?"

"I might well ask you the same thing, sport."

"Damn it, sir, there is no time for explanations, they have gone to kill him!"

Worley frowned. "Kill whom?"

"Will! Will Shakespeare!"

"Shakespeare? You mean your poet friend?"

"Aye! I heard them! The stranger in the cloak has paid those men to go help murder him! 'Twas all done on Gresham's orders, I am certain of it!"

"Bloody hell!" Sir William swore. "They are after the wrong man."

"What?"

"They have mistaken your friend Shakespeare for Chris Marlowe."

"*What*? But why would they want Marlowe dead?"

"Because he works for me. Now come on, get on your horse! There is no time to lose if you wish to save your friend."

Smythe needed no encouragement. He quickly backed the horse out of the stall and swung up into the saddle. Sir William had already gone outside. As Smythe came out, Sir William was running across the courtyard. Near the entrance, a man was holding two horses. Sir William spoke to him quickly as he mounted one of them and Smythe saw the man nod emphatically, then mount the other and set spurs, kicking up into a gallop.

As Smythe came riding up, Sir William shouted, "I have sent for help. But we shall get there first. Come on! Ride like the Devil himself is on your heels!"

13

THOUGH SMYTHE WAS THOROUGHLY PERPLEXED about Sir William's part in these events, there was no time for any questions as they galloped through the streets of London, scattering all those before them. Sir William led the way on a bay barb, riding switch and spurs as he set a breakneck pace, his cloak billowing out behind him. Smythe was hard pressed to keep up. He had grown up around horses and could ride almost as soon as he could walk, but he was no match for Sir William, who rode as if he were a centaur. As they galloped like berserk cavalrymen in a charge, Smythe knew that on these often slippery, refuse-strewn city streets, if either of their horses fell at this pace, chances were that neither horse nor rider would survive. As for anyone who happened to be in their way, Lord help them if they did not move quickly enough.

As they approached Shoreditch, Smythe realized that it was later in the day than he had thought. He could hear the final trumpet blowing from the Theatre, and it struck him that he had been so intent upon following Gresham that he had lost all track of time. He had completely forgotten about that afternoon's performance . . . the very performance that was to have been his debut upon the stage with his one line.

It made no difference anymore, he thought with resignation. It was much too late to worry about that now, and missing his first performance was now the least of his concerns. Those killers had a head start on them, though it was doubtful they had ridden as quickly. Smythe wondered if there was any chance that they could catch them. And for that matter, if they did, Smythe wasn't sure how much help he would be. Like a fool, he had left his sword back at the Theatre, in the tiring room. Carrying his dagger was second nature to him. He simply tucked the sheath into his belt without even thinking about it. But having never worn a sword before coming to London, he could not seem to get into the habit and he kept forgetting it. And even if he had remembered it, he was under no illusion that he was any kind of swordsman. He had received instruction from his uncle, but he would be no match for a trained mercenary, an assassin. He recalled that set-to in the tavern with those drunks during the street riot. If Marlowe hadn't been there, things might have gone quite badly. These were not taproom bravos they would be up against, but sober and clear-headed killers. Sir William had his own fencing master. All Smythe had were some lessons from his uncle . . . and no sword.

As they raced across the field toward the Theatre, in the distance, Smythe could see the people gathering for the play. By now, most of the audience would have already gone inside. The groundlings would be packing the yard and the galleries would be almost full. Ahead of them, he thought he saw the four riders they were chasing, but he wasn't certain.

"There they are!" Sir William shouted, pointing.

Yes, it *was* them! Smythe could see the long black cloak on the lead rider. But they would never catch up to them before they reached the Theatre. Even now, Smythe could see that the four riders had reached the gate and were dismounting, handing their horses over to the ostlers by the gate. Once they got inside, it would be difficult, if not impossible, to find them in the crowd. He had not been able to get a good look at any of them, save the one ostler to whom he gave his horse back at the inn. That one man, whom he had seen only briefly, was all that he would have to go by, aside from the black cloak of the leader, whose face he had never even caught a glimpse of. Smythe felt his heart sink. His best chance would be to reach Will first and warn him of the danger.

As they came galloping up to the Theatre, a couple of the ostlers came running up to meet them, doubtless thinking they were late arrivals hurrying to catch the opening of the performance. They recognized Smythe at once and reacted with surprise.

"Smythe! Odd's blood! Where have you been? You're late!"

"Aye, Will's been asking everybody if they'd seen you. The play's already started!"

"Never mind that," Smythe said. "There were four riders who arrived ahead of us, big, tough-looking rufflers, led by a man in a long black cloak. Who took their horses?"

"Dunno. Never saw them."

"Wait, I think I did! Tommy got one of them, I think."

"Where's Tommy?"

"In the stables, I should imagine. Why?"

"Those men came here to kill Will."

"What, *Kemp*?"

"No, no! Shakespeare! They are going to kill Will Shakespeare!"

"What? Are you joking?"

"I am in deadly earnest! Run and get Tommy, right away! Find out who got their other horses. We have to find those men in there before they get to Will!"

"God blind me!"

"*Go!*" said Smythe. "Get all the other ostlers, too! And tell them to get weapons! These men are killers! *Hurry!*"

"*Wait!*" Sir William said, sharply, as both ostlers started off. "Not both of you, for God's sake! You, stay here and hold the horses. Now, listen to me. There will be men arriving shortly. Tell them that Sir William gave strict instructions to close off the playhouse and make certain no one leaves until I give the word. And then to stand by for further orders. Understand?"

"Aye, milord!"

"Good man," Sir William said. He turned to Smythe. "Now, did you get a good look at any of them?"

"I caught a glimpse of one of them," said Smythe. "I think I would recognize him if I saw him again."

"For your friend's sake, you had damn well better hope so. Where is he now? Is he in the production?"

"He is the book-holder for this play," said Smythe. "He will be inside, backstage, in the wings."

"Would these men know that?"

Smythe thought quickly, then nodded. "Aye, 'tis very likely. Dick Burbage brought Will over to meet Sir Anthony this morning at rehearsal. Dick said that he was interested in plays and was a possible investor, and so he puffed things up a bit and told Sir Anthony that Will was about to make his mark as one of England's greatest playwrights."

"And he signed his death warrant in the process," replied Sir William. "Gresham has your friend confused with Marlowe."

"But . . . why would Sir Anthony make such a mistake?"

"Because he is *not* Sir Anthony!"

"What? Not Sir Anthony? What do you mean? You called him Gresham."

"Aye, *Alastair* Gresham. Anthony's twin brother."

"His twin brother?"

"I shall explain later. There is no time now, we have to find those men. The guard will be arriving shortly. We need to get to your friend, Shakespeare, in the meantime, and keep him out of sight. 'Tis doubtful that they shall try anything during the play, but afterward, when everyone is leaving, would be the perfect time for them to make their move. Or perhaps during the break between the acts. Then they could slip away in the confusion. How long is the first act? When does the break come?"

Smythe was at a loss. "I . . . I cannot remember! After the second act, I think. Aye, after the second act. But as to the time . . ."

"Never mind. Get to your friend. Warn him and tell him to stay out of sight. When your ostler friends arrive, have several of them stay with him to protect him, then take the others and get out among the groundlings in the yard. 'Tis where those men will be. If you recognize the one you saw, point him out discreetly and have your ostler friends get as close to him as they can. Watch to see with whom he speaks, that will help us to spot the others. I will look for the one in the black cloak. With any luck, we shall have them before they can make their move." He glanced down and frowned. "Where the devil is your sword?"

"I . . . I left it in the tiring room."

"Well, there's a useful place for it," Sir William said, wryly. "Be a good lad and get it, will you? I suspect you may have use for it before too long."

As they went into the crowded yard, they separated and Sir William made his way around to the far side, heading toward the stairs leading to the upper galleries. Smythe made his way along the railing of the lower gallery toward the stage, which projected out into the yard.

The groundlings, those members of the audience who had paid the cheapest rate of admission and stood in the dirt yard to watch the play, had packed the yard so completely that there was scarcely any room to move. Under any other circumstances, Smythe would have been pleased to see that, for it meant more money for the ostlers, more revenue for the company, more profit for the Theatre, and a boost in Shakespeare's reputation for having so improved the play that the size of the audience had nearly tripled. The groundlings stood shoulder-to-shoulder in the yard and as Smythe looked up, it seemed to him that every seat in the upper galleries was filled, as well. Good news for the company, bad news for anyone trying to pick out four men amongst this crowd . . . four men who could easily have split up by now.

It occurred to Smythe as he tried to make his way through the crowd that none of this was as he had imagined it would be. Back home, somehow, he had always pictured the London stage as being so much more elegant, so much more . . . refined. Actually, quite the opposite was true. All around him, coarse and common-looking people were shifting their weight from foot to foot, changing position to avoid discomfort or else in an attempt to get a better view. They talked amongst themselves and laughed and belched and farted boistrously and called out to others they recognized among the crowd, even while the play was already in progress. A steady drizzle had started to come down into the open yard, which so strongly resembled the courtyards of the country's inns, upon which the design of the Theatre had been modeled, with only the galleries upon the upper stories covered over with wood and thatch roofing. The light rain was soaking into the thick thatch and making the rushes strewn over the hard packed dirt of the yard slippery underfoot, the wet smell of the straw mingling with the steamy smell of bodies in damp woollen cloaks and the acrid odor of urine from theatregoers relieving themselves into the scattered straw. The briny smell of the Thames blown in upon the breeze hung over everything, occasionally bringing with it on the air the shouts of the rivermen in their boats not too far distant. Together with the creaking of the floorboards on the stage and on the walkways of the galleries, it all had a strangely nautical feel, as if the entire edifice were some sort of crudely constructed ship, its timbers sagging wetly as it floated at its moorings.

Smythe looked for Sir William and spotted him after a few moments, heading up the back stairs to the uppermost gallery, where he would have a commanding view of the stage and the entire courtyard. Smythe quickly swept the galleries with his gaze, but saw no sign of the mysterious man in the black cloak.

He continued to make his way up toward the stage, shouldering through the crowd and getting some shoves and surly remarks back as he went. It was maddening. They simply would not get out of his way and a couple of times, he almost got into fights as he pushed and bulled his way through. Then, with a sudden burst of inspiration, he started coughing, bringing a handkerchief up to his mouth, as if he were spewing every time he coughed. Ever mindful of the Plague, people suddenly shrank back from him, turning their faces away with expressions of alarm, and he made much quicker progress. Soon, he had reached the front of the stage, which projected out into the courtyard like a wooden pier into a river of churning flesh.

The crowd was packed so thickly, people were even sitting on the edge of the stage, watching the performance, so close to the actors that they could reach out and touch them. Smythe tried to determine at what point in the play they were. The production ran about two hours long, with the acts divided into roughly equal parts. Two acts in the beginning, two acts at the end, with a break in the middle. They were at least halfway through the first act, perhaps a little more. He wasn't sure. He had enough trouble remembering his one line, much less everybody else's. All he knew was that his line had come a short way into the second act, right after Kemp announced, "I would give a king's ransom for a horse!"

He grimaced. *Now* he remembered his cue! And, inexplicably, he remembered his line, too. "Milord, the post horses have arrived!" Of course, now that it made no difference, he remembered. Well, clearly, someone else would have already been picked to play his tiny part. It would only mean an extra line for one of the other hired men. Something as insignificant as that would pose no difficulty for the production, and would probably improve it, Smythe thought, since he could never seem to get it right and only managed to succeed in getting on Kemp's nerves. But just the same, it rankled him that he remembered now, when it no longer mattered.

As he had made his way toward the front of the stage, he kept looking at the faces all around him, desperately seeking the man that he had seen back at the inn, but from where he was, he could not see much more than several feet around him in the yard. The killers could all be within fifteen or twenty feet of him and he would have no way of knowing. He would need to get some height so he could see better.

He had now reached a spot roughly parallel to the middle of the stage. A bit further and he could get backstage, into the tiring room where he had left his sword and where he could warn the other members of the company about what was going on. He continued to push his way through, coughing hard and hacking like a man on his last legs, trying to get the people to make way for him. It worked, and soon he was even with the rear of the stage and then climbing up and going through into the backstage area. The fist person he ran into was Robert Speed, costumed and waiting to go on.

"Tuck! What the devil! Where in God's name have you been?"

"There is no time to explain, Bobby. We've got trouble."

"You mean *you've* got trouble. Shakespeare was furious when you simply took off in the middle of rehearsal. And now Kemp wants you out of the company entirely."

"Never mind all that," said Smythe. "Will is in terrible danger. Four men are here to kill him."

"What, *Kemp?*"

"No, Shakespeare!"

"Why would anyone want to kill him? What has he done?"

"Nothing. 'Tis a mistake. They think that he is someone else."

"Well, then, explain things to them, for God's sake. I have

no time for this sort of nonsense now, I have to go on in a moment!"

"Damn it, Speed. . . ."

"Hold on, there's my cue!" He drew himself up, raised his chin, and swept out onto the stage.

Smythe swore in frustration. Toward the end of the first act, most of the company were onstage in a scene that took place at a ball, with everyone who was not delivering lines engaged in milling around and dancing. Several of the hired men would be making rapid entrances and exits, changing pieces of their costume to make the cast seem larger than it was. Smythe rushed up to one of them as he came off the stage and ran to make his change.

"Miles!"

"Smythe! Bloody hell! You're late!"

"Never mind, where's Will?"

"Kemp? He's out on stage, of course."

"No, no, Will Shakespeare!"

"On the other side, standing in the wings and prompting."

"Miles, listen, you must tell him—"

"No time now, I'm off!"

"Miles!"

But he had already rushed out of the tiring room and back onstage.

"Damn!" Smythe swore and looked out through the curtain, toward the back of the playhouse, where he saw his fellow ostlers all standing at the rear, holding staves and clubs and pitchforks, looking around for him to tell them what to do. *"Hell,"* he muttered, through gritted teeth. He could see no sign of Sir William, or the killers, or the man in the black cloak who led them. But they were all out there, somewhere. He had to warn Will, and then get back to the ostlers and let them know what they had to do.

He found his sword, which was fortunately right where he had left it earlier that day, buckled the scabbard around his waist, then quickly made his way around across the backstage area and to the other side. Will was standing just offstage, in the wings, holding the book, following the action and making certain everyone picked up their cues and made their entrances on time, with the right props.

"Will! Thank God!"

"Tuck! Damn you, where the devil did you get to?" Shakespeare said, angrily.

"Never mind that. Listen to me, your life is in danger. Four men are here to kill you."

"*What?*"

"Look, I do not have much time to explain—"

"*Phillip! Now!* Your cue! Go *on!*" said Shakespeare, to one of the young boys playing one of the female parts.

"Blast! Sorry," said the lad, and lifting up his skirts, he rushed out onto the stage.

"Will—"

"Not *now*, Tuck, for heaven's sake! I cannot be distracted! You are getting in the way! The act is almost over. There is still time for you to change and do your part if you hurry."

"Will, have you even heard what I said? There are people here to *kill* you!"

"*What?* Why would anyone wish to kill *me?*"

"Because they are acting on Gresham's orders!"

Shakespeare rolled his eyes. "Oh, what rot! What sort of nonsense has that damned girl filled your head with now? I told you to stay away from her! Burbage told you to stay away from her! You are just going to cause everyone a lot of trouble!" He reached out and grabbed one of the hired men as he was rushing past. "Wait, Adrian, the *tray!* Do not forget the tray!"

"Shit. Thanks."

"Will, please . . . listen to me, Elizabeth has nothing to do with this—"

"She has everything to do with it! That girl is out of her

bloody mind. Sir Anthony is a perfectly decent man who deserves a lot better than her, if you ask me. Now forget this nonsense and get back there and change. The first act is ending any moment . . . no, 'tis done, they are coming in."

"*Will*—"

"I have no time now! We can discuss this later! Right, come on, now, everyone! Costumes and places for the second act! Check the pegboard for your props and cues!"

As the refreshment vendors plied their wares out in the courtyard among the crowd, the other players all came rushing back offstage, heading for the tiring room. The second act followed hard upon the heels of the first, with no break in between. Will Kemp, as one of the leading players, had to go back out on stage almost immediately, along with young Michael Jones, who was playing the lead female role. Kemp's gaze fell on Smythe and his lip curled down in a sneer.

"Oh, so you finally decided to grace us with your presence, did you, young prodigal?"

Smythe ignored him. "Dick!" he said to Burbage, as he hurried by. "They are going to try to murder Will!"

"What, *me*?" said Kemp, astonished.

"No! *Shakespeare!*"

"What?" Shakespeare said, turning around.

"They are going to try to kill you, you fool!"

"What is all this about killing?" Burbage demanded, insistantly.

"*I* am going to kill someone if you do not all keep quiet!" Kemp said. "I am listening to Fleming for my cue!"

"And you just missed it!" Shakespeare said. "Kemp, Jones, you're on!"

"Oh, *bollocks*!" Kemp said, as he and Jones rushed out on stage.

"Tuck, what *is* this talk of killing?" Burbage repeated.

"Oh, Sir Anthony Gresham wants me dead, it seems," said

Shakespeare, wryly. "You know . . . Elizabeth." He made a circling motion with his forefinger by his temple.

"Oh, God's wounds!" said Burbage, looking heavenward. "Smythe, did I not tell you to keep away from her?"

"Is Smythe going to give his line or do you still want me to do it?" Miles asked, glancing from Smythe to Shakespeare.

"Smythe can do it, now that he's here," Shakespeare said.

"Smythe never came on time," said Burbage, curtly, over-riding him. "You do it, Miles."

"Well, I really do not mind stepping aside," said Miles, trying to be considerate of his fellow player.

"He was late," said Burbage, "and he is not even in proper costume. You do it."

"*Somebody* damn well do it!" Shakespeare said, in exasperation. "There is the cue!"

"I *said*," Kemp raised his voice from centerstage, repeating the cue, "I would give a king's ransom for a *horse!*"

Smythe and Miles both stepped out on the stage together. Realizing what they'd done, they glanced at one another, trying to decide which of them would say the line. There was an awkward moment of silence, and then suddenly, from out in the audience, somebody neighed loudly.

For a moment, the audience was stunned. Startled, Smythe and Miles both looked toward the sound and, in the same moment, Will Kemp, staying totally in character, turned to face the audience, flung out an arm expansively and pointed in the direction of the offending heckler, crying out, *"Never mind the horse! Saddle yon' braying ass!"*

As the audience exploded into laughter and spontaneous applause, Smythe saw who had made the sound. Incredibly, it had been Sir William, standing in the uppermost gallery! He was gesticulating wildly. Smythe turned and looked in the direction he was pointing and there, in the middle gallery clear on the other side, stood the black-cloaked stranger!

"Ostlers!" Smythe shouted, stepping to the front of the stage and pointing up. *"Get that man!"*

Abruptly realizing that Smythe was pointing straight up at him, the black-cloaked stranger bolted toward the stairs. The ostlers in the yard below moved to intercept him. Sir William ran toward the stairs on the other side. The audience, thinking it was all part of the play, laughed uproariously and applauded.

"Milord," said Miles, picking up the cue belatedly, "the post horses have arrived!"

"Just in the nick of time!" said Kemp, returning to the script, "Then I am off, to spur on toward my fate!"

They all left the stage together to thunderous applause.

"What in heaven's name was *that?*" demanded Burbage, as they all came off.

"Dick, you're on!" said Shakespeare, pushing Burbage out on stage before he could receive a reply. "John Fleming, stand by!"

"I am bloody well going to kill you!" Kemp turned on Smythe furiously, shaking his finger in his face.

"What did *I* do?" Smythe said.

"You and that idiot friend of yours up there in the gallery just absolutely *ruined* my scene!"

"Ruined it?" said Shakespeare. "Damn it, Kemp, you were *brilliant!*"

"That 'idiot friend' of mine just happens to be Sir William Worley," Smythe said.

"Sir William Worley?" Fleming said, with astonished disbelief. "You mean the master of the Sea Hawks?"

"John, your cue," said Shakespeare.

"But . . . he is an intimate of the queen!" said Fleming.

"Fleming! Your *cue!"*

"Oh! Good Christ!" Fleming rushed out on the stage.

"You really think I was brilliant?" Kemp asked.

"Your improvisation was not only brilliant, it was absolutely inspired," Shakespeare said. He turned to Smythe. "That was *Sir William* neighing? You cannot be serious!"

"Will!" someone called out from behind them. "Will Shakespeare!"

"What *now*?" Shakespeare turned around.

"Look out, Will!" Smythe shoved Shakespeare hard. The poet fell, sprawling, to the floorboards. The dagger sailed through the air where he had stood an instant earlier and buried itself in a wooden beam right by Kemp's ear.

"HELP! MURDER!" Kemp cried out and, without thinking, ran straight out onto the stage, where he had no business being until the last scene of the act.

Smythe reached for his sword, but before he could draw it, the man who'd thrown the knife, the burly ostler he'd recognized from the inn, bellowed like a maddened bull and charged him. He struck Smythe hard, wrapping his arms around him in a bear hug, and his momentum carried them both backward, out into the middle of the stage, where they both fell heavily with a resounding crash. The second man came right behind him, charging with a large Florentine stiletto, but before he could reach Shakespeare, Miles kicked his legs out from under him and the man fell, impaling himself on his own blade.

Burbage and Fleming, onstage in the middle of their scene, suddenly found themselves rudely interrupted as Kemp came shrieking out onto the stage from the wings. Seconds later, Smythe and the hired killer came tumbling on, as well, to the immense amusement of the audience, who cheered and applauded the spectacle.

"Defend yourself!" Burbage cried to Fleming, improvising. "We are attacked!"

He drew his sword, just as Shakespeare came running out onto the stage, with the third killer in hot pursuit with a drawn blade of his own. Seeing Burbage with his sword, the man hesitated and then struck. Burbage parried, and in the next instant, what appeared to be a young girl came flying out from the wings and tackled the hired killer as young Mick Jones bravely leapt into the fray to defend his fellow players.

Smythe broke the grip of his antagonist and dislodged him, scrambling to his feet. They both got up at the same time. The man swung, but Smythe blocked the blow with his left forearm and with his right fist knocked the man clear off the stage and into the audience.

"Groundlings, don't let him get away!" Fleming shouted to the audience. "The man's a *pickpocket*!"

That one word galvanized the groundlings into action. Now realizing this was not part of the production, they surged around what they believed to be the scourge of playhouse audiences everywhere and proceeded to stomp and kick the man repeatedly. Meanwhile, Smythe drew his blade and went to aid Burbage, but by now, a number of the ostlers had reached the stage and they came storming on, brandishing clubs and pitchforks, and the man threw down his weapon and surrendered as the audience cheered loudly and kept up a sustained applause.

The man Smythe had knocked off the stage was hauled up to his feet, badly battered and bleeding profusely, barely even conscious. And the third man had not survived the fall onto his own knife. Smythe hurried to check on Shakespeare.

"Are you all right, Will?"

"Aye, I think so," Shakespeare replied. "Odd's blood, they really *were* trying to kill me! But *why*?"

"I am not entirely sure of that myself," Smythe replied, "but I think I may have an idea. Stay here with the others. And watch yourself. Their leader is still unaccounted for. I must go and find Sir William."

He jumped down off the stage and struggled to make his way through the throng of groundlings to the entrance. There he found Sir William, waiting for him along with several of the ostlers.

"Did you get him?" Smythe asked, anxiously.

"No, curse the luck," Sir William said. "But we got his cloak." He held up the garment. "A couple of the ostlers found it on the stairs."

Smythe exhaled heavily. "Damn it! So he got away, then?"

"Not yet," Sir William said grimly, shaking his head. "Come with me."

They moved toward the theatre entrance. Outside, Smythe saw the guardsmen in their helms and breastplates, posted at the gate. Sir William smiled. "I do not think he had a chance to slip past them," he said. "They arrived not long after we did."

The Captain of the Guard came up to Sir William and saluted. "We stand by for your orders, milord."

"No one has been allowed out past you?"

"No, milord, no one. Only the lady."

Worley's eyes narrowed. "*What* lady?" he said, sharply.

"Why, the one you told to leave, milord."

"The one *I* told to leave? What the devil are you talking about? I told no one to leave! I gave strict orders that no one was to be allowed out! *No one!*"

The captain looked concerned. "Aye, milord, that was what I told her. I said that Sir William gave strict instructions that no one was to leave, but she said that you had sent her home, because it would be too dangerous for her to remain. There would be trouble and you did not wish to see her placed at risk—"

"You damn fool!" Sir William said. "Where did she go?"

"Why, she . . . she left in the coach, milord."

"*What* coach?"

There was now panic in the captain's eyes. "Well, the one she said you sent for her, milord! A very handsome coach, 'twas, milord. She . . . she said it bore your crest—"

"Gresham!" Smythe said. He looked out and across the field. "Look! *There!*" He pointed.

"*Damn!* Where is my horse?"

"Right here, milord," the ostler who had been holding both their horses all along called out to him.

"Mount up!" Sir William shouted to the guard as he and Smythe ran to get their horses. "There'll be a gold sovereign for you when we return," he said to the ostler, as he swung up into the saddle. "And Captain, if you do not catch that coach, you shall be a stableboy by sunset!"

"Aye, milord!"

They all set spurs and galloped off full speed across the field. The coach was well ahead of them, but the driver could not match their pace and they closed the distance rapidly. Before long, Smythe, riding up front with Sir William, could see the driver of the coach whipping up the horses, glancing back nervously over his shoulder. That would be Drummond, surely. But who was in the coach?

If Sir Anthony was not Sir Anthony, as Sir William had said, but his twin brother, who then was the woman? Smythe hoped it wasn't who he thought it might be. She could not possibly be part of this, he thought, could she?

They had nearly closed with the coach as they reached the city limits and the chase continued through the cobbled streets. But here the coach was even more at a disadvantage. People scattered, crying out in fear, as the black coach careened wildly through the streets, and then the inevitable happened. Another coach was coming the other way as Drummond whipped his horses round a bend. In a desperate effort to avoid a collision, Drummond swung wide and tried to go around the other coach, but there simply wasn't enough room. The horses screamed as they collided and the coaches struck one another with a tremendous impact. Gresham's coach overturned and the horses fell in a horrible, thrashing tangle.

As the pursuing guard reined in, Sir William dismounted and went with several of the guardsmen to see if anyone was injured. There was only one occupant of the smaller coach, a young gentleman, but though he was shaken up and bruised, with a cut lip and a bloody nose, he seemed otherwise unhurt. Gresham's coach had not fared nearly so well.

Drummond had been thrown from the seat with such force that he had flown through the air more than a dozen feet and struck a building wall, snapping his spine on impact. His battered body was twisted and bent at an unnatural angle when they found it lying in a puddle on the street. Inside the coach, they found Gresham, with his neck broken. But there was one survivor.

She was badly bruised and bloody when they pulled her out, but Smythe immediately noticed the striking resemblance that he had not marked before, when he had glimpsed her only very briefly at The Hawk and Mouse, on the road outside of London. She looked up at Sir William with a venemous gaze and spat right into his face. *"Heretic pig!"* she snarled.

"Well, I'll be damned," said Sir William, wiping his cheek with his handkerchief. "Triplets."

EPILOGUE:

"So then Sir Anthony really *is* dead?" asked Shakespeare.

"I am afraid so," Sir William replied. He turned to Elizabeth Darcie. "What you must have seen that day was his actual murder, the very murder that enabled his twin brother, Alastair, to take his place once and for all, after trying out his impersonation upon you to make certain he could pull it off."

"And here I was convinced 'twas all some sort of trick," said Smythe. "I thought Sir Anthony had staged his own death to undermine Elizabeth's credibility and make it seem as if she were losing her mind."

Elizabeth bit her lower lip at the thought and shook her head.

"An interesting theory," said Sir William. "And you were not very far from truth, save that 'twas Alastair Gresham and not his brother, Anthony, who was trying to make it seem as if Elizabeth were mad."

They were sitting at a table in The Toad and Badger with Sir William. It was very late and everybody else had long since gone to bed after discussing the day's tumultuous events. It had been quite a day for all concerned. Sir William had only recently arrived with some wine, and an exceedingly fine wine it was, and now Smythe, Shakespeare, and Elizabeth, who had arrived along with her father, Henry Darcie, were finally discovering the whole truth behind the strange events they had become caught up in.

"So then Sir Anthony never knew that he had a twin brother? *And* a sister?" Smythe shook his head. "How could that be?"

" 'Tis a long and complicated story," said Sir William. "The sister, Allison, confessed it all to me. And I heard the rest from their aging father, James, earlier tonight. When they were children, they were all on a sea voyage together and there was a storm, which caused a shipwreck. Anthony and his father were picked up by a passing ship after drifting for two days, clinging to some wreckage. They were convinced that there were no other survivors. But as it turns out, there were. Alastair and Allison, together with their mother, had also survived and were picked up by another ship, which took them not to England, but to Spain. Their mother, Helena, never fully recovered from her ordeal. She lingered for some time, and finally died, leaving her two children orphans. Or so 'twas believed, since no one knew that their father and brother had survived and were in England."

"Incredible," said Henry Darcie.

"It grows even more so," said Sir William. "The children were raised by Jesuits, and so of course, they were raised as devout Catholics. Anthony and his father, needless to say, were Church of England. And for years, they were all unaware of one another. Until Drummond came upon the scene. Or, perhaps, I should call him Brother Andrew."

"Brother Andrew!" Smythe said. "You mean he was a *priest?*"

"A member of the Jesuit order, and a fanatic," Sir William said. "A diabolical provocateur if there ever was one. For years, ever since King Henry broke with the Church of Rome, the Papists had been sending agents into England, many of them priests, in an attempt to undermine the Church of England and eventually bring what they saw as our heretic nation back into the fold."

"For which reason, of course, 'tis a crime to give aid or shelter to a priest," said Shakespeare.

"Precisely. Well, Brother Andrew was one such agent, and he

traveled often between England and Spain, though secretly, of course, for 'twould have meant his death if his true identity were known. He knew Alastair and Allison quite well, because when he was younger, he had been their tutor. Alastair, raised in the strong traditions of the Catholic Church, had wanted to be a priest himself, but Brother Andrew found a better use for him when he learned, apparently quite by accident, that Alastair and Allison had a twin, or perhaps I should say a *triplet* brother back in England."

"So then he turned them against their own family?" said Shakespeare.

"And quite successfully, it seems. He played upon their sense of loss and fanned it into hatred. He made them believe their father had abandoned them, together with their mother, and that he and Anthony were now living a life of privileged position, having turned their backs on God along with the rest of heretic England, save for those loyal Catholic souls who still maintained the true faith in secret, at risk to their very lives. And he convinced Alastair and his sister that they both could best serve the Church by coming back to England, taking their rightful place, and working in secret for the cause. And thus the plan was hatched.

"As Andrew Drummond, he managed to secure a position as a servant to Sir Anthony. With his manners and his education, 'twas probably not difficult at all for him to do. Then, once he was secure in his position, he proceeded with his incredible plan to substitute Alastair for Anthony. But there were two obstacles in his way. One was Mistress Darcie, who had been betrothed to Anthony. Well, you have already surmised what they must have planned for her." Elizabeth shivered in her cloak and her father clenched his fists upon the table. "The other impediment to their plan," Sir William continued, "was a spy who appeared to be very effective at exposing Papist agents who were being sent to England. The identity of this spy was not known to Brother Andrew, but he had managed to discover 'twas a poet, a gifted poet who had achieved considerable acclaim among the players."

"Marlowe!" Smythe said.

"Aye, Marlowe," said Sir William, nodding. "Only they did not know his name." He glanced at Shakespeare. "Alastair was posing as his brother Anthony, by then already slain, when Burbage, anxious to secure some patronage, rather bombastically introduced you to him as a man about to make his mark as England's greatest poet, so Alastair thought you were the one. And there are some other similarities between you and Marlowe. You are both roughly the same age, both poets, both involved with companies of players. . . . Well, Alastair at once went to meet with his sister and report what he had discovered. And they hired those men to kill you."

"They very nearly did," said Shakespeare.

"Indeed. 'Twas fortunate that Tuck, here, became involved and followed them, or else they might well have succeeded."

"But what puzzles me is what *you* were doing there, Sir William," Smythe said.

"I was following you," Sir William said.

"*Me?*" Smythe was astonished. "You followed me? But why?"

"Because, I am sorry to say, I had suspected *you* of being the one sent to dispose of Marlowe."

"You thought that *I* was a hired killer?" Smythe said, scarcely able to believe it.

"Well, to borrow your theatrical terms, if I were to cast the role of an assassin, you would fill it admirably," explained Sir William. "A stranger come to town with no connections, young, very fit, powerfully strong, and you at once sought employment with a company of players. Black Billy the brigand is an agent of mine who often enables me to keep track of who is coming to the city at certain times, when information reaches me through other sources that a spy or provocateur may be en route to London. If soldiers were to stop every coach and wagon coming into London along certain routes, there would be repercussions, and a spy might be prepared for that sort of thing. On the other hand, if a highwayman accosts them . . ."

"Then no one thinks twice about it," Shakespeare said, realizing that Sir William had bent the truth a bit because of the Darcies' presence. "And it does not alert anyone that coaches and wagons en route to London are being checked. Very clever, milord. Very clever, indeed."

"But . . . you mean to say that you suspected all along that I might be an agent sent to murder Marlowe?" Smythe asked, incredulously.

"Or at the very least to discover who he truly was," Sir William replied. "And then, perhaps, either dispose of him yourself or else oversee the task."

"But you told me about Marlowe yourself!" said Smythe. "And you revealed . . ." he caught himself just in time. "You revealed certain other things to me, besides! Why do those things if you suspected me?"

"Because by then I had begun to have my doubts," Sir William said. "I had begun to have them even before I had you investigated, Tuck, and I found out about your uncle, and about your childhood, and your father's difficulties, and your burning desire to become a player. None of that seemed to fit the portrait of a hired Papist assassin. Most especially, you had never been abroad to Spain or France. And I also had another suspect. You see, Black Billy had robbed Sir Anthony's coach shortly after he encountered you. And when his report reached me, I thought 'twas quite a curious thing to find Sir Anthony on the road to London, when just the previous day, I had seen him at court. Of course, 'twas not Sir Anthony at all, but Drummond bringing Alastair to London, probably from Bristol, where he had arrived by ship. So I surmised that Gresham had a double, perhaps a twin, but I still needed to be certain about *you*. And so I took a risk, and dangled Marlowe before you as bait to see if you would rise to it."

"Was that not taking a dreadful chance with Marlowe's life, milord?" asked Shakespeare.

"Aye, indeed," Sir William said, "but when you play this sort of game, and for these sort of stakes, then you cannot afford to have much in the way of caution or scruples. And the truth of the matter is that Marlowe is as much of a liability as he is an asset. The things he says and does make it difficult to overlook his indiscretions. Especially since he brings so much attention to himself. He is a clever young man, and quite resourceful, but he is also very difficult, if not nearly impossible to manage. The Papists came to him while he was pursuing his studies at university and recruited him into their cause. He, in turn, came straight to us and offered to work against the efforts of the Counter-Reformation.''

"Us?" said Smythe.

"Her Majesty's Secret Service," said Sir William, "under Sir Francis Walsingham. And now, you realize, you are privy to knowledge that would cost you your heads if you were ever to reveal it.''

Elizabeth gasped and her father nodded gravely, to indicate that he understood the severity of this responsibility. "Neither my daughter nor I shall ever tell a soul!'' he said, somberly.

"Nor I,'' said Smythe, uneasily. Shakespeare swallowed nervously and nodded in agreement.

"Had I any doubts upon that score, then I should not have told you any of this," Sir William said. "Besides, I have a feeling that you may all prove useful, should it ever come to pass that Her Majesty has need of you.''

"Angels and ministers of grace defend us!'' Shakespeare said. "I would make a dreadful spy, milord! I fear I have not the mettle nor the constitution for it!''

Sir William smiled. "Then we shall try neither your mettle nor your constitution, Master Shakespeare. But we shall assay your constancy, methinks. There are many ways that one may serve.''

"If the queen should ever require my service, then it goes without saying that I am Her Majesty's to command," said Henry Darcie.

Shakespeare grimaced, wryly. "Aye, as are we all.''

Sir William turned to Smythe. "As for you, Tuck Smythe . . .

we already have ample evidence of both your mettle and your constitution. And of your constancy, I have no doubt. Be a player, if such is your desire, though 'twould seem to me that you have little talent for it. I think I may have work more suited to your skills. At the very least, there is still the matter of that sword you promised me."

"I am at your service, milord," said Smythe.

"Good. Then we shall speak again." He stood to leave. "And now, 'tis very late, and I shall leave you to your beds."

"But, milord," said Shakespeare, "what shall we tell the others of this matter on the morrow? They shall be full of questions about the causes behind all these strange events."

"And I have no doubt that you shall have suitable answers for them that will satisfy their craving and yet still mask the truth," Sir William said, putting on his hat and cloak. "After all, as Richard Burbage said, you are 'soon to make your mark as one of England's greatest poets,' Master Shakespeare." He chuckled. "Look to your muse to serve you. And now I bid you all good night."

As Sir William closed the door behind him, Henry Darcie and Elizabeth stood to leave, as well. "I must thank you for your service to my daughter, Mr. Smythe," he said. Elizabeth, standing beside him, met Smythe's gaze. "You believed in her when even her own mother and I did not."

"Well, under the circumstances, sir, who could blame you?"

"I blame myself," said Darcie. "I should have taken more trouble to examine the suitability of the match, to make inquiries, to . . . to . . ."

"Consider your daughter's feelings?" Shakespeare suggested.

"Well . . ." Darcie grunted, clearly feeling that the poet was presumptuous, but not feeling in a position to say so. "That, too, I suppose. Again, my gratitude to you . . . gentlemen." He gave them a curt bow and left. With a lingering glance back, Elizabeth followed her father.

Shakespeare shook his head, then turned to Smythe and

shrugged. "Well . . . I shall come up with some sort of story to explain all this, I suppose. Though at the moment, Lord only knows what it shall be." He shook his head. "This has all been the most curious and unsettling affair. Odd's blood, I need a drink."

"Here," said Smythe. "Have some more wine. We can take the bottle up with us."

"To think of it," said Shakespeare, as they headed up the stairs to their room, "two brothers, identical in every way, to say nothing of a sister, and then a servant who serves both, innocents caught up in strange misapprehensions . . . you know, with a few small changes here and there to mask the truth of these events, there may well be a story for a play here."

"Nonsense," Smythe said. " 'Tis all much too fantastic. Who would ever believe it? What audience could be so credulous?"

"Perhaps if 'twere done as a sort of farce, a comedy," said Shakespeare, musing as he paused at the top of the stairs. " 'Tis not really a bad idea, you know."

"I'd leave it alone, if I were you," said Smythe, with a grimace. "You'll get both our heads chopped off if you do not have a care."

"Well, 'twould be just a play, you know . . . a foolish thing of very little consequence." Shakespeare shrugged. "After all, in a hundred years, who do you suppose would care?"

Smythe snorted as he opened the door and plopped down into bed, fully dressed. "Not me. I am much too tired. Good night, Will."

"Methinks I shall work awhile."

"Well, don't stay up too late. Remember, we have another performance tomorrow. And do not forget to blow the candle out when you are done."

"Good night, Tuck. Sleep well. Flights of angels and all that rot. Hmmm. Now where did I leave my inkwell?"

AFTERWORD

> "What I claim here is the right of every Shakespeare-lover
> who has ever lived to paint his own portrait of the man."
> ANTHONY BURGESS
> (In the foreword to his biography, *Shakespeare*)

IT MAY BE THOUGHT THE height of arrogance to use William
Shakespeare as a fictional character in a novel, and I imagine
there will probably be those who will curl their lips with disdain
at the idea, but at the same time, I have a strong suspicion that
Shakespeare would have approved, or at the very least, been rather
amused by the whole thing. After all, it is precisely the sort of
thing he did himself.

I do not, I should say right up front, make any pretense to
being a serious literary scholar or critic on the subject of the Bard.
While I have some knowledge and I have done some research, for
my own enjoyment and as part of working on this book and teaching Shakespeare in college level English courses, there are numerous authorities whose knowledge of Shakepeare and his plays far
exceed my own. My purpose here was really just the same as
Shakespeare's, no more, no less—to entertain.

I am by no means the first to use the Bard in such a manner
nor, I am sure, shall I be the last. In this regard, I am certainly

no less derivative than Shakespeare was himself when he based his works on other sources, such as the *Chronicles* of Holinshead, when he chose to borrow from history, or the works of Greene or Nashe or Marlowe, when he chose to steal outright. What I have tried to teach my students in order to help make Shakespeare more accessible to them is that if he were alive today, William Shakespeare would probably be known unpretentiously as Bill to his friends and there's a good chance he'd be on the writing staff of some prime-time television show like *Melrose Place* or perhaps a soap opera such as *The Days of Our Lives*. I really do believe that. He would doubtless fit right in at a Hollywood power lunch with Steven J. Cannell and David Kelley, with whom he would feel very comfortable talking shop, and he might script for Spielberg or Lucas or whoever hired him to write a screenplay. In short, he would be exactly what he was in his own time, and what Dickens was in his—a working writer, without any literary pretensions, one who simply practiced his craft, as Balzac said, "with clean hands and composure."

This is not to say that I am trying in any way to denigrate Shakespeare by comparing him to Hollywood scriptwriters, which many scholars would probably consider blasphemy, nor necessarily elevate them by a comparison to him. Marshall McLuhan, I think, was wrong. The medium is *not* the message. Genius will always transcend the medium, or else exhalt it, much as Paddy Chayevsky and Stanley Kubrick and Orson Welles did. From everything I know of him . . . and to a large degree, subjectively, from what I feel . . . I think that Shakespeare would have been amazed beyond belief at the effects he has produced and the impact he has made, at the immortality he has achieved. Certainly, he never sought any such thing.

I know writers today who never throw anything away, who obsessively keep copies of every marked-up draft and every note ever scribbled on a napkin in a bar on the off chance that, someday, these things may be worth something, if not in a material sense, at least in an academic one as papers to be donated to some university for future bibliographical and biographical research. Future doctoral candidates need never worry, for there will be no dearth of manuscripts and notes for them to sift through en route to stultifying dissertations. Shakespeare, on the other hand, never saved a thing. If not for his printers, we would probably have nothing, for immortality was the last thing on his mind, and I doubt that the idea would even have occurred to him. He knew that his medium was an ephemeral one and he regarded it accordingly. He wrote his works to be *performed*, not deconstructed in a college classroom or analyzed with pathological precision for every possible nuance and interpretation. He understood, without a doubt, that his was a collaborative medium, that actors would bring their own contributions to the table, that plays were a dynamic group effort of the entire company, not a showcase for an individual writer's talent and/or ego.

Students who are forced to sit through agonizing lectures by monotonous professors who drone on and on about iambic pentameter and heroic couplets never truly learn to appreciate the Bard, and more's the pity, because Shakespeare himself would have been aghast to learn that his words were putting young captive audiences to sleep. He wanted, more than anything, to make them laugh, or weep, or rage . . . to make them *feel*, for that was why Elizabethan audiences went to the theatre. They went looking for a bit of escapism, some amusement, a little entertainment. They wanted, simply, a good time. And Shakespeare *became* Shakespeare because he knew just how to give it to them.

The irony of his career is that while he became, indisputably, the best known storyteller in the world, he is one of the least known when it comes to the story of his life. Much has been written and surmised about him, both biographically and fictionally, and it is not my purpose to go into any great detail about that here. I shall not dwell upon the so-called "Authorship Debate," other than to state briefly my own opinion, which is that Shakespeare's plays were written by Will Shakespeare, not Bacon or De Vere or, for that matter, Kilgore Trout. I shall not make any attempt to analyze anything he wrote, other than to comment for the purpose of this afterword where I stretched the truth somewhat (at least so far as it is known or might be justifiably inferred) and where true "congressional rhetoric" begins.

Shakespeare was born in 1564, the exact date is unknown, one of eight children (only one of whom, his sister Joan, was to survive him), in Stratford-upon-Avon, as is well known. His father, John, the son of a Snitterfield farmer, was a tradesman, a glover, and his mother, Mary, came of aristocratic Arden stock. He had the basic grammar school education (there is no record of his ever having attended any university and considerable circumstantial evidence that he was not a "college man") and it is likely that he learned at least something of the glovemaking trade from his father, though there is no evidence that he ever formally entered upon the trade himself.

Much is made of the so-called "Lost Years" (the time in which this novel is set), the period from roughly 1586 to 1592, during which time nothing is known about his life. No record exists from the time his name was mentioned in a legal document in Stratford in 1587 to the time he was mentioned in a book by Robert Greene in 1592, at which point he was apparently already a successful playwright. There has been much conjecture, however, based on inferences and deductions from circumstantial evidence. There have been various proposed scenarios of varying credibility that have had him working as an apprentice glover, a butcher, a law clerk, an ostler, an actor, a tutor, even a poacher. The one thing that is clear is that only a few years after his marriage to Anne Hathaway on November 28, 1582 and the birth of three children (a daughter born only six months after the marriage and twins born about two years later), he left his family in Stratford and moved to London, where he "resurfaced" as an actor/playwright and member of the theatrical company of Lord Strange's Men almost a decade later.

Among all the theories about Shakespeare's activities during these "hidden years," I gravitate toward the scenario proposed by Anthony Burgess in his spare and highly readable biography, *Shakespeare*. Burgess suggests, with some good evidence to back up his arguments, that Shakespeare had a "shotgun wedding," that his plans to marry a girl named Anne Whateley, of Temple Grafton, were derailed by his being forced to marry Anne Hathaway, of Shottery, an older woman whom he had obviously impregnated. For a more detailed explication, I refer interested readers to Mr. Burgess, who as a writer is far more lucid and entertaining on the subject than are most scholars and literary critics, some of whom tend to be agenda-driven apologists. But suffice it to say, as far as history and this novel are concerned, that everything that happened to William Shakespeare from the time he left Stratford until he resurfaced as a member of the company known as Lord Strange's Men (eventually to become more famous as The Lord Chamberlain's Men) is pure conjecture.

Consequently, there is no historical counterpart (at least so far as I know) to the character of Black Billy/Sir William Worley. That character is made up entirely of a dash of Errol Flynn, a pinch of Oliver Reed, a measure of Peter O'Toole, and a whole bunch of personal wish fulfillment. It is not, however, entirely out of the realm of possibility that someone like Worley might well have existed in real life, for the modern British Secret Service had its beginnings in the time of Elizabeth I, with Sir Francis Walsingham, her minister and chief hatchet man, so to speak.

The members of the company known as the Queen's Men, as portrayed here, are fictional with the exceptions of Dick Tarleton (who is only referred to in this novel and does not actually appear), Edward Alleyn, Will Kemp, Richard Burbage, and his father,

James, who are all based on real people, with a considerable amount of dramatic license, needless to say. Alleyn did, in fact, quit the Queen's Men for the Admiral's Men, probably for reasons very similar to those depicted here, and Kemp eventually left, as well. (Tarleton fell ill about the time of the setting of this novel and died.) It should be noted that while the Queen's Men really did exist, there is no proof that Shakespeare had ever actually joined that company. He might have, but if he did, he was not with them very long and probably left around 1587 to join Lord Strange's Men, along with Will Kemp.

Christopher Marlowe, of course, is not a fictional character, but my treatment of him is entirely fictional, based loosely on what is known of his life. He was, to say the least, a flamboyant character, Shakespeare's only real competition at the time, a sort of Elizabethan Oscar Wilde with a bit of Harlan Ellison thrown in, if one can imagine such a thing. Marlowe, as some of my students might say, was very much "in your face" and probably would have left behind an even more brilliant literary history if he had not been savagely murdered in a bar. It is generally assumed that Marlowe was, indeed, engaged in some sort of espionage activity. Though no hard evidence for this exists, there seems to be some strong circumstantial evidence. It has been suggested that he was murdered in revenge by agents of Spain or else by his own government, to prevent him from testifying before the Privy Council and revealing inconvenient associations when he was accused of heresy and blasphemy. However, it is also entirely possible that he was simply murdered for being what and who he was. That Shakespeare admired Marlowe is a matter of historical record, but it seems doubtful, given their very different personalities, that they hung out together.

Smythe is, of course, entirely my own creation and I hope that you enjoyed him. My treatment of Shakespeare, likewise, is pure conjecture based upon subjective inference. I painted him, to paraphrase Mr. Burgess, the way I would have liked to see him. Most readers will, I hope, find it merely harmless fun. As Shakespeare might have said himself, and did:

> If we shadows have offended,
> Think but this, and all is mended,
> That you have but slumbered here
> While these visions did appear,
> And this weak and idle theme,
> No more yielding than a dream,
> Gentles, do not reprehend.
> If you pardon, we will mend.
>> *A Midsummer Night's Dream*
>> (Act V, Scene I)

SIMON HAWKE
Greensboro, North Carolina